PHIA
and the
WOLF

Other adventures by DL SIGLER

CIGALA (Fiction)
The Last Fraction (Historical fiction)
Dancing with Bigfoot (Fantasy fiction)
The Last Voyage of the Ratatouille (Fiction)
Nike Wolf (Historical Fiction)
A leap of Faith (Mystery Fiction)

PHIA *and the* WOLF

DL Sigler

ISBN 978-1-957582-48-1 (paperback)
ISBN 978-1-957582-49-8 (eBook)

Printed in the United States of America

DEDICATION

The inspiration for this novel came from my Grandaughter. Actually, it was more of a request. She wanted me to write a story about a teenage hero. It was a little different direction for me, but I accepted the challenge.

Sophia Burdick, this is for you.

ACKNOWLEDGMENT

I would like to thank my friend Crabman for his help in editing my story. His legal name is Stu Ashley and he is my neighbor.

The above Grandaughter fondly gave him that nickname. (His wife Linda, she calls, the Artichoke Lady.) Because of the bounty of their garden and of the sea, they have shared many a good meal with us.

Between growing his garden, checking his crab pots, and flying his plane, he took time to redline the grammar and spelling mistakes in my story.

Thank you again for sharing some of your precious time, for me.

CHAPTER 1

Ray, what the hell just happened?"

Captain Raymond Phillips took a moment to flip through several of the switches on the panel of the Boeing 737 that he was flying. He was trying to figure out just why his instrument panel lights went dark, as did the overhead lights.

"I don't know, Dale." He turned to his copilot, "Find me a flashlight."

As Copilot Dale Wilson fumbled his way around the cockpit, a soft knock vibrated the cockpit door.

"What the hell just happened?" It was flight attendant, Autumn Fisher.

The passenger sitting in seat 14A, who was a school teacher, was awake and gazing at the stars when this happened. She saw the brilliant Northern Lights suddenly appear in front of her. And when the plane flew through the fluorescent green and red curtain, she watched the colors explode into a dazzling display of light. "Wow," she exclaimed. "That was even prettier than a rainbow." When the few remaining cabin lights went out, she didn't think anything of it. She slouched back down in her seat and got comfortable, and closed her tired eyes. "That was sure good luck!" she thought to herself.

She went back to sleep. But unfortunately, because luck can also be bad, it will be the last thing that she ever saw.

Alaska Airlines flight *AS1125* from Newark, New Jersey left on time in a cloudless sky. It was the night flight, the redeye. The mid-fall outside temperature was quite mild. In this part of the country, this was commonly referred to as an Indian summer.

As the plane climbed its way up into the upper atmosphere, the stars began flooding the heavens, and the waxing moon watched and smiled at the planet below him. He seemed to be circling the earth and shining his dim light on it like a night watchman. The Boeing jet leveled off and headed home. It was flying towards winter, an Eskimo winter, with the temperatures already showing negative numbers on its thin glass tube. Their destination was Fairbanks, Alaska.

Drinks and snacks were served shortly after takeoff. After about an hour into the flight, the overhead cabin lights slowly began switching off as passengers slumped back into their seats and gradually slipped into their own personal dreams.

The first-class section had twelve seats in it, the premium-seat section contained eighteen seats, and the coach section had over ninety narrow seats that were tightly packed into it for the maximum capacity. The plane was less than half-full so, most of the passengers had vacant seats to curl up on and catch a few z's.

Passenger 2A and passenger 2C sat beside each other in the first-class section. There was no seat 2B to allow for the extra room between them, although they each paid enough extra to cover the cost of the missing seat. These two men were oil executives and good friends. They were returning to their important office jobs in Fairbanks. Passengers 2D and 2F were the wives of passengers 2A and 2C.

In the premium-seat section, the seats were four inches narrower than first-class, but at least they reclined four degrees more than the ones in regular coach class. The passengers in this area were a small group of teachers that went to Washington DC to lobby for more money for Alaskan bush schools.

Passenger 15D and 15C were also in this area. They were an older couple visiting their son who just got a job working on the Pipe Line as a security guard.

Then came the coach seats, which were in the largest section and the back half of the plane.

Passengers 18A and 18B were returning home after their connecting flight from a vacation in Florida. In fact, most of the passengers in coach were returning from vacations or visits to friends and relatives back in what Alaskans referred to as the *lower 48*.

Passenger 22A was an old man returning to Alaska after spending two years in Florida with his daughter and her husband and their three kids. When his wife died he tried living in that hot climate but he was just a fish out of water, a polar bear out of snow.

Passenger 23E was a 23 year old exotic dancer looking for the big money in Alaska. Her friend, passenger 23F was also looking for a better life. She also danced around a pole and had a side job that involved customers and a very controlling pimp.

Passenger 24B was running away from an abusive man, her husband. She was traveling with her 14 year old daughter, who was sitting beside her in seat 24C. She had also suffered the wrath of the man that her mother had remarried, and she became very despondent after the cruel treatment. Her eyes were glazed in total withdrawal and she became deaf to the world.

Passenger 25D and 25E were on their honeymoon and the newest members of the mile-high club. Fortunately, they sat near the back of the plane and discretely kept to themselves.

Passenger 26A enjoyed his window seat. This was his first time on a plane. He was going to visit his older brother who had run away from home. Alaska was as far as he could drive his Mustang to get away from the farm and its never-ending chores.

Passenger 27E was a depressed factory worker with five kids and a nagging wife. He told her that he was going for a pack of cigarettes and would be right back. He drove to the airport in New Jersey and bought a ticket on the first plane leaving the state.

Passenger 28A was cuffed to his seat. Seat 28B was empty and passenger 28C was a plainclothes Fairbanks cop. He was the only one with a concealed weapon on board. They were in the last row of the plane, which was close to the restrooms and the rear exit.

The flight was smooth. The engines vibrated gently and hummed quietly. And without a care in the world, the unsuspecting passengers dozed off peacefully. But little did they know, an act of God was about to change their lives forever.

The sun, like the earth, rotates on an axis. It has a North Pole and a South Pole. One Sun day, or one rotation, is between 24-1/2 to 38 earth days. This difference is because the sun is a giant ball of gas and it rotates faster at its equator than it does at the poles. This peculiar difference of rotation causes chaos, and in turn, sunspots, which generate severe electromagnetic storms. These storms can shoot charged proton particles far into space and these shooting particles are called the solar wind, which can be mild, or not. Like the one that happened on September 11, 1859, which interrupted telegraph communications, literally shocked telegraph operators, and created sparks hot enough to ignite the top of telegraph poles.

Fortunately, for the most part, these protons particles do not penetrate our atmosphere and are harmlessly absorbed by it. But these proton events can be seen when they come in contact with the earth's magnetic poles. The effect is the aurora borealis, the northern lights. Yes, most are harmless and they come with an amazing light show.

But not today.

One such solar storm slipped through a thin spot in the upper atmosphere right over Hudson Bay. The area is unpopulated and the villages along the Bay's west coast consist of the First Nations' people of Canada, and they are very limited in electronic devices. When the few that had computers crashed, no one seemed to notice, or for that matter, even cared.

But flight *AS1125*'s captain became quite concerned when his lights went out, and his plane's computer crashed. He worried that his plane would be next.

"What the hell just happened?" demanded Flight Attendant Autumn as she knocked harder on the cockpit door.

After Dale found the flashlight for his captain, he quickly opened the door for Autumn and calmly explained to her, "We had a power surge and it burned out our lights, and it seems to have fried some of our gauges too."

"Well, that doesn't sound good." She uttered nervously.

The engines were still running smoothly and the auto-pilot was maintaining a course that was locked in on 330° degrees true north. Captain Raymond remained calm, but concerned. Autumn flipped down a seat that was fastened against the back wall and sat on it. As she tucked her legs under it she asked, "Is it some kind of a breaker that tripped?"

"I don't think so," replied Raymond. "This plane has a backup on it for everything."

"He's right," added copilot Dale. "Hence me."

"Well, why are the backups not back upping?"

"Well, apparently, they are burned out too."

"Do you still have control of the plane?" she nervously asked.

Captain Raymond handed his flashlight to his copilot and sat back in his seat. He flipped the toggle switch for the autopilot to its off position. Its light stayed dark and the course stayed on

330° north. He firmly put his hands on the wheel and eased it back. Nothing happened. He pulled harder and the plane slowly responded.

"The autopilot wants to hold its last position," commented the Caption calmly. "Fortunately, the plane has a manual override. But the electric motors that assist in moving the flaps and rudders are not working. At least, I can still control the plane with physical force. This works fine up here, but landing could be a problem."

Copilot Dale handed the flashlight to Autumn and he slid back in his seat. He reached for the radio and keyed the mike. It was dead. He turned on the emergency locator beacon. Its little yellow flashing light never winked.

With the autopilot permanently set at 330° north, the captain let go of the controls and got up from his seat. He went to a small storage locker and retrieved a Boeing 737 Pilot's Operating Handbook. Autumn held the flashlight while Captain Raymond looked through the Troubleshooting section for power outages.

While he quietly sat there reading the manual, everyone was becoming quite concerned. They now realized that they were flying in complete darkness, and the Captain had very little control of the plane, and they had no way to communicate with the rest of the world. They were in quite a pickle.

Meanwhile, somewhere on the ground and in close proximity of the distressed plane, sat the watchful eye of an air traffic controller.

"Mark, I just lost flight *AS1125* from Newark!" nervously replied air traffic controller Andrew. It was his first day on the job.

"What do you mean, you lost flight *AS1125*?" replied controller Mark who was sitting at the monitor next to Andrew. He was tracking the air space west of Andrew's. He was also Andrew's personal advisor and instructor until he felt Andrew was completely up to speed. They were working in the airport tower at Gillam Airport in Manitoba.

"The plane just disappeared from my screen," said Andrew as he shrugged his shoulders.

Mark quickly got on the radio and tried to call the missing Boeing jet. Andrew began calling other airports to see if they had them on their radar. When Mark received no response from the missing plane, he went to the monitor showing satellite images of all of Canada's air space. He typed in *AS1125*. The satellite was not receiving any signals from the plane, but it did show where it was when it received its last signal. It was over the west side of the Hudson Bay.

Mark quickly called the Manitoba Coast Guard and had them send out a search plane. He also asked them if they had heard any recent distress signals. "Only from an offshore fisherman," replied the dispatcher and added, "We will listen for the ELT (emergency locator transmitter) and let you know if we get a signal."

Meanwhile, somewhere over the Hudson Bay,

Captain Raymond Phillips looked up from his technical manual and asked, "Who has the time?"

Autumn reached for her cell phone and punched the bottom button to light it up. Alas, nothing. It was fried along with the other now useless important electronic devices onboard. Then she remembered the little silver watch around her wrist. She bought it as an accessory for her professional attire. She had been impressed how well its tiny little hands had kept such good time. Although, she still was in the habit of using the cell phone's perfectly accurate digital time. "It's almost 9:00 PM." She said slightly confused since it was indicating two hours before they left New Jersey.

Raymond paused as he realized that the watch was mechanical and didn't change with the time zones as the cell phones do. "You're on Fairbanks time, aren't you?"

"Ah," nodded Autumn, "Yes, I am."

"Well if I have to land this thing manually, I will need to see my runway." Raymond looked at his copilot. "What time is sunup in Fairbanks these days?"

The sun's not up until late morning. But it starts getting light around seven-ish if it's not too cloudy."

"Ten hours from now." Raymond shook his head and went back to his manual, the airspeed section. "Okay, let's see. Cruising speed is 430 knots, and landing speed is 150 knots, and the stall speed is 136 knots empty, and 146 knots fully loaded. And that is with the flaps fully extended."

His crew was beginning to lose hope.

"I think it might work. We know we have enough fuel for a seven-hour flight. If we back the throttle off to half power, subtract the two hours we have been in flight, it will give us nine hours of flight time.

"Even if we don't make it to Fairbanks, at least I will be able to see the ground and find a road to set this thing down on." He rubbed his chin while he mentally calculated his speed at half throttle. "That's 330 knots. We are good."

That was cutting it pretty close but it was hope.

Raymond set down the manual and climbed back into his seat. He eased down on the throttle. The plane slowed. But he had no idea how much. His speedometer was blank. He tried to lower the flaps and nothing happened. He looked at his copilot, "We need to lower the flaps a little at this speed for more lift. Have you ever manually lowered them?"

Dale nodded and said, "Once, in training."

"Good." He looked at Autumn. "I need you to go with him. And take two flashlights, just in case."

After they left for the hatch that led down to the baggage area and to the hand crank that controlled the cables to the flaps, Raymond started playing with the throttle some more. He kept easing it slower, trying to feel when the plane started losing altitude as it approached its stall speed. He was now flying by the seat of his pants, just like most bush pilots do. It was going to be a long night.

Even with the flaps lowered just slightly, the plane lost efficiency, and time made good. And this, versus fuel consumption, did not equal enough gas to make the trip to Fairbanks. Raymond knew this. He was just stalling for daylight. All he needed was a highway, a field, or even a frozen lake to set her down in, and maybe, just maybe, he could pull it off. If Captain Sully could land in the Hudson River, a landing on treeless tundra should be a cakewalk.

CHAPTER 2

An unobstructed Siberian winter wind, carrying a burly blanket of snow, charged across the Bering Sea, and into Alaska on its way to the Yukon Territory of Canada. On its journey east, it brought with it blizzard-like conditions as it crossed this desolate and barren country. The storm was not fit for man, beast, nor bird. And it was about to meet up with flight *AS1125*, a crippled metal bird.

The autopilot was stuck at 330° north because its electric satellite positioning system was not speaking to the autopilot. It didn't really matter because the electric autopilot was not listening, anyway. The plane's steering system was set to fly straight and level in its last received direction. So, now the plane was winging it at the whim of the wind.

Captain Raymond sat at the wheel of his plane trying to stay calm and get control of the situation. The night sky was clear except for a billion stars, a smiling moon, and an excellent display of the aurora borealis. The snow-covered ground below him showed a few twinkles of lights from villages sparsely scattered over this desolate country. With the white snow cover and the half-moon, he figured he might be able to land if he could just find an airport with its runway lights on, and one that was long enough for a Boeing 737. But he had no idea where he was, or even if such a runway existed in the direction that he was flying.

The Big Dipper constellation got his attention and with it, the bright North Star that hung above its ladle. He now had a reliable direction to follow. Now he could line the star off of the center of his right window and this would keep his course west towards Alaska. So he firmly overrode the autopilot and did just that. When he let go of the wheel, the plane again began flying straight and narrow, thinking it was still on 330° north. The captain was feeling much better. His odds had greatly improved. He took a relieved breath and leaned back in his padded leather seat. There was now nothing more he really could do but hope and wait.

A quick double-tap sounded at the cockpit door followed by a loud whisper. "Hey, guys, what's going on?" It was flight attendant, Cheryl.

Autumn quickly got off her seat and open the door for her.

"Why is it so dark in here?" asked Cheryl.

Nobody spoke. The pilot and copilot were looking intently ahead and Autumn just shrugged her shoulders. No one wanted to be the bearer of the bad news.

Cheryl glanced impatiently around the dark cockpit. "What? Is everybody deaf?"

Raymond moaned and said, "You tell her, Autumn."

Autumn carefully and gently explained to Cheryl that they were in dire straits, but not to worry, because the captain was going to land this plane like a toboggan somewhere on the snow, kind of like Captain Sully did with his plane on the river."

"You're kidding, right?"

Autumn shook her head and sadly sighed.

"Oh, shit!" said Cheryl as she reached into the tiny purse strapped to her side and pulled out a pack of cigarettes. "I need a smoke!"

Copilot Dale spun in his seat. "You can't smoke in an airplane. It's against the law."

Cheryl glared at Dale. "Watch me." She lit up and blew smoke in his face. "Go ahead and arrest me and take me to jail… one that's on the ground."

"Captain!" Dale was now facing Raymond. "Say something to her."

Raymond took a breath and turned to the attendant. "Cheryl, I know this is a bit irregular, but may I have one of your cigarettes?"

"Sure," she handed him the lit one. As she reached into her pack for another one, she asked, "Does anyone else want one?"

"May I, please," said Autumn.

After Cheryl lit Autumn's cigarette, she looked at Dale and offered him one.

He hesitated.

"Come on. You can do it."

"Fine." He said. "I guess getting cancer is now the least of my worries."

Cheryl snickered and handed him a cigarette.

For the next two hours, the captain kept his plane north by northwest, approximately. He was beginning to understand the value of a sextant. It was an instrument that didn't break down. But planes stopped using those years ago and they have become museum pieces. It wouldn't have mattered anyway, Raymond had no idea how to use one.

Copilot Dale studied the Boeing 737's manual. It helped to distract him from their hopeless situation. He was looking in the technical part of the manual that was written in fine print for a way to restore power, and become a hero.

Flight attendant Cheryl decided to make coffee for everyone. It would not be hot because the coffee makers were electric. She poured the lukewarm water through the coffee filter and filled four cups. She added a little vodka to hers.

Flight attendant Autumn assisted Cheryl in the coffee-making but refused the vodka for her coffee. She preferred whiskey.

Dale looked up at the North Star to check their position. It was still good. He checked the horizon ahead and noticed it had changed. "Ray, we are losing our stars."

Raymond leaned forward and studied the dark sky ahead of them. "They're storm clouds! We should have been above the weather patterns. We must be losing altitude." Raymond pulled back on the wheel and raised the nose. The plane responded and climbed, but lost airspeed. Raymond was concentrating on getting above the storm and neglected to add throttle.

About the time the stall alarm would have sounded, if everything was in proper working order, Dale felt it. And very concerned, he voiced, "**Ray**…"

Raymond heard and instantly felt it too. He pushed the wheel forward which put the nose down, and quickly increased the throttle. The plane accelerated to a safe airspeed and right into the blinding snowstorm. The cockpit darkened.

Autumn looked up and gasped, which interrupted Cheryl's nervous chatter. When she looked up and saw the white flakes flooding the windshield, she cursed and discretely added a little more vodka to her coffee. After which she nudged Autumn and pointed at the small vodka bottle and then to her cold coffee. Autumn nodded.

The snow was cold and dry, and it created a strong headwind. Raymond let go of the wheel and the plane's autopilot kicked in and reset to flying straight and level. Its airspeed remained the same but the ground speed was forty knots less. Raymond throttled up a bit and slowly pulled back on the wheel. He looked down at his coffee and could see that the black liquid in tilting to the backside of the cup. He was climbing. He could use it as a crude gauge.

Fifteen minutes later, the plane climbed up and into the stars. Both Autumn and Cheryl clapped. Raymond smiled and let go of the wheel. It adjusted back to straight and level. Now it was time to pray that the fuel supply would last longer than the night sky.

As the hours sluggishly flew by, the temperature slowly dropped and the oxygen level followed suit. The cabin was losing pressure. And with the thin high altitude air, exhaustion followed. Pretty soon the two attendants leaned forward in their seats and rested their tired eyes. They fell sound asleep. Dale was next. The reading of a technical manual would have probably been enough anyway. He leaned back in his chair to rest his eyes and dozed off.

Raymond looked at his sleeping crew and began to wonder if something was wrong. The brain, deprived of oxygen, does not think clearly. He blinked his eyes several times to clear his head and called to his copilot, "Da…" was as far as he got.

It looked like everyone on board was going to get their last wish, that is, 'to die in your sleep.' But fortunately, Ray had backed off the power to save fuel, and the plane again began losing altitude. It was dropping back into the thick atmospheric air of the earth.

Flight *AS1125* eased back into the Siberian storm straight and level while everyone continued sleeping peacefully. It slowly slipped lower and lower. It was now flying west towards the Wernecke Mountains, which have an average height of forty-five hundred feet, and it has a few pinnacles a lot higher. The big silver bird seemed to feel the precious life that it had in its belly, and as it dropped to five-thousand feet, it seemed to lean away from the tall peaks as it maintained the course that it was commanded. It was running out of fuel and out of elevation. Even if Captain Raymond woke up now, he would be flying blind between mountain tops. The plane continued to shy away from the tall peaks and it seemed to gravitate towards the valleys, or maybe it was gusts of wind swirling through the mountains that moved the plane, or maybe it was God answering their prayers. But whatever it was, the plane somehow made it through the mountains and into the wide plains, which were the high tundra area of north-eastern Alaska.

The plane coughed and it lost the engine on its left wing. It had run out of fuel. The plane now, with only one engine running, slowed to near its stall speed. Its autopilot was still trying to fly straight and level, but it didn't have enough power to correct its descent. At a little over 150 knots, the plane nosed down onto a snow-covered hill. Its right-wing engine was still running, as it and gravity drove it towards the wide valley below. It was not slowing down. When it dropped into a snow-filled creek bed, the wings started ripping out black spruce trees and alders. The running engine started igniting the trees with its hot exhaust. The plane was lopsided. The one working engine began to spin the plane, causing the left wing to dip into a side stream. It was promptly torn loose along with part of the fuselage and a section of floor under six seats. With the loss of weight on the left side, the right wing dropped to the ground and its heavy engine inhaled snow and it was torn off the wing. The hot engine spun to a stop in the ravine. What was left of the plane was traveling at 100 knots.

It was now an awkward sled, sliding towards the far end of the wide valley. The remaining wing dropped into a drift and spun the plane sideways and it slid out onto a smooth snow-covered area, a shallow lake that was frozen solid. The plane's speed was down to eighty knots as it slid on with its one wing dragging behind it like a tail.

With the missing wing, the fuselage was structurally damaged and it split into two halves. Both sections began spinning like a top, causing its sleeping passengers, which were not seat-belted in, to be thrown out its open end like human cannonballs and instantly killing half of them. The debris was scattered for a mile down the lake before everything finally came to a stop and it became deathly quiet.

The Siberian snowstorm continued over them on its journey east.

As the storm blew itself out, the moon appeared on the western horizon. The eastern horizon was beginning to turn pink in anticipation of the shy winter sun. It was going to be a beautiful day, well at least, weather-wise.

CHAPTER 3

S cattered across a frozen shallow lake were the bits and pieces and bodies of flight *AS1125*. The largest section of the fuselage was still were intact. It was the front section and it still contained four people. They were the ones in the cockpit, which was spun, rolled, and tumbled like a demolition derby car. Its occupants did not fare as well as some of the passengers that were thrown into the snow. They were brutally battered against the walls and bounced off the bolted-down seats in the cockpit. At least when the fuselage finally came to a stop, it was right-side-up.

The temperature outside was cold.It was a sunny -1° F.

Flight attendant Cheryl, just before she dozed off, fastened her seatbelt to keep from sliding off of her seat for her quick nap, so she pretty much rode out the unscheduled, brutal landing unscathed.

Dazed and confused, she was the first to regain consciousness. She stared blankly out the cockpit windscreen while waiting for her brain to focus into reality. When a raven landed on the nose of the plane, it startled her. "What's he doing up here at this altitude?" The last thing that she remembered was chatting with Autumn as the plane flew in darkness. She vaguely remembered closing her eyes for a quick nap.

She blinked a few times and focused on the raven. "Shoo! Get off my plane." The raven cocked his head, croaked a curse, and flew off. Cheryl tried to stand up. "**Ouch!**" The seatbelt was still fastened around her waist. Her muscles were tender and bruised from the life-saving seatbelt. She unfastened it, took a deep breath, and stood. That was when she saw her three friends crumpled in a heap on the floor. She quickly ran to Autumn. Her face was swollen and bleeding, and when she eased her on her back, Cheryl heard a slight moan. She put a cushion under her head and then went to the captain. His head was at an odd angle and he wasn't breathing. Dale was wedged between the cockpit chair and the console. He was unconscious and still breathing. She was afraid to try and move him and decided to go for help.

The cockpit door was wedged tight and refused to open. **"Help, somebody, help me, please is there anyone out there?"** she screamed. It remained deathly quiet. She rummaged around the cockpit and found a screwdriver. She slipped it between the door and the metal jam and pried. The door squeaked and finally rattled open with a pop. When she stepped through, she felt a blast of cold air and saw an empty plane with a large opening in the other end of it. Half of the plane was missing. **"What the hell happened?"** she screamed in terror.

She took a deep breath and calmed herself. She went to the small locker where she stashed her coat and boots. It was undamaged and it opened. She put on her thick fur coat and her boots, grabbed a scarf, and donned her wool hat. It was time to look for help. The plane section was sitting fairly level and upright. This meant that the seating section was still above the cargo hold. She discovered about a seven-foot drop to the snow on the severed end.

Cheryl went back up front and opened the hatch to the cargo space. She crawled down the ladder. She found the cargo area was completely empty. The suitcases and the baggage that were in it had been jettisoned just like the passengers. At least now, she was at ground level and had an unobstructed walk out of and into the scene of the disaster.

"Oh my God," she uttered as she stepped out of the plane and onto the windswept ice of this subarctic lake.

Cheryl Long was thirty-five years old. She was a handsome woman that never had any kids. She married young and when she divorced, five years later, she got a job with Alaska Airlines. She liked the travel and the different people that she met along the way. She stood five-foot-six inches in heels. Her hair was a dark red, *Revlon Colorsilk Bright Auburn #45*, to be exact, and she had a sturdy well-shaped body. She had a lot of male friends but had enough of marriage. The job of being a flight attendant suited her quite well.

The only signs of life that Cheryl could see were circling ravens. She took a deep breath, formed her hands into a megaphone, and yelled at the top of her lungs. **"Hello, is there anybody alive out there?"** She listened and muttered, "Please God, I need help on this one." She held her breath and hoped for any sounds or signs of life.

Seconds turned into minutes, and suddenly there it was. A hand came up out of one of the lumps in the snow. She was not alone and with tears in her eyes, Cheryl ran towards another living human being. Before she got to him, the passenger sat up and gazed blankly towards Cheryl. It was passenger 26A.

Passenger 26A, Jesse Reed, was traveling by himself. He was meeting his older brother who had run away from the farm five years ago. Jesse had just finished high school and decided it was time to make his own way in the world. He had sandy hair, blue eyes, and a very friendly smile.

By the time Cheryl got to him, he had climbed to his feet. "What happened?" He blankly smiled at Cheryl and she couldn't help but give him a long hug. After she let go of him, she wiped her eyes and grinned. "What's your name?"

"Jesse," he said shyly. He was not used to being hugged by strangers. "It sure is cold here." He paused and looked around. "How did I get here?"

"We had engine problems and crashed." Cheryl kept her answers as simple as she could. "Are you okay, can you walk?"

Jesse nodded, "Yes, mam."

"Good. Okay, Jesse, we need to look for other survivors."

"Well, okay," he blankly said. His young brain was working in overload, and he just stood there.

Cheryl took his hand and began leading him down the crash-cluttered frozen lake. His hand was very cold. "The luggage," she said to herself. Suitcases and plane parts were scattered everywhere. She quickly led Jesse to the nearest one. It was locked but its stitching had separated on impact. Since these people were going to Fairbanks, Alaska, she figured they would have some winter clothes in them. And they did. She pulled out a hoodie and a down vest. "Here put these on." She found a ski hat and handed it to him. Jesse put on his new ensemble and gave Cheryl a warm smile. She wanted to kiss the sweet young man.

Cheryl could see that Jesse was calming. It was time to put him to work. "Jesse, we need to spread out and look for more survivors. You keep going this way and I will work my way down the other side."

He nodded and took one step, paused, and his eyes swelled in panic. "What do I do if I find a dead body?"

Cheryl grabbed him by both shoulders. "You will. Leave them. It is the live ones that we need to find. They are the ones that need us now."

"Okay," nodded Jesse who was still a little overwhelmed. He straightened up and headed for the next crumpled lump in the snow. It was a deceased male victim. It was the first dead person he had ever seen. He stared at the cold face for a minute and said a quick prayer, and he moved on.

Cheryl's next find was an older man lying on his back. He had a gray frost-covered beard and his hazel eyes were open in a frozen stare of the sky. She remembered him as passenger 22A. She had served him several glasses of scotch. She looked at the poor dead man and wondered about his life. Was he going to Alaska to fulfill a lifelong dream that was now cut short? "Hmmm," she sighed. In the blink of an eye, both dreams and lives can be instantly snuffed out. She bowed her head and said, "Sorry, rest in peace." As she turned to leave, the dead man blinked an eye.

He looked at a very surprised Cheryl. "Am I in heaven?"

Cheryl's startled jaw dropped, but she remained speechless, she shook her head.

The old man raised one eyebrow. "Well, then I must be in hell. This sure don't feel like it, miss. And you sure don't look like no devil. Where's your pitchfork?"

Cheryl finally got her mouth moving. "Oh no, this is not hell either. You're still alive."

"Oh, Christ." He shook his head. "What the hell did you do?" He reached his right hand towards her. "Help me sit up." When he got to a sitting position he looked around and scoffed, "What the hell happened?"

"You were in a plane crash."

He rubbed his scruffy beard for a few seconds, and then he looked Cheryl in the eye. "I remember you. I don't suppose you have any more of them little scotch bottles with you. I could sure use a drink bout now, miss…?"

"Cheryl, my name's Cheryl." She reached for the small purse under her thick coat and felt the pack of cigarettes and a small single-serving bottle of alcohol. "No sir. All I have is rum."

"That will work, Cheryl. Oh, and my name is Jackson, Frank Jackson. People just call me Jackson."

Cheryl opened her purse and retrieved the bottle and handed it to Jackson.

"Thank you kindly," he said as twisted off the cap.

Cheryl pulled out her pack of cigarettes and lit one up. She took a quick puff and then offered Jackson one of her cigarettes.

Jackson shook his head. "I'd be hoarding those if I were you. I'm guess-en it is a long way to the nearest 7-Eleven." He took a swallow of his little bottle of rum and laid back down. "I came back to Alaska to die in peace. You should go and look for more survivors. Ones that have something to live for." He finished the bottle and continued his ice stare of the heavens.

Cheryl didn't have time to argue with the stubborn old codger. She looked over at Jesse and he was helping a young woman to her feet. She left Jackson and continued her search for survivors.

Jesse heard Passenger 23E sobbing. He quickly went to help her. She was lying curled up on her side. She was shivering and her lips were turning blue. After Jesse helped her to her feet, he quickly took the hooded sweatshirt and the down vest that he was wearing and put them on her. He took off his ski hat and wrapped her hands in it. "Are you okay?"

She nodded but looked very dazed.

"What's your name?"

"Barb."

Barbara White, Passenger 23E, was the twenty-three-year-old pole dancer.

"Hi, Barb. My name is Jesse. Can you walk?"

"I think so. What happened?" She suddenly focused and began looking around. "Where is Kayla?"

"Who's Kayla?"

"She's my roommate. We are going to Alaska to… Where's the plane at?" She looked around quite confused.

"We crashed," said Jesse. "Let's look for your friend." He was just as confused and was blindly doing what was asked of him.

"Okay, Jesse." She said, still in shock.

Jesse rummaged through more suitcases for more warm clothes for survivors. He found a thick woman's coat and had Barb put it on. She thanked him profusely for the expensive gift. Jesse didn't bother to try and explain it. He put his hoodie and down-filled vest back on.

They did find Kayla next. She had been sleeping next to Barb when they were thrown from the plane. Kayla was Passenger 23F. She was also a dancer and part-time hooker with a sleazy pimp. She was lightly dressed and shivering uncontrollably from the cold. While Barb helped her to her feet, Jesse found another suitcase with men's clothes in it. They slipped the oversized blue jeans over her thin pants and put her in a heavy Carhartt jacket. That was followed by three pairs of socks and a wool hat. Barb hugged her tightly until the color returned to her face.

Jesse could see that they were very confused and lost and needed a leader. So he had them help in his search for more survivors. And it seemed to help. The poor girls now had an important job to distract them from the surreal situation that surrounded them.

Cheryl's next two passengers were already dead. Their crumpled bodies lay in an undignified heap. She stretched them out, folded their hands over their chests, and covered their faces. She shook her head with a heavy heart and wanted to weep for them, but she didn't have time. "Sorry," was all she could do.

She had so much frozen terrain to cover and was afraid that more survivors would die of hypothermal before she could find them. She straightened up and continued on. She saw that Jesse had found more help.

A hundred yards in front of her, a man stood up, looked around, and staggered towards her. "Thank God." Cheryl quickly ran up to him.

"Are you okay?" She remembered him as passenger 28C, one of Fairbanks' Finest, the cop. "Boy, am I glad to find you. We really need someone to take charge and tell us what to do until rescue arrives." Cheryl was now feeling much better. "What is your name?"

"Steve," he said as he looked around still confused. "Where's Bobby?"

Steve Murphy was pushing forty, divorced, and between wives, which was a plague that affected a lot of police officers. He was trained in hostage situations and other crises, training that covered what to do at the scene of a plane crash. But unfortunately, it didn't cover what to do if one happened to be in the plane crash.

"Who's Bobby?" asked Cheryl.

Murphy turned and looked at Cheryl. His spinning brain was organizing his surroundings. He was taught not to panic and to survey the situation that was laid out in front of him before taking any course of action. "Bobby was my prisoner. I was taking him back to Fairbanks to stand trial... What's your name?"

"Cheryl," she said and became a little concerned. "Is he dangerous?"

"Not really. He's just a petty thief. He jumped bail and left the state. I was bringing him back to stand trial. I don't think he will get very far, if he tries to run in this country." Murphy regained his composure and looked around. "How many casualties are there?"

Cheryl shrugged her shoulders and was losing a little confidence in the distracted cop. "I am still looking for them. I could sure use your help, and maybe we can find your Bobby."

"Good idea. Which way do you want me to cover?"

Cheryl, alas, was still in charge. She pointed and sighed, "You take the center."

It was decided that they should put the survivors in the front half of the plane as a temporary shelter; it was the largest section of the fractured plane.

As Cheryl and Murphy helped passenger 15D, Bill Parker, who was injured and needed help walking, they passed poor old Jackson. He was still lying there with his frozen stare towards the cold blue sky.

"Are you dead yet?" asked Cheryl.

Both Murphy and Bill looked down at the inert man. He did look quite dead. Jackson never moved.

"He's dead Cheryl, let's go," said Murphy curtly.

"Just a minute." Cheryl had picked up a walking stick and used it to poke Jackson on his chest.

"**Confound it, woman**! I was almost there. Why can't you just let a man die in peace?"

Bill shrieked and Murphy almost jumped out of his shoes, which made him let go of Bill who promptly dropped to the ice. Murphy quickly helped him back up.

Jackson focused on Cheryl. "I don't suppose you have any more rum?"

Cheryl shook her head, "Sorry."

Murphy, a little embarrassed, decided to take charge and flex his authority. He unholstered his gun. "Sir, if you do not get up this instant, I will shoot you."

Bill looked up at the officer of the law incredulously. Cheryl snickered and Jackson chuckled. "What's your name sonny?"

"Officer Steve Murphy, sir."

"Are you always this funny?"

"No sir."

Cheryl looked at Murphy. "Leave him be, Steve. We have more passengers to save, ones that actually want to live."

"I guess you're right, sorry." Murphy looked back down at Jackson. "I am sorry, sir. I apologize for interrupting your untimely death."

Jackson nodded and went back to his cold stare of the heavens.

Cheryl and Murphy went back to helping Bill to the fuselage. After they made him comfortable, they continued their search for survivors. Murphy was especially aggressive in his search. He had a fugitive out there, and he planned to dog him to the ends of the earth, if that is what took. And, actually, he was searching for him near the north end of the earth.

CHAPTER 4

By late morning, the sun was fairly high in the southern sky, and the temperature rose up into the double digits, barely. The survivors were made comfortable in the fuselage that was once the front half of the plane. Spirits were high, as they waited for rescue. They ate what was left in the plane's galley, and they expected to see a rescue helicopter at any moment. What they didn't know was that all of the electronics on board were fried, and that there was no emergency locator signal coming from the plane. The plane's last signal was over Hudson Bay, and they were over a thousand miles from the search area. By spring the lake would melt, and all evidence of their existence would sink and become the unsolved file of flight *AS1125*.

The four surviving passengers that rode first class were not really suited for camping. The men were dressed in thin slacks, white shirts, and ties. And their wives were in tight skirts. The men were fairly amiable about it. They were happy to be alive. But the privileged women weren't quite so sporty. They immediately sent their husbands shopping for warmer clothes through the scattered debris. The poor husbands had to make several trips in order to find acceptable matching sweatpants and tops.

These two women stayed huddled up in the fuselage where it was warm and comfortable enough, that was until one of them had to go pee… and possibly the other. When they found out that the bathrooms were not on the section that they were congregated in, they were quite beside themselves. They made their important husbands take them to the section that had the small restrooms in it. When they got there, they found that this part of the plane was upside-down. And the facility that they urgently needed was quite unusable.

Passenger 2A, Edward, could not help himself and he chuckled. But it was cut short when his wife, Debra, gave him the look.

"It's okay honey. You can pee behind that bush."

Debra clenched her fists and glared at her stupid husband.

"Oh," said Edward. "You have to poo."

"Yes, you idiot. And I need some TP."

The wife of passenger 2C, Stephanie, volunteered her husband. "Ron, for Christ's sakes, go get her some toilet paper."

Ron sighed, "Sure thing, sweetie."

Since the rear fuselage's ceiling was now at ground level, he was able to walk in it without climbing. The aisle was empty so he had plenty of headroom. He made his way to the rear of the plane. When he reached for the door latch, he held his breath. Since the toilets were now up-side-down, he was uncomfortable with this part. He had to open the door or face his wife. He chose the lesser of two evils and pulled the doors latch. As the door swung open, he leaped out of the way. Nothing came out. It was amazingly clean in there. The vacuum mechanism in the toilets worked surprisingly well. Ron was pleasantly pleased.

After he retrieved the sacred paper, a little light went on in the business-box part of his brain. He now had access to a commodity that would soon be in great demand. He found a black garbage bag and stuffed it with all the TP that he could find. He hurried back to the poor waiting women.

After he handed Debra the emergency roll of paper, he took Edward aside. He showed him his sack of white, soft gold.

"Jesus, Ron. You're going to charge people to wipe their ass? Why don't you just twist the knife too."

Ron lowered his shameful head, "I suppose your right. It probably wouldn't have worked anyway."

"Look at this way. Now you will be a hero. Think how proud your wife will be. She might even…you know."

"A hero!" said Ron. "You're right. No wonder you're the senior executive."

The last two to be found alive were passenger 24B, Amy Nelson, and her fourteen-year-old daughter, Sophia. Her mother called her Phia for short. Amy was the one escaping a very abusive husband. The last time it happened, her daughter was traumatized and locked out the world around her, and she now stays somewhere deep in her head.

Phia was as tall as her mother, and she had dark wild eyes that now focused on nothing. Her long hair was black, cobalt black.

Cheryl found Amy curled around her daughter to protect and keep her warm. In her search for survivors, Cheryl had collected some warm clothes. When she found them, she dropped the clothing, knelt down, and felt for a breath. Amy squirmed and looked up at Cheryl. She shivered and tried to smile at her.

"Can you stand up? I brought you some warm clothes. Is this your daughter?"

Amy nodded and sat up but kept her daughter close to her.

Cheryl noticed her black eye and a bruised face. She assumed that it was from being tossed from the plane. She handed one of the heavy jackets to her. Amy immediately put it on her daughter. The daughter seemed complacent to Cheryl, maybe brain damaged. She helped Amy put the wool pants on her, and then she put a pink ski hat on her dark head, which made her look quite exotic.

"My name is Cheryl. What is your name?"

"Amy. And this is my daughter, Phia." Amy added, "She's autistic," which was a lie to cover up her traumatized daughter and the fact that they were running away from her husband.

Cheryl smiled at the girl. "Hi Phia." The girl seemed to ignore her.

"She's very shy," explained Amy.

Cheryl was becoming suspicious, but she had more important things to worry about. "Well, let's get you two back to our shelter. We have some food back there. It's not hot but it is edible."

Cheryl and Amy walked back towards the large plane section with each holding one of Phia's hands. As they walked past Jackson, Amy gasped when she saw him. "Oh, that poor man is dead."

Cheryl scoffed, "He's not dead."

Jackson scoffed. "Well, I could be! Well, I would be if you would stop interrupting my death, woman." With a disgusted sigh, Jackson sat up. "Who's your friend?"

"This is Amy and this is her daughter Phia."

Jackson grunted. "What kind of a name is, Phia?"

"It's short for Sophia," defended Amy. "Well, it just kind of morphed into Phia. When she was young, she was always getting into something. And I would yell, 'So…Phia, what did you do?' and so the name just shortened. She then asked, "What's your name?"

"Jackson, Frank Jackson, mam. Most people just call me Jackson."

Amy nodded at the old man. "Frank, well it does kind of describe you."

Jackson studied Phia for a few seconds and asked, what's wrong with your daughter?"

"She has autism."

"Autism? Hmm, can it be cured?" Jackson didn't wait for an answer. He turned to Phia and shouted, **"Sophia, child, be healed."**

"Jackson," shouted both Cheryl and Amy. "What are you doing?"

"Ah, I thought it might be worth a try, since that I was so close to meet-en God." Jackson slowly climbed to his feet.

"Be-ins that you two screwed that up, I might as well join you."

Phia regained her focus for a second and looked at Jackson with very curious eyes. Jackson was the only one to see it. He smiled and turned to Cheryl. "Maybe we can find another one of those little scotch bottles when we get back. I've developed quite a chill in me bones." Jackson looked up into the heavens and sighed, "Maybe tomorrow will be a better day to die."

CHAPTER 5

Bobby Walker, passenger 28A, was handcuffed to his seat when the plane made its unscheduled stop on the small frozen lake that lies somewhere above the arctic circle. When the plane broke up into four pieces and scattered its loose contents all over hell and high water, he stayed with the plane. He was handcuffed to his seat by his wrists. On the final violent spin of the rear half of the fuselage, his seat was ripped from its bolts and left the plane, passenger and all.

Our little lawbreaker landed at the far end of the frozen lake and disappeared into a snowdrift, and was, mercifully, knocked unconscious. A few hours later, he regained his senses and tried to move. Both wrists exploded in pain and he damn near passed out.

Moments later, and with tears in his eyes, he looked up at the sky. "What the fuck happened?" He was hypothermic and in extreme pain.

"Help, somebody, help me…please help me." His voice was weak and the plea was lost in the cold air. He listened for anyone out there. And he heard nothing. He realized that he going to die if he did not find help. He gritted his chattering teeth and got to his knees. When he looked down the lake, he could see people standing around a large section of the plane. His chest warmed with relief. He was not going to die alone out here.

He tried yelling again, but his voice was raspy and hoarse, and it was reduced to a loud whisper. The sun was now low on the horizon. It would be dark soon and the temperature was falling.

His wrists were still tethered to seat 28A. He was going to die if he did nothing.

And with excruciating pain, He got to his feet, and he slowly walked backward, dragging the seat with him.

Officer Murphy was still concerned about his missing prisoner. That was the one thing that he was responsible for. The cluttered chaos around him came second. He was confused and his rational mind was working like a squirrel in the center lane of a highway and unable to decide. So, this left Cheryl, as still the one in charge. And Cheryl was a deer in the headlights on the same highway.

After Cheryl got Amy and her daughter, and old Jackson, with the rest of the refugees, she went up the ladder to the seating area of the plane to check in on Autumn and copilot Dale. She found them unconscious but still breathing. By now it had become very cold in there. She went into the first-class section and retrieved blankets from the overhead compartments. When she returned, she slid her two friends close to each other to share body heat. They seemed to be spooning. She carefully covered them and sighed, "Now, you two behave yourselves."

As she left the cockpit, she remembered Jackson's request. She rummaged through the serving area of the plane and found two small bottles of *Cutty Sark*. She put them, and two bottles of rum, in her purse next to her cigarettes. She climbed back down and walked to the open end of the plane.

She discretely handed Jackson the scotch bottles.

"Bless you, Cheryl."

"What do you think we should do now, Jackson?"

"Well, mam, this country gets a might cold at night, and it's already getting close to dark. We should build a fire. You need to send every able-bodied man and woman to look for firewood and gather up all the clothes they can find to cover themselves tonight to keep from freezing."

Cheryl gave Jackson a relieved smile. She now had a direction. She was the only conscious representative of the airlines out here, so she was the one that had to take charge.

"Listen up everyone." Cheryl waited until all eyes were on her. "It will be dark soon, and it looks like we are not going to be rescued until tomorrow. We will need a fire. So, I want all you men to gather firewood. Since we will be sleeping here, I will need all you women to gather up all the clothes you can find so we can cover ourselves tonight." She paused. "Are there any questions?"

Passenger 27E, Albert Evans, raised his hand.

"Sir, what is your name?" asked Cheryl.

"Al."

"And what is your question?"

"Do we have radio contact with anyone?"

"I am sorry Al; the radio was damaged when we crash-landed."

"Um, mam…"

"My name's Cheryl."

"Um Cheryl, is there a locator beacon onboard?

"Yes Al, we have one on board. And if by chance it was damaged, we still have the black-box in the tail section. It automatically sends out a signal upon a crash. And it is virtually bulletproof." She turned to the rest of the passengers. "Are there any more questions?" No one raised their hand.

"Okay now, chop, chop. We are running out of daylight."

Albert Evans began mumbling to himself as he walked towards the scrub trees that lined this Godforsaken lake. He was the one that told his wife that he was just going out for a pack of cigarettes. Instead, he bought a plane ticket because he thought his life was too much to bear. He now wished he could go back to that previous life. He wished that he had bought the cigarettes instead. He really needed to smoke a cigarette.

It was passenger 23F, Kayla Adams that first saw poor Bobby Walker staggering backward towards her. The sun had gone down, but the twilight on the white snow-covered ground made the visibility good. She dropped the bundle of clothes that she had gathered and quickly made her way to the poor last survivor.

When Kayla reached Bobby, he collapsed on the ice-covered lake with tears in his eyes. Tears of intense pain were frozen on his cheeks. Both of his wrists were broken and bleeding.

"Why are you dragging that seat?" she asked. Bobby lifted his hands and exposed the cuffs. "Oh," she said. "You poor fucker." She turned and waved to her friend, Barbara. "Barb," she hollered. "I need some help here."

Barbara had an armload of nice fabric; she had gotten distracted by a suitcase that one of the women in first class had packed. She could hear the urgency in Kayla's voice and started to set down the clothes. But then she had second thoughts. She kept them under her arm and ran towards her friend.

"What do you need?" asked Barbara when she saw Kayla kneeling in front of a young man whose face was as white as a ghost. She gasped, "What the hell happened to him."

"He was chained to his seat."

"Why?"

"There're handcuffs."

"Oh…Is he dangerous?"

"No…I don't think so." Kayla looked down at Bobby. "Are you dangerous?"

"Are you both blond?"

They both nodded.

"What do you need me to do?" asked Barbara.

"I need you to drag his seat while I help this poor convict walk."

"Okay."

"Barb, what are you carrying?"

Barbara grinned and as she glanced around to make sure no one was watching. "Look at this." Out of her pile, she displayed a blue cocktail dress of smooth satin, which was low cut and sparkled even in twilight. Kayla stood up and took the dress, and she pressed it against her body. She twirled in it. "What do you think?"

Bobby groaned. "You know what I think, I think you should try on the dress, while Blondie here, runs and finds Officer Murphy and gets the keys to these damn cuffs. That's what I think. Oh, and let's try and do it before *the poor convict* **freezes** to death."

The two looked at each other and decided that the key would be a lot easier. "I'll get the key," said Barbara. She turned to leave and stopped in her tracks. "Don't try on that dress until I get back."

Jackson gathered what he called squaw wood. It was thin dry tree branches used as tinder for starting fires. The arctic tundra has thick vegetation, but the spruce trees never get very tall. The winters were too long and too harsh, and the growing season too short. If one were to take a sample of the tree rings, one would need a magnifying glass to count the rings. A tree five inches in diameter may well be a hundred years old. Firewood was going to be a precious item, if they were not rescued soon.

When Jackson returned with his kindling, he placed his bundle inside the cargo-bay area near the severed entrance. The floor was metal and fireproof, and he needed the heat inside the plane. Most of the smoke would follow the ceiling and exhaust out the open end. Hopefully, it would heat up the place enough to keep the survivors from freezing to death at night.

Jackson climbed up the ladder to the seating area. He rummaged through its serving area looking for paper towels, or napkins, or any loose paper to start his fire. He also really needed a decent knife, which is a very important survival tool. All he found was plastic eating-ware, since knives were forbidden on planes. The coffee pots were heated on an electric pad, but for the most part, they were metal and glass. They could be used to heat water on a fire. He started opening cupboard doors and he found some coffee. "Thank you, Jesus." He gathered it all. The last door he opened revealed a full bag of Reese's Peanut Butter Cups, and with a chuckle, he stashed them in his pockets.

He walked into the first-class section. The overhead bins were open and empty. He reached into one of the little magazine holders behind the seats and found what he was looking for, the Alaska Airlines Magazine. He now had plenty of paper to start his fire, something to read, and he would have hot coffee in the morning. Life was starting to sound…livable. After all, he now was almost back home and away from that insufferable heat, noisy traffic, and incessant city noise of Florida. He loved his daughter and his video-game playing grandchildren, but he just could not live there anymore. He was an old dog and not interested in any new tricks.

Jackson peeked into the cockpit before crawling back down to the cargo area. He saw the two covered lumps on the floor. He could see slight movement. They were still breathing. The third lump, the captain, was uncovered and quite dead. Jackson was pretty sure the other two would join him in death by morning.

Jackson climbed back down the ladder and began building his warm fire. And like moths to a flame, the light, and the warmth brought all the living passengers in a circle around the fire. They perked up and began chatting with each other. Surely, they would be rescued in the morning.

The last to join them around the fire was Officer Murphy with his criminal and the two young women that apprehended him. They had just gotten back. When Jackson saw Bobby's arms, he tore a T-shirt into strips and wrapped his bleeding wrists. He then placed two short sticks of firewood as splints on both wrists and wrapped them tightly with the remaining strips of T-shirt. He made a large sling out of another shirt and placed both of Bobby's arms in it. When he finished, he helped the poor man up close to the fire where he could sit and thaw. Jackson took one of his scotch bottles and placed the opened end next to Bobby's lips.

It took both bottles to relieve his pain and Bobby finally warmed enough to relax. With a relieved smile on his tired face, he thanked Jackson and promptly passed out.

Later that night, and after everyone had finally slipped into their own dreams, Jackson heard the howl of a lone wolf. He was starting to feel at home again. He added a little more wood to the fire and walked outside. The Northern Lights were dancing under the North Star. He inhaled the fresh cold air. He had also forgotten how much he had missed this cold country.

The wolf wailed again somewhere between him and the moon. When Jackson turned he could see the wolf on a distant hill. The proud animal stood with his nose pointed towards the winter moon and he howled again.

Suddenly Jackson chilled. He could feel it. Something wild was watching him. Instinctively, he reached for his hunting knife, but it was not on his belt. It was forbidden baggage on planes, all because some stupid terrorist took over a plane with a box cutter.

Helplessly, he quickly spun and saw two, wild, dark eyes staring back at him.

It was Passenger 24C, Phia.

CHAPTER 6

Sophia Nelson was born in a small farming community in Ohio. She came into this world kicking and screaming, bright-eyed and bushy-tailed. She was the apple of her father's eye. But sadly he died on her fourth birthday. She never got to know him, and her mother found it too painful to talk about him.

Amy remarried a couple of years later to a man that seemed to love her and her daughter. He took them to New York and life in the big city. It was good at first. But when things didn't go right at his job, Amy's new husband started drinking, and after that, he began taking it out on her. Soon that wasn't enough, and he began abusing Sophia.

The beautiful headstrong girl wilted into a shell. She shut down the human side of her brain and lived in the animal side for survival. That was when Amy decided that she and her daughter should disappear. She figured that her husband would never find them in Alaska. And as fate would have it, it looked like neither would anyone else.

When Jackson turned and saw Phia, she was looking at the distant wolf. His lone wail woke up something wild in her brain. The animal side of her heard the calling. She sniffed the cold night air and her dark eyes seemed to glow when she looked at Jackson.

He shivered. "Hello Phia. What are you doing out here?"

Phia ignored him and kept staring at the wolf's silhouette.

"We should go back by the fire. It is pretty cold out here, child."

She relaxed and went back to being a broken child. She lowered her head and just stood there.

Jackson slowly reached down and took her left hand and led her back to her mother. Her hand was surprisingly warm, very warm.

Jackson didn't bother sleeping that night. He made it his duty to keep the fire going, and to closely watch her, as he wondered about what was going on in this young girl's head. She was different.

Morning found the surviving passengers of flight *AS1125* in good spirits. They slept fairly comfortably and woke up with the smell of hot coffee. As they got up and warmed their hands by the fire, Jackson handed them a white cardboard cup of his coffee. Jesse Reed, who was going to Alaska to visit his brother, was the next one to amble his way. Jackson handed him a cup.

"Thank you," said Jesse. "How soon do you think we will be rescued?"

"I expect any time now," replied Jackson.

Jesse cradled his cup with both hands and smiled. Shortly, he asked, "Can I have another cup for Barb?"

Barb was the first girl that he had found and helped. After that, she stayed quite close to her hero. They kept each other warm last night. He was smitten, as was she.

Jackson handed him the second cup for his female friend and glance towards Phia. He caught a glimpse of her eyes as she quickly turned away. Jackson smiled and reached into his pocket and pulled out one of his Reese's Cups. He tossed it her way.

She ignored it.

"Well, if you don't want it…?" Jackson walked over and retrieved it. He took a step back towards his fire and stopped for a second. He opened the wrapper and bit the candy in half. She never looked at him. He laid the other half just out of her reach and went back to serving coffee. He watched her closely, but she never moved or looked his way.

Jackson served coffee and chatted with his customers, but always had an eye on the Reese's Peanut Butter Cup. Office Murphy was the next one to drift in for a cup of his coffee.

"How's the criminal this morning, Murph?" asked Jackson as he handed him his cup.

"Still sleeping. I got his legs tied. He ain't getting away again."

"Really?" scoffed Jackson.

"I'm just kidding." Murphy chucked. "I mean where could he go?"

"Here," Jackson handed him a second cup. "Take this to your prisoner."

As Murphy reached for the cup, Jackson glanced at the chocolate and peanut butter bait. It was still there. He blinked and it was gone. He looked at Phia and she was still motionless sitting next to her mother, Amy. He studied Phia's jaw and waited. And, nothing. She was quicker than a weasel. Game on.

He poured another cup of coffee and brought it to Amy. She was still sleeping. He looked at her daughter. She stayed still stoic. Jackson gently nudged Amy with his foot.

Amy blinked a couple of times and focused on Jackson. "Is something wrong?"

Jackson shook his head. "I figured you could use a cup of coffee this morning. Made it myself." Jackson raised his eyebrows, "Oh, did I wake you?

"No," lied Amy. She took the coffee and held it with both hands. The warm cup felt good on her cold fingers. She looked up at Jackson, and with a warm smile said, "Thanks." She sipped it slowly. She could tell that he had something on his mind. "Good coffee," she commented and waited for his question.

Jackson was very curious about her daughter and did have a couple of questions. But they were personal. He had no right to ask about their private lives. He decided to wait and watch.

The awkward silence was interrupted by passenger 2F, Stephanie. She was married to Ronald, the oil executive. She was also the one that had packed the expensive, blue cocktail dress. "Excuse me," she said with a hint of impatience.

"Yes, mam?" Jackson was relieved by the distraction.

"Would you please pour me a cup of coffee?" It wasn't really a question.

Jackson reached for one of the disposable coffee cups. He inspected it and blew out any dust or ashes that may have fallen in it.

Stephanie gritted her teeth with a little disdain.

Jackson poured and then he handed her the coffee.

"Thank you." She took the cup and politely ask, "Do you have any cream?" That was a question.

"Sorry, mam. We are out of cream." Actually, there might have been a lot of cream up in the plane's serving area. Jackson just never bothered to look.

Stephanie took a sip and pruned her face. She never drank it black before.

"Pretty good coffee, ain't it?"

Stephanie forced a nod and left.

Officer Murphy softened and seemed to take a liking for his little sarcastic prisoner. He held the coffee cup to Bobby's lips so he could drink, and between sips, he would ask questions about his life and where he went wrong. He was starting to feel a little sorry for him. That was until they both had finished their coffee, and Bobby informed him that he had to pee.

"Go ahead. You're not cuffed. Besides I trust you."

Bobby rolled his eyes and looked down at his useless hands. He looked back up at Murphy and shook his head. "I may need some help here."

"Oh, no," gasped Murphy, "No fucking way. You're just going to have to figure it out on your own."

"Awe, come on Murph, you can do it."

Murphy folded his arms and shook his head.

They were both interrupted by a chuckle. It was passenger 23F, Kayla the hooker. She was sleeping beside her friend, Barbara, who had just recently acquitted a nice blue dress. "I'll do it for ten bucks."

Bobby looked over at Murphy. "I don't have any money."

Murphy pulled out his wallet and found a twenty.

"Here," he handed Kayla the bill. "That should cover… two trips. Oh, and I will be needing a receipt." He helped Bobby to his feet. "Pee somewhere, where no one can see you."

Bobby nodded.

Kayla slipped her hand under Bobby's left arm and led him to a discrete spot. She gently unzipped him and reached in. Bobby, by this time, became a little gun shy, and his little tool shriveled in fear.

Kayla's hand finally retrieved the shy digit. "You know, I usually get paid a lot more to handle jobs like this."

"Please don't talk." Bobby suddenly couldn't pee.

"What are you waiting for?"

"Please look away and don't talk."

"Sorry," she snickered.

"And no laughing."

And with a very serious and solemn voice, she said, "I am very sorry." And then she burst out laughing.

Jackson was not as optimistic as his fellow passengers were. He was beginning to suspect that the locator signals were not signaling.

If rescuers were not here by now, something was wrong. There should have been high aircraft flying over them pinpointing their signal. He heard nothing. So he began anticipating a longer stay and really needed what was in his suitcase, or rather in his old, faded-green duffle bag. He finished drinking his coffee, buttoned up his mackinaw coat, and began his search.

The temperature was bitterly cold that morning. Without a blanket of clouds to hold the ground heat, the nighttime temperatures had plummeted. He could see his breath and his beard began frosting up.

He began walking towards the scattered debris on the lake. Most of the suitcases were opened and empty. Anything soft in them was taken to the fuselage to sleep on or under. None of them were his. His old duffel bag had to be buried in the deep snow in the tundra somewhere around the lake. He was wearing regular shoes and even with three pairs of socks on, his feet were becoming extremely cold. He began worrying about frostbite. He really needed to find his duffle bag with the winter clothes that he had packed in it.

He pulled out one of his Reese's Cups and tore off the wrapper and bit the round candy bar in half. It was frozen. He needed the energy. As he chewed, a set of tracks caught his eye. On further inspection, they revealed several sets. It was the pack of wolves that came through here last night. He was guessing they had caught a whiff of the dead. And then he heard a soft crunch in the snow behind him.

He was okay with death when he thought he was going to die from freezing, which is relatively painless, once the shivering stops, but being eaten alive, not so much. He turned slowly to see what predator was behind him. And there, crouched in the snow, was Phia. She was staring at his uneaten half of the chocolate.

"Hi Phia," said Jackson with a relieved smile. "What are you doing out here?"

She looked at his eyes.

Jackson held up the Reese's. "Do you want this?"

She kept her wild eyes on Jackson and remained silent.

"Can you speak?"

Her head shook ever so slightly.

"Do you understand me?"

The same negative head shake.

Jackson grinned. "Well, that's too bad. I was going to offer you this last piece of candy." Jackson threw it in his mouth and chewed in front of her.

Phia's eyes went cold.

"Oh, wait a minute, I just remembered." He reached into his pocket and pulled out another Reese's Peanut Butter Cup. "I was going to give this to you if you would help me find my bag. But since you can't understand me, I guess I will just have to eat it myself and look for my own bag."

Phia lowered her head and held out her hand.

"So, you do understand me."

She nodded.

Jackson placed the candy in her hand.

Phia clenched it tightly and said nothing. She backed up and started to walk in a tight circle as she sniffed the air. She began walking further onto the tundra. She walked and leaped through the deep snow like a deer. Her long thin legs were as strong as oak. Jackson trudged through the deep snow and broke into a sweat while trying to keep up with her.

Phia stopped to wait for the old man. When Jackson finally caught up, she was sitting on his faded-green duffel bag and eating the candy. She looked up at him and smiled, and her teeth were covered in a disgusting, chocolate-brown, gooey mess.

And, it was her first smile in over a year.

CHAPTER 7

Like a child at Christmas, Jackson hurriedly opened his old green duffel bag. He stood up and shook its contents onto the tundra snow. Phia watched curiously as she finished her peanut-butter-chocolate reward.

"Ah, there you are," sighed Jackson as he reached for his caribou mukluks. He hugged them to his chest like a long-lost love. He quickly kicked off his thin hiking boots and put on the mukluks. Instantly his feet warmed. The next item he fancied was his wolf-trimmed muskrat parka. He took off the Mackinaw jacket he was wearing and handed it to Phia. "Here put this on over your jacket."

Jackson put on the parka and pulled the hood over his scruffy face and grinned from ear to ear. He looked down at Phia and asked, "Don't I look handsome? This outfit is the rage in all the thriving igloo cities up here." He gracefully spun in a circle.

Phia cocked her head and just stared at him with an incredulous look on her face.

"Jesus, child. Ain't your mother ever taught you how to laugh?"

Phia ignored the question. Suddenly a light went on in her eyes. She padded the pocket of the red Mackinaw that she was now wearing and felt the Reese's. She formed her second smile. And a devious one it was.

Jackson gasped. "Now hold on there, missy. We have to ration those, and above all, they must be shared. Please hand them to me."

When Jackson reached for his stash of Reese's Peanut Butter Cups, Phia leaped like a gazelle. "Come back here, you little weasel."

Phia shook her head and opened one of the Reese's and tossed it between them.

Game on.

Jackson leaped for it, but it was gone before he got close. Jackson regrouped, as he watched her proudly munch away.

Phia tossed out another teaser.

Jackson looked his little opponent in the eye and folded his arms. "As my old friend, David Mamet once said, 'Old age and treachery will always beat youth and exuberance,' we shall see who has the last laugh."

Phia had no idea what the old man was talking about, but she knew that she was a thousand times faster than he was. Her eyes dared him to make the first move.

Jackson just shrugged his shoulders and stepped back. He turned and rummaged through his pile of stuff. Phia figured he was distracting her before he made his move. She watched cautiously. Jackson squatted with his back to her and began humming.

"This will do nicely." Jackson stood up holding something.

Phia quietly moved to her right. She kept a careful eye on the chocolate-covered bait.

Jackson had picked out a thick, red-flannel scarf. He put it over his head, around his neck, and with a flamboyant toss, he threw it over his shoulders. He turned towards her and proudly smiled. The scarf did look quite fetching on him. He motioned for her to come his way. She obliged. She knew the bait was still safe.

Jackson removed his beautiful scarf and put it over Phia's head, wound it around her neck, and carefully draped it over the front of her shoulders. He adjusted it and padded it so that it looked perfect on her. "That sure looks a lot better on you than it did on me. Turn around."

When Phia turned, Jackson laughed and dove for the prize. "Ha!" he said as he clenched his right hand on the snow-covered Reese's. He stood back up with a smug grin on his face. He opened his hand to show her that he had won. But alas, his hand only held packed snow. He looked back up at Phia, and now she had his smug look on her face.

"Ha!" she said as she started chewing Jackson's Reese's. It was her first word in over a year.

"Curses," he cursed.

Phia finished eating her prize and reached for another one. She really liked this game. But to her dismay, her pocket was empty. She looked at Jackson, who was now holding a fist full of prizes. While he was adjusting her scarf, he discretely picked her pocket. His fingers might be old but they were still in good working order. Once again, "Old age and treachery, love," chuckled Jackson.

Jackson went back to sorting his gear. He found what he really needed to survive out here. He fastened his hunting knife around his waist. He now felt fully dressed and completely at home. He put the rest of his stuff back into his duffle bag. "I think it's time we head back and get a cup of coffee. "Do you like coffee?"

She just snarled and refused to look at him. He wasn't nice like her mother. But something about him was different. He had a wild nature or attitude. She felt strangely intrigued and drawn to him.

As the day wore on, the group of survivors started to lose hope that they were soon to be rescued. They silently sat around the warm fire as they wished and longed to be home. By day's end, they had eaten up all the mixed-nut packages and the small condiment envelopes of sugar, and creamer, and ketchup, and even the mustard. They were becoming rather hungry, a little agitated, and very worried.

"Well don't you look authentic," remarked Cheryl, when Jackson returned wearing his fur parka.

Jackson smiled at her, "And pretty too."

Cheryl laughed. "We are getting a little low on firewood, and it looks like we will be spending another night out here."

"I noticed that. I will fetch some right now. You might want to send some of the men out to help me. It will give them something to do, and it will occupy their unhappy heads."

"That's a good idea. How about the woman?"

"I'm thinking that the woman should look for suitcases." Jackson pointed up at the hazy sky. "There could be a storm a come 'en. After they gather them, they need to fill them with snow. We will use them to build a wall in front of the opening in the plane. That will give us a little more security and help to keep the wind and snow from blowing in, and it should hold in a little more heat."

Cheryl nodded and sent the men out for firewood and the women out for their project.

Jackson motioned to Officer Murphy to follow him.

Murphy nodded and left the circle of fire. He followed Jackson to the end of the frozen lake. He could see the serious look on his face. "What are you thinking, Jackson?"

"Can you hit anything with that shooter that ya got strapped to your side?"

Murphy nodded. "Why?"

"I fear that rescue might be a while or they would have been here by now. We need to find something for these people to eat. I saw a moose track near this end of the lake."

"This pistol is only a .38 caliber, Jackson. That's a little light for a moose, and it is only accurate at a pretty short range."

"The tracks were made by a cow moose. They're smaller, and a moose is a big target. You will have to sit and wait for her to come to you. Put a round in her chest area behind her front legs and centered it on her body. If you're lucky you might hit the heart, but most probably the lungs. If you hit the animal, do not move, or it will panic and run. You wait until it drops; it could take a couple of hours."

"Do you want me to go hunting now?"

Jackson studied the northern sky. He could see a dark cloud forming on the horizon.

"Not today. There's a storm coming. The moose will be hunkered down soon and won't start browsing until after the storm." Jackson looked back at Murphy "Say, Murph, how many rounds do you have for that thing?"

"Just what's in the revolver, six."

"Geese, Murph. You didn't pack any ammunition?"

"Of course I did. I packed half of a box in my overnight bag. And when I found it, its contents were scattered in the deep snow. Believe me, I looked a long time for them. But I did find my toothbrush."

"Your toothbrush!" laughed Jackson. "Without bullets and nothing to eat, you're not really going to need that toothbrush, are you?"

Murphy chuckled at Jackson's comment. "I still have six bullets. That's six moose, if I do it your way. That's a lot of meat." Murphy noticed a concerned look on Jackson's face. "What's wrong?"

Jackson stroked the gray, curly hair flowing down his chin. "You see that mountain range over there?"

Murphy looked to where Jackson was pointing. "Yes."

"I am pretty sure that is Alaska's, Brooks Range.
"Sooo?"

"I am thinking of heading that way after this storm is over. That's my home and I'm sure I can find help and rescue. If you keep everyone in meat and firewood, you should be fine."

"How long do you think it will take you?"

"Maybe a week, maybe a month, maybe more. Depends on the weather and…" Jackson paused. There were a lot of things that could happen between here and there. "…and how soon I find anyone, or a cabin with a radio where I will call for help.

"Another thing Murph, I don't think our plane is sending a signal. I think I am your best bet."

"I was beginning to think the same thing."

"Let's gather some firewood and get back to the plane."

As the woman packed the suitcases, pillowcases, backpacks, and any hollow container with snow, the men began building the crude wall at the open end of the their fuselage-shelter. The mood perked up with everyone now busy improving their refuge. A blanket was used as a door, and a small opening was left at the top of the wall to let out the smoke from their warm fire. When it was finished, the survivors went inside and thawed out. Their round, metal cabin in the middle of nowhere, was now surprisingly warm and snug.

Cheryl climbed up the ladder to the seating area of the fuselage to check in on her two unconscious friends. She found that they had died, and this brought a flood of tears to her eyes. She said a quick prayer over them.

"I guess you don't really need your blankets anymore." She said to her friends with a sincere apology. "The living will need them a lot more." She gently removed their coverings and climbed back down to the cargo hold. Cheryl distributed the blankets.

Jackson and Murphy made their way through the blanket-door. Both were carrying an armload of firewood. Jackson was impressed with the wall and the amount of wood the other passengers had already gathered. They placed their bundles on a neat pile near the entrance. It looked like two days' worth of firewood or better. Murphy joined Bobby who was in a one-sided conversation with

Kayla, the hooker. She was doing all the talking. Jackson went to his spot between the fire and Phia.

Jackson took a long log and put one end in the fire. They had no way to cut them, so they just slid them onto the hot coals as the ends burned off. It was a lot less work this way, and the logs had plenty of room in the long fuselage-cabin for the unburned ends. As Jackson warmed his hands, he realized how much he had missed these warm fires on cold days. Although if he had a comfortable rocker and a bottle of single malt, it would have made it a little better. Survivors can't be choosy.

Cheryl joined Jackson and warmed her hands.

He looked over and smiled at her. He saw her red eyes. "What's the matter, Cheryl?"

"Dale and Autumn have died." She continued her stare at the fire.

"Sorry," was all Jackson could think of to say. He put an arm around her. She turned and put her arms around his waist and began sobbing on his shoulder.

The storm came in fast with thirty-mile-an-hour wind and with thick heavy snow. It was a typical arctic blizzard. The snow was blinding and stung like tiny white bees. The storm will last over a day and a half, and it will completely bury all signs of the crash site. They will be completely invisible from the air. And, there will be no moose hunting, until the weather has cleared. And their food situation was already critical.

Jackson slept comfortably that night. Cheryl curled up against his back and they kept each other warm. It had been a while since Jackson had a warm body next to his. He missed his wife and the simple life they had on that nameless stream south of the Brooks Range.

After seven hours of sleep, Jackson's old body ached and it told him that it was time to get moving. He eased out of their nest. Cheryl groaned from the chill. Jackson smiled and covered her with his parka. She relaxed and disappeared under the extra covering like a hibernating bear.

Jackson took her flashlight and climbed up out of the cargo hold and into the plane's cabin area. He began another search of the serving area for whatever might be left. He hummed and he hawed as he searched. "Jesus, this galley is barer than Mother Hubbard's cupboards." His search did produce a few teabags, some instant coffee packages, some pepper, and a little salt. He also found a plastic washtub in with the medical supplies. He put his stash in it and went back to his fire.

He dumped yesterday's used coffee grounds into the tub. He emptied the tea bags and instant coffee packages into it and added some of the pepper, and a pinch of salt. He went to the firewood and gathered spruce needles off the smaller branches. He added those to his strange blend. He mixed the concoction with his bare hands and then he added a little of it to each boiling coffee pot. He was the first to taste his witch's brew.

"Hmmm, not bad. I shall call my coffee blend, *Arctic Grog*." He took another sip and nodded his pleased head.

Shortly Phia joined him. She was chewing away on a Reese's Peanut Butter Cup. Jackson had left the parka that covered Cheryl, unguarded. "Oh, you're a sly one." He said as he poured her a cup of *Arctic Grog*. "Here, this will put a little hair on your chest."

Phia took the cup with a confused look on her face. She took a small sip. She found it not unpleasant. She nodded and retrieved another Reese's Cup from her pocket and handed it to Jackson.

"Thanks," said the scruffy old sourdough, as he touched his cup to hers. "Good morning."

CHAPTER 8

The blizzard howled and growled all the next day. Jackson's Grog kept hunger at bay, and most of the surviving passengers found it quite acceptable. Although Stephanie, from first-class, still complained that she needed creamer.

Jackson noticed that Phia's mother, Amy, did not come to the fire and share a cup of his famous grog. He poured her a cup and took it to her. "Good morning, Amy. I brought you a cup of coffee. Are you feeling okay?"

Phia helped her mother to a sitting position.

"Thanks," said Amy as she took the hot drink. "I feel fine." She sniffed the hot brew. "I just seem to be tired a lot lately." She took a sip. "Humm…Maybe I am sick. This doesn't taste much like coffee." She took another sip. "It's not bad. What blend is it?"

Jackson grinned. "It's my own personal blend. Most of it is homegrown right here, and it is organic."

"Homegrown?" she took another sip and lowered her eyebrows in thought. "What's your secret ingredient?"

"Scrub-spruce needles, mam, the scrubbier the better."

Amy laughed, which ended in a cough. "Sorry," she said and wiped her mouth with her sleeve. "I noticed my daughter has been following you around. She has not spoken or even made eye contact with strangers for over a year now. What's your secret?"

Jackson shrugged his shoulders. "It must be my puppy-dog smile. Well, that and Reese's."

"Reese's?"

"The candy. You know, the chocolate-covered peanut butter cups. I would show you one, but I seem to be out of them." Jackson looked at Phia and lowered his bushy eyebrows.

Phia ignored the insinuation.

Amy chuckled, followed by a small cough. She took another sip, which seemed to soothe her throat. "Has she spoken to you at all?"

"No mam. But I do find that a good quality in a woman."

Amy smiled. "Are you married?"

Jackson shook his head. "My wife died five years ago."

"Sorry. I take it that she did not speak much."

"Not much in English. She was half Athabaskan."

"Any children?"

"I have a son and a daughter."

"Grandchildren?"

"Three, my daughter moved to Florida with her military husband. She has three kids. They spend their time pecking away at their cell phones. I just came from there. I got claustrophobic and began missing the open country."

"What about your son?"

Jackson inhaled a sad breath. "I had a falling out with my son years ago and he left. All I know is that he is living in a small house near Fort Yukon with an Athabaskan woman and he races sled dogs."

"Oh, I am so sorry. Sounds like you two might be alike. Are you going to try and find him?"

"I don't know." Jackson sighed.

But deep down, while his aching gut was screaming, 'Yes,' his stubborn brain was saying, 'No,' and his big heart was siding with his gut.

"Maybe."

Amy finished her grog and laid back down. Her breaths were short and a little ragged. Phia made eye contact with Jackson.

"She will be fine, little girl. We have all been through a lot." He could see the fear in Phia's eyes. He felt helpless and wanted to do something, anything for her. As a strong, independent man, this helplessness made him very angry.

That evening, Murphy made his way to Jackson. "Do you hear it?"

Jackson strained his ears trying to hear what Murphy had heard. Nothing. It was as quiet as a church. "Ah, yes I do Murph. The storm has quit us. I do believe that it's time to go hunt-en."

Jackson put on his parka and crawled through the blanket door. Murphy followed.

The sky was clear and full of stars, and the Northern Lights were dancing between them and the moon. The clear night, with twinkling lights and a bright moon, would now light up their world more than the disappearing sun. The snow had drifted high around the larger plane parts and completely covered what was left. Even if a search plane flew over now, Jackson knew it was hopeless. But the good news was that the visibility on the ground was excellent.

"Yep, I think that it is time to go moose hunting, Jackson."

"I couldn't agree more, Murph." Jackson sniffed the air. It was still above zero. "Do you have your gun?"

Murphy padded his right hip. "I never leave home without it."

Jackson led the way.

The small lake was still windblown and smooth. Once they reached the end of it, the snow deepened making the progress slow. They worked their way over the tundra, trudging and tripping over snow-covered tussocks as they worked their way up a small hill. Once there, they scanned the moon-lit patches of willows looking for a browsing moose.

In this country, ptarmigan, snowshoe hare, and arctic fox are invisible with their white feathers and fur. Whereas, the moose stays a nice dark color year-round, and he is a lot bigger. But, he is elusive and moves slowly, and in the brush, with the twilight sky, he is very hard to spot. It takes patience.

Jackson studied a large patch of willows not far from them. A miniature fog rose out of its center. It could be nothing, or it could be the frozen breath of a bedded moose.

"Do you see anything?" whispered Murphy

"Shhh," whispered Jackson, as he pointed towards the frozen vapor.

The willows under the frozen breath moved, and a large bull moose climbed to his feet. He shook the snow off his back, and then he spread his back legs, and with a grunt, he relieved himself. After he peed he began browsing on the willows. The two hunters dropped to their knees.

Thirty minutes later the bull began browsing their way. Jackson positioned Murphy behind a small clump of spruce trees. "Wait here," he whispered. "Remember the three things that I told you. Patience, and patience, and don't miss. I will stay out of sight and downwind of him."

Jackson turned to crawl down the backside of the hill. He looked back at Murphy and whispered, "Not to worry you, but everyone's life depends on this shot, Murph."

Murphy tightened his lips and pulled his hand out of his pocket and gave Jackson the appropriate sign language. Murphy then put his hand back in his pocket to keep his trigger finger warm and ready.

Jackson crept out of sight as he worked his way around the moose. He wanted the bull to be between him and the lake. He took a slow peek occasionally to stay on track.

A bone-chilling hour dragged by, as the moose browsed back and forth around Murphy. Murphy held his stance. He didn't panic. He patiently waited for the right time. Jackson took another look. The moose was close. Jackson quit breathing, as he waited for the shot. It had to be only seconds but it felt like an eternity, and finally the shot rang out as it shattered the frozen silence across the tundra.

Jackson climbed to his feet. The bull moose leaped into the air and spun in a circle. He was confused and angry at what had stung him. He huffed, but saw no enemy. A trickle of blood dripped from his nose. It was a lung shot. He went back to browsing.

"Perfect," Jackson said to himself. This animal weighed over a thousand pounds. It was too big to drag back. It would have to be cut up into small pieces and packed back a little at a time, leaving it available to the wolves between trips.

Jackson began walking slowly back and forth without making eye contact. The moose looked at Jackson and studied him for a second. He could see that it was not a wolf and did not appear to be threatening. He continued to browse, but shied away from the irritating animal behind him.

Soon his chest began hurting. He now wanted to lie down, but he did not trust the annoying two-legged critter behind him. He quit browsing and began walking towards the lake. He was now losing a lot of blood from the hole in his chest and was coughing up more from his lungs. Jackson shortened the distance between them.

The moose moved out and onto the lake. Oxygen was not getting to his muscles. He knew something was wrong. He now blamed the animal that was slowly trailing behind him. He stopped and waited, and when Jackson stepped onto the lake, the moose dropped his head, laid back his ears, and charged.

Cheryl, now the last living representative of the airlines, considered it her duty to be responsible for the passengers. After Jackson and Murphy left the plane, she began making her rounds and reassure her travelers. According to the watch she had on her wrist, it was late in the evening, and everyone was retiring for the night, even though the night sky was brighter than the daytime's blizzard sky.

Amy's cough got Cheryl's attention. She quickly went to her and knelt down. "Hi Amy, are you all right?"

Phia was on her other side. She was holding her mother's hand and had a very worried look on her face.

Amy opened her eyes and forced a smile. "Hi, Cheryl." Her reply was weak as she struggled to a sitting position with Phia's help. "It's this damn cold weather. I am constantly tired and this cough won't let me sleep."

"You poor dear." Cheryl rummaged through her pockets and found a bottle of aspirin. She shook out two tablets and looked at her daughter. "Phia, please get me a cup of water."

Phia nodded and let go of her mother's hand. She quickly went to the coffee pots that had been filled with snow and were thawing by the fire. She poured a cup of the melted water and returned to her mother and gently put it in her hand.

Cheryl handed Amy the aspirin. "I think we might have some cough drops up in the serving area." She climbed to her feet. "I will be right back."

"I know that he is hoarding the creamer from me, Ron," scoffed Stephanie.

"Who is?" asked Ronald, passenger 2C, to his wife.

"That grizzled old man that makes that disgusting excuse for coffee."

"Now, now, Steph, why would he do that?"

"Because he has to ride in coach class, and he hates us in first class. We earned it. We worked hard for it, Ron."

"Yes dear, we have."

"And another thing, I found my suitcase, and I am missing a few things out of it."

Ronald leaned back and folded his hands. "Well Steph, pretty much everyone's luggage broke open and was scattered in the snow. Your things could be just lost." He tried to sound sincere, but there was a hint of a patronizing tone in his voice. "What are you missing?"

"I am missing my blue cocktail dress, Ron," she scoffed. "And I suspect a she-wolf took it."

"Why would a wolf take your blue dress?"

Stephanie leaned into her husband and said, "I'm talking about a two-legged wolf, you idiot."

"Oh!"

"I think I have to pee," pleaded Bobby to Kayla.

"No you don't," replied Kayla, firmly. She was comfortably warm and wanted to stay that way.

"Yes, I do. It is urgent. And I really need your help." Bobby shrugged his shoulders and held up his splinted wrists for emphasis.

"Hold it, pervie. It's fucking cold out there."

"I can't. Please, I need your help."

Kayla shook her head and slowly got to her feet, she then helped Bobby to his. As they walked to the blanket-door, she informed him, "I swear, if you don't pee, I will turn you into a…" She paused suddenly, when she heard it. "Was that a gunshot?"

CHAPTER 9

A pack of wolves is a group of family members just trying to make a living. You could compare them to any family. The head of the family is the alpha male followed by his mate, the alpha female. And then there are the children, the pups, followed by a few aunts and uncles. It is a close group. They play and hunt together. The older members teach the art of the kill to the young. In this society, they look out after the old and the injured, and they are affectionate to each other. They seem so nice for professional killers.

The alpha male was kicked hard and broke a few ribs during their last hunt. It was a large bull moose that the pack had taken on. Normally they do not go after an animal this large, but the caribou had migrated on, and they were down to eating snowshoe hares and lemmings. Today the alpha female was leading the hunt. Her injured mate stayed back at the den and was left in charge of last summer's pups.

She was cautious of men and tried to stay clear of them. But a new group of these two-legged species showed up in her territory, and she began watching them very closely. They were different from the others, and they had shown up suddenly from the sky. She watched their strange and unusual habits. She did not trust them and kept her family at a safe distance. Today's hunt was with her sisters, their mates, and her older daughter.

The storm had just ended and she knew that the clear skies would bring out hungry mammals, both large and small. She pointed her nose at the moon and howled, signaling that it was time. The other hunters crawled out from the den and anxiously followed her across the wide tundra.

When she had heard the gunshot, she stopped. She sniffed the air and cautiously led her group towards the sound. She saw a man and a moose not far from their strange human village on a frozen lake. She sniffed the air and detected two men. The second man was not far from them. She also smelled blood, as did the rest of the wolves. They crouched down and patiently watched.

The two men began following the moose. She and her pack silently followed the distracted men. The smell of blood overrode their caution. The moose walked out on the lake, and she could tell it was weakening, but she didn't trust the men. She had seen the devastation that followed the explosive noise that these creatures sometimes make. She crept closer.

Phia was holding her mother's hand, when she heard the shot. Being young and raised in Florida, she had never heard a real gunshot, except for the ones on TV. This one sounded a little different. She gently placed her mother's hand under the blanket. She was sleeping. Phia looked around. No one else seemed to have heard it. She put on the red mackinaw coat, pulled the hood over her head, and slipped outside.

Bobby and Kayla were standing just outside the entrance and staring down the lake. Apparently, they also had heard the shot.

"Hi," said Kayla.

Phia dropped her head and said nothing.

"She can't speak," informed Bobby to Kayla. "I think she is brain-damaged."

Kayla scoffed. "*Challenged*, is the word, dummy. She's mentally challenged."

Bobby ignored his new girlfriend, as he scanned the area where he thought the shot came from. He saw movement on the far tundra, and with his splinted arm, he pointed across the lake. "Look, there is a moose coming our way."

Kayla studied the large brown object slowly moving over the tundra. She was from New York and had never seen a moose before.

Phia discretely looked in the direction he was pointing. She saw the huge animal coming their way. And he had a very impressive set of antlers crowning his head. He looked quite dangerous.

"Look," said Bobby. "I think that's Jackson following it. He must have shot it." A light went on in Bobby's eyes. "Oh my God, doesn't a moose steak really sound good? I wish we had some potatoes to go with it… and beer."

Phia also recognized Jackson. You couldn't help it. He was the only one there with a fur parka. But he looked so small compared to that moose. Phia took off running.

"Where's she going?" asked Kayla.

"Like I said, she's brain-damaged."

"*Challenged*, you idiot."

Jackson was trying to gently herd the thousand-pound animal towards the shelter at the far end of the lake. As he stepped on the windswept ice, his eye caught a red object moving fast down the lake. It was his mackinaw, and Phia was in it, and she was running his way.

In the distraction, he missed seeing the angry moose, as it tipped his antlers forward and charged towards him. The bull wanted nothing more than to stomp this annoying animal to death. He was sure it had something to do with the pain in his chest.

When Jackson saw Phia, he began running to head her off. He became fearful for her because there was a wounded animal between her and him.

And that's when it happened.

"Waoo," howled the she-wolf to her pack, and she charged the moose. Her loyal family followed. She was the first to leap on the moose's back. And the second wolf leaped for the neck, and he sunk his teeth into it. The enraged moose violently spun and shook loose the two wolves. The alpha she-wolf landed on Jackson, knocking him to the ice. The rest of the pack instantly joined their leader and leaped as one, completely overpowering the weak moose. The moose went down and never got back to his feet. It was over in seconds.

Both the she-wolf and Jackson scrambled to their feet and snarled at each other. Each was afraid to take their eyes off the other. As Jackson slowly backed up, he was suddenly knocked off his feet by Phia.

Phia was on all fours and faced the alpha female. The wolf sensed she was protecting the old man. She had never seen this in these two-legged predators before. She accepted Phia's actions as caring. She closed her mouth and yipped, and then she went back to her pack. It was time to feast.

By this time, Murphy had caught up to Jackson with his gun drawn and pointed at the wolf. Jackson stood up and placed his hand over the revolver. "It's okay, Murph. Let them have their fill. They earned it. There will be plenty left for us."

Kayla turned to Bobby and hugged him. "Wow, did you see that? Those dogs killed that moose."

Bobby hugged her back. "Those are not dogs. They are gray wolves in the wild. You have witnessed something very few people have ever seen. And I don't think that girl is as challenged as I thought she was."

Kayla separated their hug and winked at Bobby with excited eyes. "Do you still have to pee?"

"Maybe."

In the pack was a young she-wolf, the two-year-old daughter of the alpha female. She was a little small for her age, and this was her first time on a moose. She watched carefully, as her aunts and uncles took down the moose. Her job on this hunt was to learn. The human in the red coat got her attention. Her mother had shown these two-legged animals to her and told her to beware of these cunning creatures, and yet her mother confronted one and accepted it without fear. This had made her very curious. As the rest of the pack tore into the belly cavity of the moose, she sniffed the air and the human scent. She then worked her way for a closer look at the human. When she got close, she crouched down and listened to their strange sounds.

Jackson took hold of Phia's hand and stood her between him and Murphy. "God Almighty, little girl, you could have been killed. Don't you ever do that again!"

Phia looked into Jackson's eyes, confused. She was being scolded for coming to his aid. She let go of his hands and indignantly folded her arms. She turned and looked towards the feeding pack. Out of the corner of her eye, she saw the lone wolf crouched in tufts of grass on the lake's edge. The wolf was barely visible, and it was watching her. Phia approached. Jackson and Murphy were distracted by the feeding frenzy.

As Phia edged closer, the young wolf instinctively raised the hair on its back and bared its teeth. Phia stopped and cocked her head. They both stared at each other's dark eyes. Phia squatted. Both were fearless.

The wolf stood up and added a slight growl. Phia grinned, which showed her teeth. They were flat and not at all threatening. The young wolf would have laughed, if it could. It closed its mouth and then sniffed the air for a scent of fear.

Phia stood back up and approached. The young wolf held her ground. Phia calmly walked up to it and knelt down in front of it. She held her hand close to the wolf's muzzle. The young wolf sat down and tasted the human by licking her hand. Phia scratched her behind the ears. It was friends at first sight.

Jackson glanced over at Phia and saw her with the wolf. "Jesus, Murph, would you look at that?"

Murphy's jaw dropped to his neck. "I don't believe it."

After a twenty-minute feast, the alpha female barked a command. Each wolf tore off a piece of meat to take back to the den and the waiting hungry pups. She howled, and they all began loping across the tundra. The alpha female noticed that she was missing her daughter. She stopped and howled long and hard.

The young wolf in front of Phia rolled her head back and answered the call. Each wolf has its own voice just like humans. It was her mother calling, and she called back. The young she-wolf spun in the snow and leaped onto the tundra and was soon gone.

CHAPTER 10

Jackson pulled out his hunting knife and gently rubbed his thumb across the blade. It was still sharp. He grinned and looked up at Murphy and asked, "Are you hungry?"

Murphy vigorously rubbed his tummy. "I'm as hungry as a wolf."

"Grab a leg, Murph, help me get this thing skinned."

The moose was laying on its right side. Murphy got a hold of the left back-leg and pulled it up in the air. Jackson started just below the hoof and made a long slice from there to the animal's vent. He carefully began separating the skin from the meat. Once the hide was removed from the leg, he worked his way across the body and to the front leg. When the left side was skinned, it was time to roll the moose so that Jackson could skin out the other side.

"Phia," called Jackson; she was intently watching the butcher with mixed emotions. "Grab the other leg and help me roll this thing on its other side." Murphy pulled on the hind leg while Jackson and Phia tugged on the front one. The large moose didn't budge, it was too heavy.

By this time, rumor had it that there was food at the other end of the lake. Jackets were donned and every able-bodied man was scurrying towards Jackson and real food, meat. Most of the women were right behind them. Jesse and his new girlfriend, Barbara, the exotic dance, were the first to arrive. They quickly latched onto the hind leg with Murphy. Albert, the factory worker, and Ronald, the suited oil executive, arrived next. They help Jackson and Phia with the front leg, and with a gaggle of grunts, they rolled the moose.

Jackson's sharp knife soon made short work of the large animal. When Bull Winkle was naked, Jackson cut off a front shoulder and boned it out. He sliced it up into small pieces and wrapped them in a piece of moose hide. "Here," he said to Cheryl. "I think it is time to feed your passengers." She handed the hefty package to one of the men, and everyone left for the cooking fire in their shelter.

Jackson stayed and finished cutting up the meat. Phia also stayed and silently watched. Jackson piled the meat in the snow but left the leg bones and the ribs for the wolves and ravens. He cut the hide into thin strips, while it was soft and pliable. Once he was back inside, he planned to smoke the rawhide, which would crudely cure it into stiff leather. The thinner strips, he planned to weave into rope, and with the wider ones, he was going to make snowshoes. He was getting ready to leave. He saved out a thick piece of moose-hide from the back to make a crude pair of mukluks for Phia. He was worried about the child, especially since her frail mother became sick. He suspected she had pneumonia.

Before Jackson left the remains of the moose, he removed the tongue. It was his favorite. The meat was white like pork and almost as sweet in flavor. His second favorite was the fresh liver, but the wolves had already consumed all the organs in the chest cavity.

Before he left, he found two long willow branches. These he would thaw by the fire and slowly and carefully bend them into the shape of snowshoes. With a backpack of dried meat, he was sure that he could make it to the mountains, and once there, find help and rescue for these poor air-wrecked passengers. He felt good again. He now had a purpose in life. He was needed and very much alive. It was good to be so close to home.

Jackson baked his tongue in a makeshift oven that he made from a small piece of plane metal that he covered with hot coals. He shared the rich meat with Phia's mother and she seemed to perk up. She ate it ravishingly, and when she finished the last morsel, she licked her fingers, and the color came back to her face along with a satisfied smile.

Jackson made her a cup of spruce-needle tea, and they relaxed and talked. Phia just listened.

Amy sipped the bitter but soothing, hot tea. "Mr. Jackson, do you believe in God? By the way, what is your first name, again?"

"It's Frank, mam. Just call me, Jackson."

"Frank, is that short for Francis?"

Jackson nodded. "Only my mother called me Francis."

"Do you mind if I call you Francis?"

"I guess not. There was a time, when I was grow'en up, that I fought many a school-mate for calling me that. But it does sound nice to hear it again from you."

Okay, Francis, do you believe in God?"

"You sure don't believe in small talk, do you?"

Amy smiled. "Well?"

Jackson sipped his tea. "Sometimes. I was a firm believer, when the plane was crashing. I guess I still believe in Him out here. This is definitely God's country. But when I am in the city for any period of time and see all the senseless crime and shootings, well, not so much."

Amy nodded. "I went to church every day, when my husband started having problems at work. He tried to solve his problems with his friend *Jack Daniels*. It seemed the more I prayed, the angrier he became. And he began taking it out on, first me, and then on Phia."

"Your husband, is he Phia's father?"

Amy shook her head. "Her father was part Mohawk Indian and he was a marine, special forces. He was killed somewhere in the Middle East, when Phia was a small girl."

Phia didn't like listening to this part. So, she silently put on her coat and slipped outside. The moon was just setting and the stars were the only thing lighting up this cold isolated part of the world. She could see her breath, as she walked through the soft snow. The temperature was dropping into the negative double digits. She shivered and pulled the hood over her head. She decided to look for firewood.

She heard a young wolf howl in the distance. She recognized the voice. Phia howled back, but received no response for a few minutes, and then she heard it again. It was a lot closer. She ran towards the voice. The snow deepened, as she sprinted off of the windswept lake. She kept running and leaping over the drifted snow. She stopped to catch her breath and threw her head back and howled.

She listened.

A lone distant owl was the only thing that answered her call. She was sure the first howl was the young wolf that confronted her at the moose kill.

"Where are you?" she whispered. It was the first sentence that she had uttered in over a year. She listened, and ever so softly, the snow behind her made a crunching sound. She turned slowly and faced her new friend.

The young wolf was cautious. It sniffed its new, hooded friend and approached.

Phia got down on her knees and held out her hands. The young wolf wanted to play and leaped into her lap, and they both rolled in the snow. Phia laughed out loud and hugged her new furry friend.

The young she-wolf was darker than the rest. She was more of a chocolate color, and she was mottled with silver hair rather than the gray on the other wolves. Phia smiled at her and said, "I shall call you Reese."

Reese barked her approval.

For an hour they played in the cold powder snow. In a couple of hours, the sky would brighten and the sun would peek over the southern horizon for about two hours, and then it would disappear for another twenty-two. It would be even less tomorrow. A wolf howl interrupted their play.

Reese threw back her head and answered her mother. She looked at Phia and yipped something, and then she turned and loped effortlessly through the deep snow and back to her family.

"Goodbye, Reese, goodbye," sadly said Phia to her friend, as the young wolf disappeared in the dark. Her voice was rusty, but she liked speaking again, even if it was only to her secret friend. With an excited breath, she worked her way back to her mother and the rest of the stranded and worried passengers.

Amy closed her eyes and took a short breath. She was tiring. "Francis, my daughter has pretty much not left my side for over a year now. But now in less than a week, she seems to be coming out of her shell. Has she spoken at all to you?"

"Not really mam, but she seems to communicate very well with her eyes."

"Francis, please call me Amy."

"Yes mam, I mean Amy." Jackson glanced over towards Phia. She wasn't there. He looked around with a puzzled look on his face. "Where's Phia, Amy?"

"Oh, she left about an hour ago. She seems to be getting her independence back. I blame that on you, Francis."

Jackson bowed his head. "I am sorry, Amy. I really didn't…"

"No Francis, it is a good thing," interrupted Amy. "And she seems to like you." Amy took a quick gasp of air, leaned back, and closed her eyes. Her breaths were short.

"Francis," she whispered, "If anything happens to me, promise me you will protect her."

Jackson nodded his head. "Nothing is going to happen to you. It's just this cold weather. It takes a while to get used to it. You will be fine. I bet in a couple of days, that you and your daughter will be out making snowmen and ice skating on the lake."

Amy smiled and again closed her eyes. "I hope you're right."

"I'm always right, mam.'

"Amy," said Amy.

"Right, Amy,"

When Amy drifted off, Jackson covered her with another blanket. It was his. He poked the fire and slid in a little more wood. He kept glancing at the blanket door. He was starting to worry. It was damn cold out there and she was just a little girl. He decided to look for her. As he reached for his parka, he felt a sudden draft coming from the flimsy entrance door. Phia was crawling through it. He had mixed emotions; relief and anger. He wanted to hug the little girl and then scold her for going out by herself. He had had these feelings for his own children, when they were young, especially when he let them have their wings. He thought he was through with these gut-wrenching moments.

Phia brought in an armload of firewood. She deposited it on the pile and went to the fire to warm her hands. She squatted beside Jackson. He smiled and never said a thing. All was forgiven.

"Would you care for a cup of tea?" Jackson poured her a cup without waiting for a response. He knew he wasn't going to get one anyway.

Jackson handed her the tea and studied her red face. "Did you have a nice walk, Phia?"

Phia took a sip, which Jackson translated as, a yes.

Jackson poured himself a cup and they both sat silently and watched the red and yellow flames, as they danced and swayed all along the spruce logs. Even though it was a rerun of yesterday's fire, he never tired looking at it.

Jackson yawned. "Well, young lady, I've surely enjoyed our conversations, but I am a bit tired. We can finish our chat at moon up tomorrow. I will be needing a hand with the snowshoes tomorrow. Good night." Jackson covered himself with his parka and was soon snoring like a rusty chainsaw.

Phia looked at him and smiled. She now had two new friends.

CHAPTER 11

Cheryl yawned and looked at her faithful Timex. Its small dainty hands were both pointing at eleven. It was almost time for the sun to make its short appearance. Besides eating, it was the great event of the day. It marked another day that they had survived, and made it a day closer to being rescued, at least for the optimists. The pessimists, on the other hand, considered it another day in the fucking cold. Ah, such is life.

"Good morning, Cheryl, a cup of tea? I made it fresh this morning."

"Jesus, Jackson, do you ever sleep?"

Jackson poured her a cup of spruce tea and carefully handed it to her. "I hate to waste what time I have left on sleeping. Besides I might miss something."

"I see. You mean like the two-hour wait between the sunrise and the sunset?"

"Maybe. Or maybe I just like to watch the water in the teapots start to boil."

"So, it's not true that a watched pot never boils."

"Nope, not according to my research."

"Good to know." Cheryl took a sip of her tea. "Murphy told me that you are leaving us to look for help."

Jackson nodded, topped off his cup, and put the pot back in the hot coals. "The sooner I leave the better."

"Are you going alone?"

"Yep."

"Shouldn't you take someone with you?"

"Like who? Any one of these people would slow me down, and I would just have to babysit them. I'm better off by myself."

Cheryl thought about this for a minute and had to agree. "I guess you are probably right. Just how long do you think it will take you?"

"I don't know. If I find the Yukon River, it won't take long. There are a lot of settlements all along it. But if it is south of us and I have to cross the Brooks Range, it could take me a month. Maybe more."

"What if something happens to you, then what?"

Jackson scoffed. "Nothing is going to happen to me. I am pretty tough for an old bird. And this is my country. I am quite at home here.

"So, don't worry your pretty little head over it."

But deep inside, they each were worried as hell.

"Morning, Jackson." Murphy poured himself a cup of tea.

Jackson nodded, "Morning, Murph."

Murphy took a sip and grimaced. "God, I miss real coffee." He squatted down beside Jackson. "When are you planning on leaving?"

"This evening, as soon as the moon comes up, that is if the weather holds."

"Well, I guess the sooner the better." Murphy paused and asked, "How long do you think the moose meat will last?"

"Maybe a week, Murph. But if you ration it, probably two weeks."

"So, I should go hunting next week."

Jackson shook his head. "You should go hunting today. We were lucky. It might take two weeks before you even see a moose or a stray caribou. But on the off chance that you get lucky again, the meat is not going to spoil in this weather."

Murphy nodded and took another sip.

"And another thing," continued Jackson, "when you do shoot something, the wolves will hear your shot. So, let them finish the kill. They are smart and will understand that you are working with them. Let them feed first and leave them a lot of meat on the bones. They have a family to feed. It is better that you share in the hunt. Or they will begin hunting you."

Murphy had to agree with that logic.

Jackson unstrapped his hunting knife and handed it to Murphy. "Here, you will need this."

"Thanks," said Murphy. "But what about you? Won't you need it?"

Jackson patted his pocked. "I still have a good pocket knife. It is all I need to cut up jerky, or snowshoe hare, or whittle some shavings to start a fire. You will need the large knife for big-game."

Murphy nodded and went back to his pretend coffee.

Jackson had cut up small pieces of moose meat and boiled them in one of the coffee pots. He poured some of the steaming broth into a cup and took it to Amy. She was awake and just blankly staring at the smoky ceiling. Jackson helped her up to a sitting position.

"Here," he handed her the cup. She sniffed it, and a pleasant smile formed on her face.

"Thanks," she said weakly. She slowly sipped on the soothing hot liquid.

Jackson turned to Phia. "So, Sophia, I have a gift for you."

Phia looked Jackson in the face and lowered her eyebrows. She was doubly shocked. She had not heard her full name in years, let alone from a stranger, but it was the word, *gift*, that got her full attention.

Jackson chuckled at her facial response.

Phia tried to ignore it. She folded her arm and anxiously looked at the fire.

Jackson reached behind his back and retrieved a pair of mukluks that he had crudely stitched from the moose hide. "Here, try these on."

Phia took them from Jackson without looking at him and slipped them over her feet. When she stood up, Jackson laced the tall boots and got to his feet. He walked around her admiring his work.

"Not bad, if I say so myself. I wish I had some arctic fox fur to trim the top of them with. I guess I can add that later."

Phia looked at Jackson and wanted to hug him. But, it was still too hard for her. She was still angry at the world. Just letting Jackson in this far, was a big step for her.

Jackson walked over and retrieved the long willow branches that he had thawed by the fire. He tested them. They seemed limber enough. He slowly pulled one into a circle. When the two ends met, he handed it to Phia. "Here, hold these ends together."

Phia took the willow ends and held them together, while Jackson lashed them tightly with some moose rawhide. The shape of his first snowshoe was formed. While she held the frame, Jackson weaved the wide strips of moose hide to form the bottom of the snowshoe. It was a slow process and took over an hour for the first one. The second one was a little faster.

As the late afternoon drew to a close, Phia watched Jackson fill a crude backpack with dried meat, a blanket, an empty tin can, and a rolled-up piece of carpet that he scraped up from the first-class section to use as a sleeping pad. She began suspecting that he was leaving her. Her eyes panicked, she became very upset, and that turned into anger.

Now came the hard part. Jackson had to tell Phia that he would be leaving as soon as the moon cleared the eastern horizon. He knew that she had begun to rely on him. He was afraid that she might go back into her shell. And he had grown quite fond of her. But he had to leave.

Jackson stalled as long as he could but it was time. He lowered his head and softly sighed, "Phia… child…"

She would not look at him.

Jackson wiped his nose and whispered, "Sophia, I, I must…"

Phia took off her mukluks and threw them at him, and with tears in her eyes, she stormed out of the worthless fuselage refuge and ran to the end of the lake.

She threw back her head and howled. And it was immediately answered by her other friend, Reese. Phia looked back towards the shiny shelter at the other end of this small lake and let go a fierce growl. She took a quick breath, looked up at the rising moon, and howled a bone-chilling wail. After that, she loped off like a two-legged wolf towards the sound of the young she-wolf that had answered her first call.

The moon had been up for over an hour. It lit up their world nicely. Jackson could not stall any longer. As much as he wanted to say goodbye to the angry little girl, he knew he couldn't wait any longer. He had to find help and rescue for all these survivors. It was now up to him.

He hugged Cheryl, first.

"You be careful and come back for me." She demanded.

Jackson winked at her. "I will, I promise."

"If you don't, I will kick your ass." She meant it.

Jackson clasped Murphy's right hand and hugged him with his left arm. "When you see Phia, tell her I said goodbye."

"I will do that, Jackson, and you be careful out there. I am going to miss your confounded, disgusting coffee."

Jackson chuckled.

But it was time to go. He glanced up at the North Star and began his trek east. The crowd of well-wishers stood silently as they listened to the soft sound of Jackson's snowshoes, as he paced across the powder snow. They watched until he disappeared into the cold silent night.

A very solemn group of survivors made their way back inside their makeshift shelter. Each was in prayer to his own personal God for a safe passage for their friend and, probably, their only hope for survival.

CHAPTER 12

Under the glow of the Aurora Borealis, Phia and the two-year-old wolf, Reese, ran through the vast tundra of North America, completely free. They bonded as friends, as equals. They were tireless as they romped under the full moon.

Phia stopped and knelt down and gently worked the thick fur behind Reese's ears. "Promise me that you will never leave me."

Reese cocked her head at the strange voice coming from her play friend. She studied Phia's eyes and sniffed her feelings. Her odor radiated love. She wagged her tail and said, "Yip." Phia was sitting on a large tuft of grass and Reese put her head in Phia's lap. They both rested. They happily watched the curtains of green dancing lights, as the Aurora paraded across the sky.

A long, lone howl filled the somber night. It was Reese's mother calling her errant daughter. It was time to join her family in the hunt. Reese jumped to her feet, pointed her nose at the moon, and answered her call. She nuzzled Phia's hand for a quick pet, turned, and ran like a rolling wave across the snow-filled tundra towards her den and her waiting pack.

Phia lowered her head and slowly trudged towards her people. Both of her feet and her heart were very heavy. She was not ready to return. She looked back to where she last saw Reese, but the wolf was already gone. "Damn him," she cursed when she thought about Jackson not being back there. Angrily, she stomped the white ground around her. She stopped when she saw the tracks that she and Reese made in the soft snow. Then she saw the tracks that Reese had made when she left. So, blindly, she followed them. She wanted to see their world.

This moonlit north-country was plenty bright. She could see a long ways, and so she kept following the tracks. She had no idea what she was going to find, or how far she would travel, when she found it. But, at least she had a direction.

Since bears were hibernating, the wolves were at the top of the food chain. They relaxed their caution. Phia found their den and slipped up fairly close to them undetected. She watched the alpha male playing with the four-month-old pups. His injury was on the mend, but he was still unable to hunt with the pack. Phia sat with her back against a scrub spruce tree and remained perfectly still. She wanted to see her friend's family and how they lived.

One of the pups, which was darker than the rest, caught a strange whiff of another animal. Curiously, he followed his nose. He loped back and forth trying to discover what, and where, this scent was coming from. The alpha male watched his youngest son, as he sniffed and stalked his prey a short distance from the den. He was guessing it was a lemming. Someday the pup would leave, find a mate, and become an alpha male of his own pack. He was proud of him.

Phia watched closely, as the pup worked his way towards her. She began panicking. She slid lower into the snow and out of sight.

Soon, she could hear the pup as it searched very close to her. Suddenly it stopped. She heard a soft growl, as it slowly approached. The little wolf crouched low. He was ready to leap and attack this strange animal. The largest prey he had ever gone after was a snowshoe hare. He was in for a big surprise.

The large alpha male got to his feet and watched the pup, as he crouched. He had taught him how to pounce on hares and to quickly go for the throat. The old leader silently worked his way towards the pup. He suddenly got a scent of what the pup was stalking. It was not a rabbit. It was a human. He growled and leaned back on his hind legs, which were like coiled springs, but the pain from two broken ribs made him unable to leap. He snarled in pain and started slowly creeping towards the human scent.

The alpha she-wolf and her pack had a successful hunt of squirrels and rabbits that they were bringing back to the den. She threw her head back and howled to announce that they were close. Reese was running beside her mother and howled second.

Phia recognized her friend's call and howled back. She then quickly got into a submissive position. She knew the big male was close.

Reese heard Phia's cry and dropped the rabbit that she was carrying and sprinted towards her friend. She got there a moment too late. The alpha male was now standing over her friend. He was confused. He never saw prey, or any other animal, drop into a submissive position. They either ran, or charged. He just growled at her.

Reese loped up to her father and slid her body over Phia, and also took the submissive position. The alpha wolf backed up in surprise. He was still their leader. And as their leader, he could take it from her. But he accepted that it was her prey. He huffed at her and started circling them. He became curious about why Reese protected this human. He decided to let her have it. He turned and slowly made his way back to the den.

The young pup that had found the prey first quickly ran up to his older sister and pounced on her. He considered the prey his.

Reese quickly pinned the feisty wolf on his back. She was still a lot bigger than he was. He wiggled and wined and finally accepted that this animal was hers.

The alpha female was a little more hardnosed about it. She circled her daughter and impatiently snarled and growled at her. Reese kept her friend covered and maintained her submissive position. This was hers and she was not giving Phia up.

The standoff lasted an hour. The mother was stubborn and didn't like what the young wolf was doing. Reese was her mother's daughter and just as stubborn. The rest of the pack became bored and went back to the den. There were squirrels and hares to feed on.

Phia was terrified. She slowly peeked out from under her protector and looked at the large wolf circling her. When the she-wolf saw Phia, she recognized her. She was at the moose kill and stood between the two men that had wounded the moose. She stopped pacing. She yipped acceptance of her daughter's new toy and went back to the den.

"Oh, Reese, you saved me." Phia hugged her and kissed her on her dark nose. Reese licked her face. They were now BFFs.

It was time to meet the fam.

Phia followed Reese back to the den. She kept her head down and as submissive as she could. She knew that she was at the bottom of their pecking order. Reese stopped and stood near the entrance to the den. Phia sat with her legs crossed next to her friend on the hard-packed snow.

The puppies were the first to come out of the den. They slowly circled Phia, as they sniffed and snarled and yipped at the newcomer. The little male that discovered her, was the first to slink up and touch her with his nose. The Plains Indians called this "*counting coup*.' If he touched his enemy, it showed prestige over him. He proudly backed up and let go a puppy howl.

Phia laughed, which startled the other pups. But they were brave little hunters and one by one they *touched coup*. The last was a shy little runt. He was lighter in color than the rest. As he got close, he sniffed for danger. He stopped at the new smell. He was sure that was what danger smelled like. Phia reached out her hand and he froze. She slowly pulled him into her lap and began petting him behind his ears. He decided that it was not all that unpleasant. He relaxed and yipped to his brothers, showing that his *coup* was stronger than theirs. Phia laughed again.

Before long, she was surrounded by the whole pack.

As the moon began to set, it marked the end of the night and the start of a new day. The wolf family began crawling into the den for a short winter's nap. Reese was the last to leave. Phia could tell that she wanted her to follow her into the den. "I am sorry, Reese. But I must go back to my pack. I must check on my mother." Reese voiced a small wine and crawled inside with the rest of her family.

With the moon down and the sun still hours away from rising, Phia only had the stars to light up her way home. The endless sky was filled with these twinkling lights, and she had no problem finding her way back. As she walked, she looked up at the North Star and thought about her other friend, Jackson. "I wonder where he is, and I wonder if he is looking up at this same star."

Jackson was wondering the same thing at that very same moment.

Phia crawled into the metal shelter and took off her hooded Mackinaw. The +15° temperature inside felt very warm to her. Considering that she just came in from fifteen below, it was thirty degrees warmer inside. She looked around and saw that nothing was stirring, not even a lemming.

She went to her mother first. Her breathing was slow and shallow. She was cold to the touch. Phia added more wood to the fire. She went to the stash of unfrozen meat and took a small piece of it. It was about the size of a chicken leg. She took one of the empty coffee pots, filled it with snow, and put it on the fire. She tore off a piece of the moose meat with her teeth and chewed it into small pieces. She spit them into the pot. She was making a meat-broth for her mother like she had seen Jackson make. He had a knife to cut his meat, but her broth would be a little richer as it thickened in the boiling water. After all the meat was in the pot, she added a little more wood to the fire and slid the pot on the hot coals next to the pot of spruce tea to simmer. When she was finished, she crawled under her mother's blankets and curled up next to her, giving Amy her body heat.

As Phia came out of her shell, her metabolism kicked in. She could now tolerate the severe cold temperatures with less clothing. She put her head on her mother's shoulder and listened to her mother's faint heartbeat. It was steady, and the rhythm of it calmed her, and it put her to sleep.

Cheryl was the first to stir. She opened her eyes and stared at the flickering ceiling. The fire was still going. "Good," she said to herself. She could see her breath, but her blanket had held her body heat quite nicely. She took a breath and sat up. She began wondering where Jackson was sleeping. She knew it had to be out in the elements; perhaps a snow cave. She shivered at the thought.

Cheryl climbed to her feet and put on her jacket. It was covering the blanket that had covered her. She added a little more of the precious wood to the fire. She smelled the meat broth and looked over at Amy. Phia was staring at her.

"Good morning child. Did you make this for your mom?"

Phia sat up and gave her a hint of a nod. It was the most she had ever communicated with Cheryl, or with anyone else for that matter, except for Jackson.

Cheryl poured herself a cup of the bitter tea. The hot liquid was soothing as she sipped on it. And surprisingly, it was beginning to taste a little better. Cheryl studied the young girl and wondered what had made her this way and what would happen to the poor child, if her mother died. Cheryl sighed, "I guess I won't think about that now. I have enough to worry about just getting myself through today."

Phia's mother heard Cheryl's mumbling and woke up. She looked at her daughter. "Hi, Phia, darling," she softly said. "I didn't hear you come in." Amy tried to sit up.

Phia put her arm around her mother and helped her to a sitting position.

"Thank you," said Amy, as she leaned back and got comfortable. "Is that meat broth I smell? Is Jackson still here?"

"No," replied Cheryl. "He left last night."

"Who made the broth?"

Cheryl filled Amy's cup and handed it to her. "I am guessing it was your daughter, Phia."

Amy looked at Phia. "Did you make this?"

Phia nodded and smiled.

Amy set down the cup, and with tears in her eyes, she hugged Phia. When she let go of her, she took the cup and sipped its hardy, warm contents. "Why this tastes even better than Jackson's. What's your secret?"

Phia shrugged her shoulders. She was starting to miss the old man. Her anger was replaced with sadness and anxiety. She stood up and poured a cup of the broth and handed it to Cheryl. Phia liked Cheryl. She looked out for everyone, especially her mother. She was nice.

"Thanks," said Cheryl, when Phia handed her the cup.

Phia poured herself a cup. The three of them sat silently in thought, each wondering what was going to happen next.

Fortunately for them, nothing.

Unfortunately for Jackson, something would happen, a very bad something.

CHAPTER 13

Everyone cheered, when the sun peeked its red nose over the left side of the southern horizon. It was *the* big social event of the day. After which, it became time to collect the firewood. It was becoming rather scarce. The men, and now the women, had to travel a little further each day to find anything that would burn. The woman began tightly rolling up tuffs of tundra grass to burn. It gave out a lot of light, but not much heat. The temperature sagged a little lower each morning. It was still about a month, until it was officially winter. Everyone had given up hope of an early rescue. Now they worried about enough firewood to keep themselves warm, until Jackson could find help. He was now their only hope.

Phia helped her mother outside to see the sunrise. It, like the dry rolled grass, gave out a lot of light, but sadly, no heat. Her mother had perked up, after her meat broth and the bitter tea. Cheryl brought out a blanket to wrap around Amy, so she could stay somewhat warm, as she watched the rising sun. It was bitterly cold outside of their refuge.

Murphy was the next to come out of the shelter of the plane. He was packing his revolver with the five precious bullets in it.

Cheryl joined him as they both watched the red sun crawl up out of the white horizon. "Going hunting?" she asked.

"Yep." Murphy was dressed in everything that he owned. "I saw a couple of moose tracks yesterday, but the animal that is making them seems pretty shy. I also saw a couple of caribou north of here, but they kept moving west. It gets damn cold just sitting out there waiting for something to mosey on by."

"Maybe you will have better luck today."

"How do you suppose Jackson's doing?"

Cheryl formed a confident smile. "I'm sure he's fine."

Amy began shivering uncontrollably. "Phia, honey, please help me back inside. I need to sit by the fire."

Phia nodded and whispered, "Okay."

Amy's heart warmed at her verbal communication.

Once Amy was comfortably sitting by the fire, Phia began gathering wood to add to it. Amy silently watched her daughter, as she banked the fire. She was pleased with how much she had come out of her shell. Amy knew that it was Jackson that had somehow managed to do this. He seemed to be the key to her survival.

Amy leaned back and closed her eyes. She was exhausted. Her breaths were shallow. She suspected the worst. She was sure she had pneumonia, and she knew that if anything happened to her, her daughter would slip back into her shell. She decided if she died that Phia would be better off with Jackson. And, without rescue, it would be *when* she died.

When Amy heard Phia put more wood on the fire, she opened her eyes and sat up. "Phia, darling," she softly called. "I am worried about Jackson. I think he will need your help. You should go with him."

Jackson now had been gone for two days. During this time, Amy had spent most of her hours sleeping. The fluid from the pneumonia was filling her lungs, so she was not getting much oxygen. Her awake time was very short. To her, Jackson had just left. This error put quite a burden on her daughter, but her feelings about Jackson needing help were quite accurate. Without assistance of some kind, Jackson was not going to make it.

And if he didn't, whatever happened to flight *AS1125*, was going to turn into an unsolved mystery.

...

Phia looked at her mother and shook her head. Jackson was her friend, but staying with her mother was much more important.

"Phia, honey, please come here."

Phia set down the firewood and knelt in front of her mother. She had a very stubborn look on her face.

Amy laughed at the look, which turned into a deep cough. She put her arms around her daughter and gave her a weak hug. "That look was so…so your father. It was too bad that you never really got to know him." Amy's breaths were short now, and her voice was weak. "I don't want to scare you, but I am afraid that I will soon need a doctor. You must help Jackson find one."

Phia's eyes panicked. She wrapped her arms around her mother and hugged her with silent sobs. "Okay," whispered Phia, and she mouthed the words, 'I love you.'

The faint sound of a distant gunshot got Phia's attention. She looked around the shelter, but no one moved. She was the only one who had heard it. She helped her mother back to her sleeping pad, and the exhausted Amy fell right to sleep. Phia kissed her on the forehead and said, "Don't you dare die!" She now had a very important mission.

Phia quickly put on the mukluks that Jackson made for her and her thick, hooded Mackinaw, and she started for the door. A small spruce tree, that had about six feet of it still waiting to be pushed into the fire, got her attention. The bark had been rubbed off, probably by a bull moose in velvet. The end in the fire had burned to a point. She pulled it out of the fire and went to the make-shift door and rubbed it back and forth against the raw metal floor of the plane and sharpened it. She now had a fire-hardened, pointed weapon. It was as sharp as a wolf's tooth and now she was not helpless. She was now a predator.

The sun had already reached its peak. In another hour it would be sundown. She didn't have much time. She heard the howl of Reese's wolf pack. They had also heard the shot. Phia quickly ran towards the kill. She wanted to say goodbye to her friend.

By the time she reached Murphy, the wolves had the animal down. It was a cow. It was not as big as the bull Murphy had first shot, but it still had a lot of meat on it. She could see Reese with her family, as they tore the belly apart and then began feeding on the warm organs. Phia walked over to Murphy. He had a proud look on his face.

Murphy glanced at Phia's spear. "Nice walking stick you have there, lass."

Phia shrugged her shoulders with a hint of a smile.

Before long, the men and women that had been gathering wood, and that had heard the shot, began working their way to the kill. They stopped at a safe distance, as they watched the wolves feed. When the wolves had their fill, the alpha female threw back her head and wailed. It was time to leave with as much meat as they could carry to the hungry pups waiting at the den. Reese also howled to Phia. She had seen her friend watching them feed. Phia wanted to answer her back, but didn't want to do it in front of the men in her pack. They would not understand.

As the sun set, Murphy went to work cutting up the moose, while the men and women began packing the meat back to their shelter. Phia patiently watched. When Murphy got to the last of their share of the meat, Phia tugged on his coat.

"What? Did I miss something?"

Phia nodded and then she took him to the moose head. She spread its jaw and pulled out the tongue.

"Ah, Jackson's tongue." Murphy pulled out the hunting knife and sliced it free. "There you go, lass. Hope you enjoy it." Murphy began walking back to their shelter. "You coming?"

Phia shook her head.

"Suit yourself." Murphy shivered and started jogging to warm himself. The temperature was going down with the sun.

Phia put the moose tongue in a side pocket of her coat and waited until Murphy was close to the plane. She raised her head and howled. Her call was returned instantly. Reese was quite close. She popped up out of a snow bank and excitedly bounded up to Phia, and playfully knocked her over.

"Reese, calm down, my furry friend." Phia laughed and hugged the young wolf.

Once the wolf got her scratch behind the ears, she began running circles around Phia. She wanted to play.

Phia knelt down and waited for Reese to calm down. The wolf saw the serious look on Phia's face and went up to her and sat down. They were nose to nose.

"Reese, I am sorry, but I cannot play today. My mother is sick, and I must leave for a little while. Do you understand?"

Reese stopped panting, closed her mouth, and nodded. Which to Phia, meant yes. But to Reese, who just swallowed something, she had no fricking idea what Phia had said. She just wagged her tail and again began running circles around her, indicating that she still wanted to play.

Phia stood up and said, "**No.**"

Pretty much that sound is universally understood. Reese put her tail between her legs and took a submissive position. She had done something to anger her friend. She whined.

Phia gave her a last, sad hug and left without looking back. The sun was down and the stars were out. The moon would not be up for another three hours but the starlight was enough to see by. It had not snowed since Jackson had left, so his tracks were easy to see in the dim light. She followed them at an easy jog. Jackson wore a backpack, so his tracks were fairly deep in the snow, and he was moving slow. She figured that she would catch up to him by this time tomorrow, if not earlier. The mukluks kept her feet very warm, and when jogging, she had to flip off her hood and unbutton her Mackinaw to keep from overheating. When she got into deep snow, she slowed down to a high-stepping walk. But she was making good time.

Soon the aurora borealis came out to keep her company. When the moon finally came up, she stopped to rest. And her landscape had brightened. She could now see the Brooks Range. It didn't look all that far. But because of the curvature of the earth, she was only seeing the top half of the mountains. She felt a slight chill. It was time to keep moving.

When the moon reached its high point, she stopped to rest again. She had brought a blanket. It was rolled up and fastened with rawhide, and it was slung over her left shoulder. She carried her spear in her right hand. She felt prepared and very little fear.

Again she chilled; so she ended her rest and continued following Jackson's tracks, as they took her east towards the rising moon. She found this pace tiring; she slowed to a fast walk. She was planning on catching up to Jackson before she needed to sleep. She had no idea of how to build a shelter and wished she had gone inside Reese's den to see what her shelter was like. But Phia was strong and young, and she could go a couple of days without sleep, so she continued on,

The next four hours went by quickly. The moon would not set for another three hours, and then it would be back to starlight, until the sun would come up. She hiked on, closely following the tracks, and began noticing that they were getting harder to see. She looked up at the moon, and it was hazed over by a thin cloud. A light snow began filling her world.

She trudged on, as the snow flurries that were quietly falling all around her, thickened. She looked up and the moon was gone. She looked back down and now the tracks were gone. They were covered over by the fresh snow. As the night darkened, the snowstorm completely engulfed her. Without shelter, she suddenly realized that she could die.

She buttoned up her coat, pulled her hood over her head, and slowly continued on until she found a large grass tussock. She quickly dug out the snow down to its thick grassy base. She wrapped her blanket around herself and curled up as snug as she could on its dry grass. At least she was out of the wind.

Poor Phia had lost Jackson's tracks forward, and her tracks back, and now she had no star to steer by. She tightly gripped her spear for security and closed her eyes to try and get a little sleep. She was cold. The blanket was thin, but as the falling snow covered her, it insulated her. And slowly Phia warmed up and fell into a fitful asleep.

Tomorrow she would worry about tomorrow.

CHAPTER 14

D amn," cursed Jackson, when he saw the storm coming. "I guess I better find me a place to hole-up for a while." He was still moving through the vast tundra between the Yukon Border and Alaska's Brooks Range.

His time in Florida had softened him. His old legs didn't like coming out of retirement. They bitched and cramped-up on him. He had slept very little, only taking short naps under the stars. He was looking forward to a good night's sleep under a proper shelter, or in an old trapper's cabin. But this vast tundra offered no protection against the snow and the wind. If it had held off one more day he would have been in the shadow of the Brooks Range, where actual trees grow in their valleys. He had hoped to be there by now, but he was not as young as he used to be. But then who is? As it turned out, he was only a couple of miles ahead of Phia.

Jackson worked his way into a dip in the tundra that had drifted over. He took off his snowshoes and used one as a shovel. He scooped out a small area in it and crawled in. He put the carpet-matt down on the icy floor and snuggled in. He was out of the weather. The entrance soon drifted over, and his breath and body heat soon warmed it up. He rubbed the cramps out of his legs, ate a little smoked, moose jerky, and fell asleep.

Nine hours later the noise of the wind subsided. Jackson kicked away the snow from his shelter and wiggled backed out. The sky was clearing and the moon was rising. He took a deep breath of the frigid air and laughed. It felt good to be close to home. He missed the clean space, the silence, and mostly the Northern Lights. He pulled out his gear, wrapped up his sleeping pad, and slipped on his backpack.

Jackson continued east. As he trudged on in the fresh snow, he chewed on breakfast and hummed a song that he knew as a kid. Tomorrow at this time he would be in the mountains. That was where civilized people live. There he would find a cabin and a trail leading to a settlement or a tribal village. He was close.

Unfortunately, another predator would stop his progress. Jackson was not really worried about bears, because brown bears were now hibernating and polar bears were not this far south from the Arctic Ocean. But there is a meat-eater out there that doesn't hibernate. He is always hungry and meaner than a snake. Only sow grizzlies with cubs will take on this vicious predator. And one of these predators got a whiff of the moose meat that was in Jackson's moose-hide backpack.

Phia dreamed about Reese and how thick and warm her chocolate-colored coat was. And how much she smelled like a wet dog. Only it wasn't a dream.

Reese followed her human friend's scent, but kept her distance. When she got to the edge of her family's territory, she stopped. Beyond this invisible line was the territory of another family of wolves. Their pack was larger than hers and very protective of their terrain. The line was distinctively marked with wolf urine. Both packs peed on scrub trees and bushes as a warning not to cross.

Reese squatted and peed on a small willow tree, as was her custom. Her mother and father warned her not to cross, and she was a good little girl. Well, that was until she befriended a wayward human. She paced back and forth, sniffed the air for other wolves, and then she sat down and whined. Her friend needed her. She threw caution to the north wind and continued following her. The blowing snow covered Phia's tracks, but she could still smell her snow-buried scent. She followed at a faster pace.

When she found her friend, she wormed her way through the drifted snow and curled up beside her, and protected her from the cold.

"Reese," cried Phia, when she realized that she wasn't dreaming. "I am so glad to see you." With happy tears in her eyes, she hugged her four-legged little friend. Reese just licked Phia's face, since proper wolves don't hug.

Phia scanned the eastern horizon looking for any sign of Jackson. The rising moon revealed a pristine, unblemished, black and white world. Phia walked in circles gently brushing back the snow looking for Jackson's wide, snowshoe track. The blizzard had erased it all.

Nigh on to hopeless, it was.

Reese suspected that her friend was looking for her family. Reese sniffed the red mackinaw that Jackson had given to Phia. She smelled the Jackson that was left in it. She sniffed the snow and caught his scent. She yipped at Phia and started following the smell. Phia followed. She hoped that the wolf was following Jackson and not her next meal. She had no other option.

Wolverines are weasels. They are the largest members of this savage family. They are lone travelers and always looking for an easy meal. And, since they are fearless, they will take on animals ten times their size. That makes an old man of Jackson's size fair game for the hungry predator.

The wolverine loped tirelessly out of the sparse trees of the Brooks Range and out on the tundra in search of his next meal. As he bounded across the barren land, his sensitive nose searched the air for the scent of prey, large or small. An odd scent got his attention.

The wolverine stopped and stood up on his hind legs and sniffed again. It was a human mixed with moose. He dropped back down and followed his nose. When he caught sight of Jackson, he stopped. He heard the tall prey, and it was voicing an odd gravelly growl. It was Jackson serenading in the wild.

Jackson was happily singing his song and totally unaware that he was being watched and followed.

Curiously the wolverine circled his prey as he sniffed and listened. He could smell the fresh meat in Jackson's pack. He had never attacked a human before. He never had the need to. They seemed to shy away from him. His hunger soon outweighed his curiosity. It was time to kill.

Jackson never heard a thing. The wolverine silently rushed him from behind. He leaped and ferociously sunk his teeth into Jackson's backpack. The stealthy wolverine's contact drove Jackson to the ground. He instinctively curled up and covered his head. The wolverine began shaking his prey like a ragdoll as he tried to rip lose the moose-skin pack that held the meat. Jackson slipped out of his pack and began crawling away from the vicious animal, but the snowshoes were slowing him down. Jackson tried to get to his feet and run, while the wolverine was distracted chewing on his backpack.

The wolverine suddenly stopped, cocked his head, and growled at Jackson. The old man had shed his snowshoes and was up and running. The wolverine's instinct was to chase his prey and to finish killing it. In a quick leap, he grabbed Jackson by the back of his right leg with his sharp curved claws. Once Jackson was pinned, he sunk his teeth into his calf and shook his head like a feeding shark, and severed a large portion of muscle from his leg.

Jackson screamed in pain and rolled onto his back. And with his left leg, he kicked and cursed at his attacker. The wolverine leaned back on his hind legs and snarled, showing all his bloody teeth. With a fierce huff, he leaped for Jackson's throat.

Phia heard Jackson's blood-curdling scream and took off like a two-legged antelope. Reese was right on her tail and a bit faster. The wolf weighed about the same as the wolverine and caught him in mid-flight. They tumbled to the snow just missing Jackson. Phia arrived a second later and, with both hands tightly clamped on her spear, she leaped towards the growling predators in front of her. Her spear was now inches from the wolverine's nose. The clever carnivore leaned back, snapped his jaws, and he flashed his red eyes at her. He was ready to attack. He could still taste Jackson's blood on its teeth.

Reese, who had a mouthful of wolverine hide in her teeth and a taste of his blood, sprang to her feet and joined Phia. They now both faced the angry overgrown weasel.

The three predators slowly rotated in a circle as they snarled and snapped their warnings at each other. It was a standoff of top predators.

Finally, the wolverine decided he was outnumbered. He slowly backed up, turned, snatched the backpack with the meat in it, and he ran towards the mountains. Reese gave chase.

Phia ran to Jackson. His right leg was bleeding profusely.

"Where in the hell did you come from?" winced Jackson when he saw Phia.

Phia ignored his question as she inspected Jackson's wound.

Jackson pulled off his bandana and handed it to Phia. Sweat was running down his forehead from the pain in his leg. "Here child," he said with gritted teeth. "You need to wrap my leg. You got to wrap it tight. You have to cinch it tight enough to stop the bleeding." Jackson gasped in pain, rolled his eyes, and lay back down. With short quick breaths, he blankly stared at the sky. He felt around the deep snow until he found a stick to put between his teeth. He bit down on it and waited.

Phia opened Jackson's pant leg. The muscle was shredded and half of it was gone. The artery was punctured but not severed. She instinctively wiped it clean with fresh snow. She slipped the blue bandana around the mangled calf and tightened it as best as she could. She then packed more snow around the wound and the bleeding slowed. Phia shook the old man. He had passed out. She didn't know what to do next.

Jackson would probably lose a leg to frostbite. And if that didn't get him, he would most likely die from an infection from the foul mouth of the wolverine. He needed medical attention.

Phia looked at Jackson. He was quietly laying there with a stick in his mouth. He looked dead. "Jackson, Jackson," she cried as she shook him. "Are you dead?" She got no response.

Phia shook him again and became very angry. She grabbed a hold of his ears and pulled his scruffy face up close to hers. "Damn you! If you die, I will kill you."

Jackson's eyes opened a slit. He spit the stick out of his mouth and moaned. "If I catch you swearing again, I will wash your mouth out with soap, little girl."

Phia let go of his ears and hugged him around his neck. When she finally let go, she leaned back and sat on her heels.

Jackson smiled and sat up. He studied her face and asked, "Were you talking?"

Phia shook her head.

"Liar." Jackson groaned and looked at his leg. "Oh thank God. It felt like that damn wolf ripped it right off."

By this time Reese had returned and was watching at a safe distance. At the word *wolf,* Reese growled at the scruffy, noisy human.

Jackson spun, gasped, and tried to stand. The pain brought tears to his clear blue eyes, and he passed out again.

CHAPTER 15

Phia found Jackson's carpet-pad and placed it on the ground next to him. She carefully rolled him onto it. She took her blanket and gently covered him with it. He was exhausted and had passed out. It had been a long day for all of them. She crawled up next to him and Reese curled up next to her. Phia was warm and shortly fell asleep between her two protectors. That night, they all comfortably dreamed under the swaying, fluorescent, green lights of the Aura Borealis.

When a pink haze on the southeastern horizon announced that the sun was going to rise, Phia got up. It was still pretty dark and frightfully cold. It was time to get wood for a fire. As she gathered what she could find, Reese bounded off towards the hills that lie between the tundra and the mountains northwest of them.

Phia gathered the dried moss under the Black Spruce trees as tinder, as Jackson had shown her. When she returned, she brushed the snow away from a flat spot near where they had slept to set her fire. She balled up the gray moss and carefully placed it on the center of her fire pit. Very small twigs and dead needles were next. This was followed by thin dry branches. Now she was ready to start her fire.

She gently rummaged through Jackson's vest pockets until she found his wood matchsticks. Jackson's breathing was steady. He would live. She lit one of the matches and put it under the dry, frozen tinder. When the match was half burned, the moss began flaming on its own, and then there was light, and that was followed by heat. Phia smiled, as she warmed her cold fingers. She added more wood to her very first fire. She was quite proud.

As a survival tool in primates, their ears never sleep. They are always on alert.

Jackson woke, when he heard the crackling of a fresh fire, and he opened his eyes. His leg ached, but the sharp pain was gone. He sat up and inspected the bandana covering it. The bleeding had stopped. "You done good girl," he said. "I thought that ole wolf was going to kill me." Jackson crawled closer to the warm fire.

Phia scoffed and said, "**Not** Reese!"

Jackson chuckled, as he warmed his old fingers in front of the flames. "Ah, so you can talk."

Phia shook her head and again said, "No!"

Jackson raised his thick, gray eyebrows. "No? I could have sworn that I heard you cuss-in at me last night. I guess I must have been dream-in, right?"

Phia added more wood to the fire and ignored his question.

Jackson slid his injured leg closer to the fire. "Who in the heck is Reese?" he asked, as he gently felt the wound on his leg.

Phia shrugged her shoulders and mumbled, "My friend."

"Your friend; I see," said Jackson, but clearly, he didn't. "Where did your friend come from?"

Phia just pointed back towards the direction that they had already come from.

Jackson scoffed impatiently. "Okay child where is your friend now? And if you just point, I will break your finger."

Phia balled up her right fist to protect her fingers and shrugged her shoulders.

"Is he close by?"

Phia nodded and corrected him. "Yes, *she* is."

"Please call to your, *she*-friend," demanded Jackson.

Phia sighed and threw her head back and howled like a wolf.

Jackson almost crapped his drawers. And when Reese came bounding in towards them, he did.

"That, that, that's the wolf that attacked me, child. Get away from him."

"Her," corrected Phia.

"Fine, **her**." Jackson threw his hands in the air in frustration. "And… and… Jesus child." Jackson took a breath and relaxed. "Well if your friend…Chocolate bar there…"

"Reese," impatiently corrected Phia again.

"Okay, Reese. If your friend, Reese," Jackson paused for emphasis, "If Reese didn't attack me, who did?"

Phia shrugged her shoulders.

Jackson looked at the *she-wolf* for an answer.

Reese scoffed and growled at the old noisy human.

Jackson sighed and dropped his frustrated head. He looked around at their overnight camp and studied their tracks. "Well, I'll be damn," he exclaimed, when he saw the wolverine tracks. Phia had never seen a wolverine before. In fact, very few people have seen these animals in the wild. Jackson knew what vicious and relentless fighters they were. He was lucky to still have a leg, or for that matter, to be alive. Jackson looked over at the girl and the wolf, and he saw the dynamic dual in a whole new light. "Well, well, child," Jackson smiled at Phia. "I think we need more wood for our fire."

"Okay," said Phia. She and Reese bounded off in search of firewood. Jackson crawled in the other direction and discretely disposed of his shorts.

Jackson wasn't really all that hungry, until he realized that the wolverine had run off with his backpack and all the food he had packed in it. He now became worried. He was a cripple, and he had no food. And there was an extra mouth to feed. And, he mumbled, "That damn wolf can feed himself…herself."

Shortly Phia came back with an armload of firewood. And soon, their fire was blazing hot. It was cooking fire hot. That's when Jackson really wanted to cook some of the meat that the damn wolverine got away with. Now he was even hungrier.

"Phia," called Jackson. "Help me stand up. I need to see if I can walk." Jackson knew that, if he couldn't walk, he would have to send Phia, (and that mangy wolf), to find help for the survivors back on the frozen lake. Also, help for himself! Without food and a fire, Jackson knew that he would not last long in this harsh climate. He really needed to be able to walk, no matter how painful it might be.

With Phia's help, Jackson struggled to his feet. With most of his calve muscle gone in his right leg, he would be unable to flex his foot and keep his balance. Jackson did find that he could support himself upright. It was painful, but doable. When he took a step, his ankle wobbled precariously. But with his right arm over Phia's shoulder, he could walk. His leg bone was not broken, and it did support him. All he needed her for was balance.

"This just might work," said Jackson with a hint of hope. And added sarcastically, "Now all we have to do is tighten our belts and make another pair of snowshoes." The snowshoes were for Phia, because she had to help support Jackson's weight.

Phia nodded, enthusiastically.

Jackson smiled at the sweet girl. "Well, first things, first. I need you to find me a couple of willow branches about as thick as your thumb and as long as you are tall." As much as he hated the thought, he figured he could slice up part of his parka for the webbing.

When Phia returned with the willow branches, Jackson had her warm them up by the fire, and slowly bend them in a circle. He pulled out his pocket knife, removed his fur parka, and laid it across his lap. He cringed as got ready to make his first slice.

"Reese," cried Phia. "What have you got?"

Jackson looked up from his parka when he heard Phia's call. He didn't hear the stealthy wolf, as is it proudly loped in from the tundra with a gift for her friend. But he did see a large snowshoe hare in her mouth.

Reese proudly pranced past Jackson, snarled at him, and laid the plump prize at Phia's feet.

Jackson looked up at the sky with tears in his eyes. "**Thank you, God.** I now have food and a rabbit hide to make the snowshoes. He quickly put his warm parka back on. He sighed and looked at Phia. "I don't suppose you can tell your friend to fetch another rabbit, or two?"

"Sure," said she.

And the wolf understood.

By sundown, the three had feasted, and Jackson had weaved together another crude pair of snowshoes. When the moon rose, our dynamic trio ventured into the foothills of the Brooks Range. They were back on course and a little closer to rescuing the surviving passengers of Alaska Airlines flight, *AS1125*.

CHAPTER 16

As mountain ranges go, the Brooks Range is not tall. The tallest peak barely reaches 9,000 feet. The 700 mile long mountain range runs east and west, and into Canada. It is the barrier between the North Slope and interior Alaska. This terrain contains a boreal forest of black spruces, larches, and a few birch trees. This area is at least dry, as opposed to the tundra in the flatlands south and north of this range. This tundra lies on permafrost, and when the winter snows melt, the water lies on the frozen soil beneath it. And in summer, even though it gets less rain than most desserts, it creates a mosquito-infested marsh. Winter is a much better time to travel.

If our intrepid rescuers were to find an inhabited cabin, it would only be on the slopes of this magnificent mountain range. The Chandalar River runs south out of this range and it empties into the Yukon River. And the mighty Yukon has small towns and villages along it. It now would only be a matter of time before they would find help.

Jackson's leg ached something awful. He had a high tolerance for pain, which helps if you live in this harsh country. But he was older, and his wound was quite severe. He had to rest often. Their progress was agonizingly slow. They were only making a few miles a day. Jackson prayed that they would find a remote cabin that was still inhabited by a local trapper, who had radio contact with the outside world.

"Phia, what is your favorite color?" asked Jackson.

Since they were basically attached at the shoulder, as they trudged through the deep snow, Jackson had her undivided attention. He kept asking Phia questions, which forced her to speak. She had a soft but firm voice and was beginning to relax.

"Green," she said.

"Why green? Mine is red. It is a lot better color."

Phia scoffed. "Why red? How can one color be better than another color?"

"Well child, let me explain. Red is the color of Christmas. My very good friend, Santa Clause, puts on a *red* parka, hooks up a team of Alaskan caribou to his *red* sleigh, and delivers gifts wrapped in *red* paper to children all over the world. In fact, his workshop is not far from here. And that, Phia, is why **red** is better than green."

Phia laughed at the crazy old man. "Santa Clause is not real."

Jackson gasped. "You don't believe in Santa Clause?"

"Of course not. He is a scam that toy companies use to sell their toys, silly."

Jackson sighed, very heavily. "But the whole world believes in Santa Clause. All our politicians believe in him. They have statistics that prove he is real. My God child, the whole world can't be wrong."

Phia looked incredulously at Jackson. "Are you serious?"

Jackson gave Phia a stern look and nodded his scruffy head. And that was followed by a restrained chuckle that escaped his lips and that, in turn, exploded into a hardy laugh.

Phia giggled.

"So, you can laugh," said Jackson. "Okay, your turn. Why is green better?"

"Because green is the color of summer."

When the moon said goodbye for the night, Jackson led them into a group of Black Spruce trees. They dug the snow out from under these scrawny trees and made a crude shelter. And the three of them curled up for the rest of the night.

Jackson woke up cold. The shy sun was blushing on the horizon. He could smell the fire and the sizzle of meat on the barbie. He stretched, he ouched, and he carefully crawled out from under his blanket. He hobbled up close to the fire, and with a relieved sigh, he warmed up. "What-cha cooking there, girl."

"Squirrel."

"Squirrel's good. But it would be better with eggs. You should teach your furry friend to fetch them too."

Phia looked at Jackson with lowered eyebrows.

"It was a joke, girl. Do you even know how to laugh?"

Phia nodded. "It has to be funny, first."

Jackson and Reese eyeballed each other for the last piece of skewered squirrel. Phia cut it in half and tossed a piece to each of the drooling carnivores.

"Thanks," said Jackson.

Reese just snapped it up in one bite and swallowed it. She flashed her dark eyes on Jackson and grumbled a growled.

With the sun actually up, they could see clearly the high peaks of the Brooks Range. Its snow-filled valleys and rugged peaks stood defiantly against the powder blue sky. Only God and Sidney Laurence could recreate such a scene.

For two more days, they worked their way west, and still, there were no signs of human life. Jackson knew that they had to be getting close, and they were. But on the morning of the third day, a cold north wind dumped thick snow on them. Last night's crude shelter filled with the blowing snow, and it was impossible to build a fire. The stayed hunkered down and the thick fur of Reese, as she curled up on top of her two sleeping mates, kept them warm.

On the following morning the blizzard showed a hint of weakening. The visibility was about ten feet between gusts. It was still not fit for man or beast. They continued to wait it out.

Suddenly Reese popped her head up. She caught a whiff of something. She growled.

Phia sat up. "What is it?" She listened for danger, but all she could hear was the howling of the wind.

Jackson continued snoring.

Reese got to her feet and pointed her nose into the storm. Her low guttural growl was now continuous. Phia felt around the drifting snow, until she found her spear. She got to her feet and straddled the wolf. Phia leaned forward with the point of her spear inches above the wolf. These two were ready to take on a woolly mammoth, if need be.

Whatever was out there, it was getting close. Reese's teeth were snapping a warning. Phia bent her knees and was ready to spring. Suddenly, Phia saw a slight blur in the swirling snow. Whatever it was, it was here.

The upright form staggered and toppled in front of them, and it lay motionlessly in the snow. Phia nudged it with the point of her spear. It didn't move. It was human. She got down on her knees and rolled the man over. Phia gasped. He was an old woman, and she was only wearing a thin flowered dress. Phia quickly latched on to her cold hands and dragged her to where Jackson was sleeping. She snuggled her up next to the old man, and she crawled in on the other side of the old woman.

"Reese," called Phia.

The wolf understood and curled up over the newest member of her strange pack.

It took the rest of the day for the storm to finally blow itself out. It was fate, or an act of God, that brought the old woman to Jackson and company. It was not time for her to die, and now, because of her, neither would they.

Hours later, Jackson's bladder rudely woke him up. The snow had drifted over them covering them completely. It was snug and warm in their snow-cocoon. Jackson could feel the warm body behind him. He assumed it was Phia. He tried to disregard nature's call and go back to sleep. This annoyed his full bladder, so it shot a message to his slow brain. This time, it was one he couldn't ignore.

"Crap," he grumbled and he carefully slid out of the snowdrift. The moon was up and the storm had passed. It was a clear and cold night. His leg ached, so he crawled through the snow to a nearby bush. He got to his knees and with a thankful sigh, he relieved himself.

Jackson saw wolf tracks in the snow. "Phia's wolf must be out hunting. I hope he brings back a fat rabbit this time. "Them damn squirrels were tough and stringy," he mumbled as he zipped back up. With a cold shiver, he started crawling back towards the crude snow-shelter. He wished there was already a hot fire going. That was when he saw Phia coming down the edge of the boreal forest with a load of firewood. His shivering heart warmed.

"Phia, child, you're a keeper." Jackson quickly cleared a spot for the fire. He silently watched as Phia placed the tinder and the twigs in his clearing. When she was ready, he handed her one of his precious matches. She lit her fire, and with a gentle blow on the tinder, it came to life. She looked up at Jackson and grinned.

Jackson nodded and gave her a proud smile back. He scooted a little closer to the fire and thawed his fingers. As he warmed up, it suddenly occurred to him that there was someone else here, someone still sleeping. He glanced at the mound of snow that he had slept under. There was still a lump under his blanket. He looked at Phia and asked, "Sooophia, do you have another friend that I don't know about?"

Phia shrugged her shoulders.

"Is this another wolf?"

"No," said Phia indignantly.

"Does your new friend have a name?"

Phia nodded. "I think so."

"Well, where in the hell did…" Jackson stopped talking and decided to cut to the chase and find out for himself. He crawled over to the blanket and carefully lifted it up. It was an older woman and she looked like she was an Indian.

The old woman blinked a few times and sat up.

This startled Jackson.

She wrapped the blanket around her shoulders and looked around. She looked at the bearded man in front of her and said something in the Athabaskan language.

Jackson smiled and laughed at the old woman. "Sorry, but no, you are not dead."

She sighed and dropped her head. "But it was a good day to die. Now, I must wait for another big snow." She looked at the fire and got to her feet. With short stout legs, she made her way to its edge. She warmed herself and threw more wood on the fire. She looked back at Jackson and said, "I'm hungry. What did you bring to eat?" Before Jackson could respond, she looked at Phia. "Who is girl? She looks too young to be your woman." She looked back at Jackson and scowled. "Are you some kind of pervert?"

"Jesus no, woman," gasped Jackson.

"Please, no cuss. I am good Christian woman, old man." She looked at Phia and softened. "What is your name?"

"Phia."

The old woman bit down on her lower lip in thought. "Phia, is that Christian?"

Phia nodded her head, even though she had no idea if it was, and answered, "Phia is short for Sophia."

"Ah," ah-ed the old woman. "Sophia is good name." She took Phia's warm hands and squeezed them. "My mother named me Chena. It means River. But when I was baptized, I got good Christian name. I am now Ruth." Ruth studied Jackson and saw his leg wrap. "Is old man a cripple?"

"No," said Phia. "He is injured."

"Did he fall?"

"No, he was attacked by wolverine."

Ruth gasped. "And, he still alive!" She was impressed. She studied Jackson's face. Even with that scruffy beard, he looked handsome. "Is he married?"

Phia shook her head.

"Good. What is old man's name?"

"Jackson."

Ruth let go of Phia's hands and looked back at Jackson. She studied him for a long minute. She shivered, and she added a little more wood to the fire.

"What's wrong?" asked Phia.

Before Ruth could form an answer, she was rudely interrupted by a wolf charging her way that looked like it was foaming at the mouth. She leaped out of her blanket and scampered up the hillside. The old woman was quite spry for her age.

Jackson roared in laughter.

"Ruthie, Ruthie," Called Phia. "It's alright. It's only Reese. She won't hurt you."

The deep snow impeded Ruth's escape. She panted and kept clawing her way through the deep snow. Yesterday, she was ready to die by freezing to death, which is uncomfortable at first, but virtually painless. Death by wolf, on the other hand, not so much.

Phia quickly caught up to her and stopped her. Phia put the Mackinaw coat that she was wearing on Ruth. The old woman calmed and looked at the wolf that was standing by the fire with a snowshoe hare in its mouth and relaxed.

Jackson was still laughing.

Ruth scoffed at the scruffy old man.

Phia gave Jackson the look.

Jackson stopped laughing and slid over to Reese, and he carefully retrieved the rabbit from her mouth. He opened his pocket knife and began skinning breakfast.

Phia helped the old woman back to the fire. Phia could see in her eyes that something was bothering her. The name *Jackson* had really upset her.

"What do you know, Old Woman?" thought Phia to herself.

CHAPTER 17

While the old woman gnawed on a back leg for breakfast, Jackson took Phia aside. "Phia, that old woman knows the way out of here. You must have her show you the way."

"What about you?" asked Phia.

"I would only slow you down. Once you find a phone, or anyone with communications with the outside world, you have them call the local police and tell them about the plane, where it is at, and about the people that need to be rescued."

Phia nodded hesitantly.

"Good," said Jackson. "And don't forget to include me."

Phia hugged Jackson. "I could never forget you."

"Okay, it is settled. The sooner you leave the better."

Phia took a deep breath and said, "Okay."

Phia gathered her things. She looked at Jackson tearfully and asked, "Are you sure that you don't want to leave Reese with you?"

"Nope. I think that I would feel safer with the wolverine."

Phia chuckled.

"I see you're finally finding my jokes funny." Jackson patted Phia on the head. He turned to Ruth. He took off his parka and handed it to her. "Here, you are going to need this."

"Well, what about you? You'll freeze to death," scoffed Ruth. She wasn't expecting the man to be nice to her.

"Yes, what about you?" Phia said, indignantly.

"I'll be fine. I got this here fire."

Phia looked at the small stack of wood and of how far Jackson had to hobble to find more. She knew that without his fur parka, he wouldn't last the night. "No, you won't be fine."

"Damn right that you won't be fine," scolded the old Christian woman in agreement with Phia.

"Damn it to hell," cursed Jackson. "We got no choice. I am the man in charge here, and I demand that you two go look for help."

Ruth shook her head and laughed, "Men. They can't ask for help. They can't ask for directions. They need women to think for them." She picked up her blanket and tossed it to Jackson. "Here, put that on. My son-in-law has a cabin near here. He stays in it, when he is trapping in this area. We go there. You stay there. Plenty wood. Plenty can beans."

Jackson threw the blanket over his shoulders and indignantly asked, "Well, when were you going to tell us about this cabin? And, just how far is this cabin?"

Ruth was on a roll. "What do you care? Or, are you asking for directions?"

"Maybe."

Ruth put on the nice coat and buttoned it up. "Nice parka," she said as she stroked the soft muskrat fur. "Do you have any more questions?"

"Yes I do, old woman."

"My name is Ruth."

"Okay, Ruth, What is your favorite color?"

Ruth led the way to the cabin in the wilderness. Phia supported Jackson, and Reese ran circles around them, as they worked their way into the foothills of the Brooks Range. The moon was a little smaller each night, but the visibility stayed good. If they traveled during the hour that the sun was up, they risked snow blindness.

That was when they rested and, if they were lucky, ate fat rabbits during this short time with half-closed eyes.

Ruth stomped her way through the deep snow without snowshoes and still had to wait for Jackson and Phia the catch up. She was a tough old bat. Apparently, she was not as old as she looked. "Hurry," she said impatiently. "What are you two waiting for, spring?"

Phia chuckled. She was growing quite fond of the old harridan.

Jackson scoffed. "She is killing me. You should have left me. It would have been a less painful death."

Phia again chuckled. She was also growing quite fond of Jackson's humor.

As they crested a hill, a long, wide valley opened up in front of them. Running down the valley was a long narrow frozen lake. The surrounding hills were covered in a thinly wooded Black Spruce forest. These hardy small trees grew halfway up the mountains behind them. The place was quiet and pristine and painted in black and white. And on the edge of the lake was a small cabin. It was a hermit's paradise, and if it was closer to a big city, it would have made a very nice VRBO.

They worked their way down to the frozen lake. The thick ice on it was wind-swept, and the need for snowshoes went away. It was now easier to keep up with Ruth. Jackson felt relieved that they were so close, as he hobbled over the frozen lake with Phia's help. His leg throbbed, but it was almost over. He prayed that he would find a two-way radio inside, and a bottle of whiskey.

The cabin was small. The door was boarded shut, and there were no windows. This made it bear-proof. There was no lock on it, which made it not human proof. After lifting the thick boards that covered the door off their metal hangers, and giving it a hard yank, the door opened. They went inside. The metal stove already had tinder and kindling in it. It was ready for instant fire. That was code for survival in this country. A Colman lantern hung from the ceiling.

Jackson was tall enough to reach the lantern. He set it on the rough wood table. He took out two matches and handed one to Phia. "Here you go girl, you light the stove." He took the other match and lit the lantern and hung it back up. The small space lit up bright and cheery. By the time their eyes adjusted to the intense light, the stove was turning a toasty pink. Ruth took a kettle and filled it with snow and set it on the stove. She rummaged through the cupboards and found some tea and three cups.

There were two narrow bunks and only three chairs at the small table. With the woodstove, there was no more room for any more furniture. The cabin was small and easy to heat and the nicest home Phia and Jackson had been in, in weeks.

Jackson sat with relief on one of the bunks, and Phia sat beside him. Ruth checked her melting snow, and then she sat on the bunk facing them. Reese preferred to stay outside.

Jackson spoke first. "So, Ruth, you say this is your son's cabin. Does he come here often?"

"Not son, daughter's husband. And yes, he come often with his son and my daughter. Good grayling fishing in lake."

"How old is his son?"

Ruth smiled proudly. "My grandson is seventeen and a very handsome man now."

Jackson smiled. "I have two Granddaughters and also a very handsome Grandson."

"All from your daughter and none from your son?" she asked.

Jackson nodded and paused. He wrinkled his forehead and asked, "How did you know I had a daughter?"

Ruth shrugged her shoulders. "Lucky guess, I guess." She changed the subject. "We have radio."

"Where?" gasped Jackson.

"I get." Ruth quickly went to a far cupboard and pulled out a small transistor radio. She turned it on to see if the batteries were still good. She got a lot of static, which meant they were. Radio signals were pretty rare this far north.

Jackson's heart soared when he heard that they had a radio. But when he saw that it only received signals, his heart took a nosedive. "I don't suppose you have any whiskey hidden in one of those cupboards?"

"Sorry," said Ruth as she added more snow to her melting pot. It takes a lot of snow to make three cups of tea. Ruth brought the radio and handed it to Jackson. She sat across from him and said, "Maybe we get news on Tundra Topics. "What time is it?"

Jackson glanced at his wrist out of habit and chuckled. He hadn't worn a watch in years. "I have no idea."

He slowly turned the dial of the radio and listened for any sound. Finally, a squelchy-sound warbled out of the old small speakers. It was Willy Nelson singing, *Mama, don't let your babies grow up to be cowboys.* When the song ended, the man on the other end announced, "This is KFAR, your *far* reaching voice in the bush. The time is seven PM, and it is time for Tundra Topics." He came in loud and clear. His voice was deep and quite pleasing to the ear.

"I only have one message to relay today." He paused. "This is to Frank from his wife. 'Mom took the old Skidoo and headed upriver. Please look for her. I think she is looking for dad again. Hug Francis for me. I love you.'"

The radio announcer finished with local news and village gossip. After that, he went back to playing country-western music.

Jackson switched the radio off, folded his hands, and looked suspiciously at the old Athabaskan woman. "Ruth, I am guessing that you considered yourself a burden to your family, and that is why you walked out in the snowstorm."

"Yes," said Ruth somberly. "Sometimes the old ways were better." She was staring at the cabin's dirt floor and didn't look up.

"Please tell me why you didn't take us back to your home. You could not have walked very far in the blizzard without a parka."

"Cabin closer."

"How much closer."

Ruth sighed, "Just a little."

"Remember you are a good Christian woman."

Ruth tightened her eyes and balled her fists. The bastard pulled the Christian card. "Maybe lot closer."

Jackson leaned forward and put his hands on his knees. "Was it more than ten miles?"

Ruth hesitated and nodded.

"Was it more than fifty miles?"

Another forced nod came from the Christian woman.

"Was it more than one hundred miles?"

Ruth looked up into Jackson's cold eyes. "I don't know. I ran out of gas."

"So, that was you that took the snowmobile."

Ruth nodded. "Yes, I was looking for my husband's spirit. He died on the Chandalar River, many winters ago. I wanted to join him, but I got lost and find you instead. Your Christian God works in mysterious ways. I think I will go back to Indian god."

"I have one more question." Jackson paused and waited for Ruth to look at him. "I find it interesting that your grandson was given my Christian name. Please, tell me what your grandson's last name is."

The poor old woman sighed heavily, as she looked back down at the dirt floor. She whispered, "Jackson."

CHAPTER 18

W ow," said Phia with young innocence. "What a coincidence. Ruthie's grandson has the same name as you." Phia noticed the steam coming from the kettle on the woodstove. "How about a cup of real tea." She hopped off the bed and went to the stove.

Jackson smiled at Ruth. "So, Frankie married your daughter. How is he doing?" Where does he live now?" Jackson kept rattling off questions without waiting for an answer.

Before Ruth could slow down Jackson's quarries, a low growl got their attention. It was Reese; she remained outside and on guard by the door.

Phia quickly ran to the door and opened it. Ruth followed, and Jackson hobbled as fast as he could towards.

"Look," said Phia. She was pointing across the lake. "Someone's coming."

A small team of dogs was barking and pulling a loaded sled their way. Running, and occasionally hopping on the runners, was a man in a beaver parka. The lead dog was gray like a wolf and slightly larger than the rest of the dogs. Phia watched this dog, as he led his team up the lake. When the dogs behind him swung out of line, he would pull them back on track. She stood there fascinated at the team of huskies, as they charged her way. It was such a glorious sight.

But her wolf friend didn't think so. Reese growled with open jaws, and her hair stood tall and bristled all across her back. She was ready to fight.

Phia got down on her knees and tightly held on to the snarling wolf. "No Reese, please no."

Reese wanted to ignore her friend, but she finally calmed down.

Phia pointed toward the wooded hillside behind them. "You must go. I will be fine. These are my people. Please, I don't want anything to happen to you." Phia gently turned the wolf around. "Go."

Reese didn't understand why she had to leave. She looked up at Phia and waged her tail. Phia kissed her on the nose and pointed towards the hill behind them. "Please go."

The sad wolf understood and made her way up the hillside. She found a pinnacle of rock that she could crawl out on and watch the valley below. She lay down, and patiently watched and waited for her friend. She would be there, if Phia needed her.

Jackson turned to Ruth. "Is that my son?"

Ruth shook her head. "Frankie travels by snow machine. The handsome young man coming this way is my grandson, Francis."

Phia stood between Jackson and Ruth. She felt the anticipation radiating out from the adults beside her. It was contagious. She was on her toes, as she watched the team of dogs effortlessly charged up the lake. They were poetry in motion.

She had heard of Alaskan sled dogs and had seen their pictures. But to actually watch them in action was breathtaking. As the team drifted left, she heard a gentle, but firm voice sing out, "Gee." And the lead dog swung right, and the sled straightened out, as it headed up the lake.

They were smooth and fast, and in a few minutes' time, they were at the trail that led up to the cabin. "Whoa," cried the man standing on the back runners of the wood-frame sled. The team stopped, and the man retrieved a pronged steel hook, which was attached to the sled, and he buried it in the snow behind him.

It was an anchor to keep the team from running off with his dog-powered vehicle. They were bred to run, and like a child at Christmas, they couldn't sit still very long.

While the man from the sled tied his lead dog to a stake, Ruth pumped her short stout legs his way.

"Grandma, is that you?" The man dropped what he was doing, when he saw Ruth coming down the trail from the cabin and met her halfway. He pulled back his parka hood and caught her around the waist. "Grandma, we have been looking all over for you. Mom is worried sick. How did you end up here? I saw the smoke coming from the cabin and thought someone was in trouble. What happened to you?"

Ruth smiled at the boy and all his questions. "I got lost."

"Lost?"

"Yes my sweet boy, and these nice people, found me in a snowstorm, and so I brought them here."

"You were lost in a snowstorm?"

"Yes," warily replied grandma.

"If you were so lost, how did you find the cabin?"

"I prayed to St. Anthony."

"Oh, grandma, I love you," laughed Francis. "Please don't ever run away again." After a quick hug, he asked, "Okay, who are these people with you?"

"Oh Francis, they very much need our help. Come quickly." Ruth turned and ushered the boy towards the cabin.

Phia studied the man as he tended to his dogs before anything else. She watched him meet his grandmother on the snow-packed trail and flip his parka hood to his back. The man was a boy. His thick black hair was neatly trimmed across the center of his forehead. His eyes were dark and, when he smiled at his grandmother, his teeth sparkled as white as the snow. He didn't look very tall, but she could see that his broad shoulders filled out his fur parka quite well. And he had a sweet boyish face behind his smile. Phia was smitten.

Jackson saw the same boy and was immediately proud. He could see his son in him. He suddenly became terrified and had no idea how to introduce himself to the boy.

Francis couldn't help but notice the cute girl at the cabin. And when he got close, he couldn't help but notice that she was way beyond cute. He was also quite smitten and couldn't take his eyes off her. He also became terrified, because he was hopelessly shy around girls. And he had no idea how to introduce himself to the girl.

Grandma Ruth ignored Jackson. Her grandson lived this long without him, and, as far as she was concerned, she was the only grandparent that the boy needed. "Francis, this is Phia, and she needs our help. Her plane crashed, and we need to find help."

Francis heard nothing after the name, Phia. He just dumbly smiled at the exotic creature in front of him.

"Hi, Francis." Phia reached out and shook the boy's hand. Her hand was warm and his was hot.

"Hi Phia." He gave her hand a slight squeeze. She didn't seem to notice.

The squeeze increased her heart rate a little, but she concealed it nicely. "Your grandmother says that you can take me to a phone, or a two-way radio, and call for help."

He smiled and nodded. "Yes, I can." And he added, "When do you want to leave?" Now he wished he had listened to his grandmother, as to why they were going for help, but he figured he could wing it.

"You should leave right away," said the old man next to her. Francis glanced up at him and nodded. As he turned back towards Phia, something about the old man's grizzled face got his attention. He looked back. He was very familiar looking, and suddenly he remembered where he had seen him. "You were at Grandma Rains' funeral."

Jackson backed up a step. "You were at her funeral? Was your father there?"

Francis nodded. "We sat in the back."

"Do you know who I am?"

"I asked my father who you were, and he just said you were a friend of the family. But I knew who you were. My father was very angry with you. And so we left early."

"Did he say why he was angry with me?"

"No. He said that he never wanted to talk about it. And now that Grandma Rains is dead, we never need to come back here."

Jackson wanted to hug his new grandson and tell him how sorry he was but he didn't know how. "Do you want me to tell you why he was so angry with me?"

"No," and that was all he said.

Francis looked at Phia. "Please get your things. It is a long way to a telephone." Phia quickly ran into the cabin and grabbed her blanket, which was all of her things.

Francis glanced down at Jackson's leg. "What happened to your leg?"

"Wolverine."

"You can still walk! You're lucky to be alive." Francis was impressed with his grandfather. "I know that damn wolverine. He kept robbing my traps and stealing everything that I had caught. I had to quit trapping here and go somewhere else."

Jackson smiled at the boy, he already was a man. "Do you have a number 4 trap with teeth?"

Francis nodded. "Do you think you can catch him? They are pretty wary."

Jackson laughed. "Who do you think taught your father to trap?"

Francis smiled at the old man. "Wait here. I will get you one from my sled."

While Francis hurried to retrieve the wolverine trap, both Grandfather and Grandson were one in deep thought about the other. Jackson had so many questions, and there was so little time. Finding rescue was the most important thing now.

Francis returned just as Phia came out of the cabin with her blanket. "Good luck," said the handsome boy with a smile, as he handed Jackson the trap.

"Thanks," said Jackson with a pounding heart.

When Phia joined them carrying her blanket, Jackson took off his Muskrat parka and gave it to her. "Here, trade me. I won't need it. I will be in the warm cabin."

Phia handed Jackson the hooded Mackinaw that she had been wearing. She turned to Grandma Ruth. "Please take care of that old man. I am not through with him yet."

"Yes, Grandma," added Francis. "And I have a few more questions, myself."

Ruth sighed and forced a nod.

Francis motioned for Phia to come to the back of the sled. He pointed at the runners coming out the rear. "Put your feet on these and hang on tight to the bars. My dogs are fast."

Phia grinned at the boy. "I prefer to run in back, like you do."

Francis turned to Jackson and lowered his eyebrows.

"Don't worry about her, Grandson. She's a fast one, and guard your Reese's Peanut Butter Cups, if you have any."

Francis shrugged his shoulders and turned to Phia, "Suit yourself." He retrieved his metal snow-anchor and hollered, "**Mush**." And they were off.

Phia turned to Jackson and Ruth. "You two behave yourselves. I will be back."

Phia caught up to the team in no time. The two grandparents watched, until they were out of sight. Jackson turned to Ruth, "I sure could drink a cup of tea about now.

"Good idea," said Ruth. She paused and with a shy grin confessed, "I may have lied about there being no whiskey in the cabin."

"Bless you, Ruth, bless you." Jackson put his arm over Ruth's firm shoulders for support, and they shuffled back to the cabin.

CHAPTER 19

Francis's team followed a wide trail that led to the southwest. He was coming out of the Brooks Range and running his team back down into the tundra. The dogs were tireless, and before long, Phia hopped on one of the sled's back runners. Since they were going downhill, Francis joined her. She had her right foot on the runner and pumped with her left foot, and Francis rode the other rail and pumped with his right foot. They were making good time. The ride was thrilling and breathtaking. Phia's face was frozen in a smile. She couldn't have been more delighted.

Phia watched and learned as Francis communicated with his four-legged engines. He shouted most of his commands to the lead dog. His name was Kona, and he was a beautiful creature.

When the trail made a sharp left, **"Kona, Haw,"** Francis shouted. And Kona quickly charged left. The two dogs behind him, the swing dogs, leaned into their harness and swung the team to the left. And the wheel dogs, the strongest of the group, kept the sled from hitting trees, when they turned too sharply. Each knew his job and listened for the commands.

They were running above the Arctic Circle and it was approaching the last day that the sun would shine its light at this latitude. It would then disappear for over two months.

"Whoa…whoa," cried Francis, as he brought his team to a stop. "We rest the dogs," he said, as he kicked his snow hook deep into the crusted snow. "Today is the last day that we will see the sun for a while. We will camp here."

Francis unlashed the tarp on his sled. He pulled out a bag of old frozen salmon and placed it near the sled. He found a small ax and a tall tin pot.

Phia watched in horror, as he began preparing the food. He was using the ax to chop up the whole fish… head, guts, and all. And he tossed everything into the cooking pot. She cringed and asked, "Do you want me to build a fire?"

"That would be great." He looked up at her and asked, "Do you know how?"

"Yes, your grandfather taught me. Where do you want it?"

Francis pointed towards two trees and went back to chopping fish. Some look spoiled and even rotten.

As soon as Phia had her fire going, Francis put the tin pot on the hot coals. "Nice fire," he complimented with a shy smile. She smiled back. Francis left to tend his dogs. He was not a man of many words.

He unhooked his dogs and staked them to keep them from straying, or fighting. The lead dog, Kona, stayed loose and close to his master. When he got the dogs squared away, Francis came back to the fire. He found a long stick and began stirring his gruel. Phia began wishing that she had more of Jackson's Reese's Peanut Butter Cups to eat, instead of Francis' strong-smelling fish soup.

"It smells good," she said to be polite.

"No, it don't," replied Francis. "This is for the dogs. They always eat first. We need them fat and happy. They are our life support out here. We are a long way from any village. So, they get the *good* food."

"The good food! Really?" This time her tone was not as polite.

Francis laughed. "I was kidding." He had a good laugh. "I always pack some canned potatoes and canned peaches and moose steak for me. I even threw in a small bottle of wine. I like to celebrate the coming of the dark days of winter."

"That does sound better," said Phia casually, but what she actually wanted to say was, 'I could kiss you!'

She added a little more wood to her cooking fire. "Why would anyone want to celebrate the coming of winter?"

"No mosquitoes. If you ever lived here in the summer, you would understand. They are the tiny piranhas of the north."

Francis took a rope and tied it between the trees behind the fire, and then he took the tarp from the sled and hung it over the rope. It reflected the heat nicely. He got a supply box from the sled and placed it between the fire and the blanket. "Sit," he said.

And like an obedient dog, Phia sat.

"It is almost time," he said as he unscrewed the metal cap off the cheap red wine. He sat down beside her and pointed south towards a bright light that ran red across the snow-covered horizon. The sun was rising. They watched as it slowly crawled up into their world, but it didn't quite make it all the way up. Old Sol smiled at them, and then sadly, he slowly sank back towards the southern hemisphere. This was the last time he would rise for almost three months.

"We should toast to the sun for his final encore." Francis raised the bottle towards the pink sky and handed the wine to Phia for the first sip.

Phia shook her head. "But I am not old enough to drink."

"Don't worry, I won't tell anyone, and neither will my dogs."

Phia took a deep breath and flashed him a devious smile and drank. She handed the bottle back to him, so that he could also drink to the sun's final performance of the year.

The steak and potatoes were cooking in the same pan. Francis handed Phia a knife and a fork. With a gloved hand, he pulled the pan off the fire. They both ate out of the hot skillet that the meal was cooked in.

When Francis served up the peaches, a lone wolf howled in the distance. Phia gasped, she recognized the call.

"What's the matter?"

"It's my friend. She's not supposed to be here."

Francis looked at Phia's concerned face. "There is another woman out here?" He jumped to his feet and looked across the tundra for whoever was out there. With the sun already down, all he could see were dark shadows. "Where is she?"

Again, the lone howl of a wolf filled the night sky. It seemed closer.

"That's her," whispered Phia.

Francis looked back at Phia, "The wolf?"

Phia nodded.

Francis gasped, "**Who are you?**"

By this time, Kona, who was quietly lying beside Francis, sprung to his feet with a growl. He was upset and ran to the edge of their camp. He sniffed north and continued his low growl towards the dark tundra.

"**Kona,**" shouted Francis, as he quickly ran and grabbed a hold of him. Once he had the dog restrained, he turned his attention back to Phia. He started to ask her something, but she was gone.

By this time, the other dogs, that were staked, began barking and wailing at the smell of a wolf. Kona broke loose from Francis and loped off into the darkness. Francis quickly ran to his team and tried to calm them down. They were leaping at their tethers, which were only anchored in the deep snow. As they loosened, Francis quickly re-anchored them. His hands were full. He was worried about his lead dog. But since he was half wolf and in his prime, he knew he would be alright. It was Phia that really worried him the most.

The rising moon shed a little light on the matter. It was enough for Phia to see by. So she raced across the tundra in search of her friend. She hadn't gone very far, when she was suddenly broadsided by a very excited wolf. Phia landed on her back and her view was obstructed by a face-licking wolf.

"Reese," cried Phia as she sat up and hugged her around the neck. "What are you doing here?" Phia kissed her on the nose and said, "Bad dog." But it sounded sweet to Reese, and she just wagged her happy tail.

Their fanning moment was rudely interrupted by a low growl. Kona was slowly circling them with drool dripping from his sharp teeth. The whites around his dark eyes glowed in the dark.

Reese turned towards the aggressive lead dag. She was as tall as him and weighted close to the same. She stood between him and Phia and flashed her teeth at him. She was not backing down. It would be a fight to the death, if need be. She grew aggressive and took a step towards Kona.

Kona huffed and accepted her challenge. He leaned back on his powerful hind legs and was ready to leap.

Reese was not intimidated. She shortened the distance between them. It was do, or die. She was so close now that their noses were almost touching.

Phia was beside herself. As scared as she was and as much as she wanted to run, she had to stay and help protect her friend.

Once Francis finished securing his team, he grabbed his lever action 45-70, and ran in the direction that he had last seen Kona. The tundra was rough, and he stumbled and fell a few times. He kept going and prayed he would find the girl before it was too late. **"Phia,"** he desperately hollered.

"Over here."

As he ran towards the sweet voice, he pumped the lever on his rifle putting a live round in the chamber. It was too quiet. "Phia," he called again.

"We are over here."

Francis looked towards the sound and saw her waving her hand. His heart fluttered and he took off running. But unfortunately, a tuft of tundra snagged his ankle and he face-planted into the deep snow. He quickly recovered and ran up to Phia. He was completely covered in snow. He looked like a ghost.

"Are you all right," said the ghost.

Phia laughed so hard that she almost wet herself.

The indignant ghost brushed the snow off. "What's so damn funny?"

While Phia regained her senses, Francis looked at his dog. He was staring back at him, and a large wolf was standing next to him. He looked back at Phia. "What happened?"

Phia shrugged her shoulders. "I thought they were going to kill each other. But when they finished sizing each other up, they didn't" Phia giggled. "I think they fell in love."

Francis looked at the odd couple and shook his head. He looked Kona in the eye. "I thought I could trust you."

Francis gave out a relieved sigh, and he began laughing hysterically. Phia joined him in laughing and wanted to hug the sweet snow-covered boy. These feelings were new to her and she liked them.

CHAPTER 20

After about six hours of sleep in his tent, Francis quietly slipped out of his sleeping bag. Phia was wrapped in her blanket and softly snoring away. Francis slipped on his parka and crawled out of the flimsy shelter. He was greeted by a dazzling display of the Northern Lights. He never tired of seeing them.

The dogs were already up and chomping at the bit. He knelt down in front of each dog and affectionately stroked its back and talked softly to each, as he took them to their position in front of the wood sled. He loved each one a little differently. Kona was the last to be snapped into his harness.

Hours earlier, when he and Phia got back to their camp, Reese was introduced to the team. It was a loud and a frenzied convention. But finally, a pecking order was established, and they all settled down and became canine friends. Kona was still the alpha male, and now they accepted Reese as the alpha female. She would run with them unharnessed.

The excited dogs woke Phia up. She folded her blanket and rolled up Francis's sleeping bag, and she put them in the sled. She turned north and smiled at the tall green lights, with their flashes of red, in the star-studded sky. After that, she began taking down the tent and added it to the rest of the cargo on the sled.

When Francis finished hooking up the dogs, he made sure that everything was loaded into his sled and lashed down good and tight. At the back of the sled was a large plastic bag filled with dried salmon. It was breakfast. He handed a piece to Phia. She stared at it for a minute. She wasn't sure to trust her new friend.

Francis pulled out another piece and stuffed most of it in his mouth and began chewing it enthusiastically, followed by a ghastly smile.

Phia took a small bite, and she became pleasantly surprised. She was hungry and stuffed the rest of it in her mouth. Her smile was also disgusting.

Francis gave her another piece and tossed a little of the smoked salmon to each dog. When he finished, he stuffed the bag back in its handy compartment and retrieved the metal hook out of the snow. It was time. He motioned to Phia to hop on to the left runner and said. "Would you like to do the honors?"

Phia nodded and hollered, "**Mush**."

And they were off and back on their rescue mission. It was up to her, with the help of Francis and a team of huskies, to find help for her mother and the surviving passengers of flight *AS1125*.

The tundra was like a white ocean. Its rolling expanse was like the swells of the sea. The sled flowed down the white valleys and over the crests of frozen-grass waves. It was thrilling. It was exhausting. And it was damn cold. The temperature dropped into the basement. The hoar frost covered the sparse trees like white foliage. It was beautiful. It was scary. And it was a typical winter night above the Arctic Circle. And on they rode to fulfill their rescue mission.

They finally came to a wide river, the east fork of the Chandalar; it was the main winter road in this region. The dogs could now run even faster down this flat, winding road of ice to the small town of Fort Yukon on the Yukon River. But, it was still over a day away.

"**Whoa…whoa,**" commanded Francis, as they pulled out on the river. The team heeded and came to a stop. It had been a long run and they needed a rest.

Francis secured his snow hook and broke out the smoked salmon. He tossed a small piece to each dog, after which, he and Phia sat on the sled and also ate some of the dried, high protein. It was their midnight lunch.

"How much longer, Francis?" asked Phia.

Francis finished chewing the thick wad of salmon in his mouth before he answered. "If everything goes right, we should be in Fort Yukon by tomorrow at this time."

"Good. Do they have rescue helicopters there?"

"I don't know. They have a decent airport and a few bush planes."

Phia took another bite of her dried salmon and suddenly stopped chewing. "I hear something." She paused and pointed. "Look there is something coming down the river."

Francis looked to where she was pointing. It was a snow machine, and it was charging their way. Francis smiled. "It's Dad."

Phia looked at the noisy machine and the hooded driver of the vehicle sitting behind its frost-covered, plastic windshield. Phia could not see his face. "Wow, you must have really good eyes. It could be an old woman for all I can see."

"Old woman?" Francis laughed. "I recognized the machine by its sound. Every snowmobile has its own voice. That's dad's."

Frank Jackson, Francis's dad, roared the machine right up to them. He stopped and shut off the noisy engine, and swung off the seat he was straddling. He looked over at Phia and sagged. "Oh," he said as he walked up to his son. "I thought you found Grandma."

Before Francis could tell him, Frank turned to Phia. "Who are you?"

"That's Phia, dad. And I did find Grandma Ruth."

Frank spun back to his son. "Where? Is she okay? Your mother is worried sick."

"She's fine, dad. She's with Grandpa."

"But Grandpa is dead," explained Frank. "Are you telling me that she finally found his spirit?"

"No, Dad," chuckled Francis. "She's at our cabin on Whitefish Lake with my other Grandpa."

"I thought he was in Florida with my Sister. What in the hell is he doing here?"

Phia knew that answer. "He told me he came back to Alaska to die."

"And," added Francis. "He was the one that actually found Grandma Ruth. Well, him and Phia."

"How did he get to the cabin?"

"He walked."

"All the way from Florida?"

"No, silly." Phia decided to answer that question. "From the Yukon."

"Interesting! May I ask how he got to the Yukon Territories?"

"We flew."

"Are you from Florida?"

Phia shook her head. "We are from New York."

"Who's *we*?"

"Me and my Mom."

"Where's your Mom now? And aren't you a little young to be gallivanting around with strange boys?"

"She's back at the plane with the rest of the survivors. And I am not gallivanting around. Your son and I are on a rescue mission."

Frank gasped. "Dad was in a plane crash? Is he okay?"

"He's fine, dad. He's with grandma and she is nursing his leg."

"What happened to his leg.?"

"He was attacked by a wolverine."

Frank sat on his snowmobile and rubbed his head. "Let me get this straight. Your grandfather came back to Alaska to die, and he survived a plane crash, and then he was attacked by a wolverine and survived, and now he is with Grandma Ruth."

Both Phia and Francis nodded their heads.

Frank laughed and just shook his head. "I guess he really had a couple of bad days. Well, if your Grandma tries some of her special weeds, that she calls her herbal medicine, on him, he might just get his wish."

Frank jumped back to his feet. This was an emergency. He dug through the saddlebags on the snowmobile and found his first aid kit. He handed it to Francis. "Here son, take this back to the cabin and put a lot of disinfectant on your Grandpa's wound. Wolverine bites are nasty. I will take…what's your name again?"

"Phia," said Phia.

"I will take Phia with me and head into Fort Yukon."

Phia wasn't sure she wanted to change partners. "Will that machine that you're riding, be any faster than Francis' dogs?"

Frank looked at his son and grinned. "A little." They both laughed at his sarcasm.

"Hop on missy and hold on tight."

Phia straddled the seat behind Frank and latched on to the sides of the seat.

"You need to put your arms around me, Phia, and hold on to me real tight."

Phia forced her arms around the strange man. A year ago she would not even look at one. But she needed to get help for her mother, and so she trusted him. She heard the engine throttle up and the machine took off like a rocket. Frank ran a few Iron-dog Races with his snowmobile, so it was really fast.

He was going sixty by the first turn in the river, and that was the slowest he would go, until they hit the streets of Fort Yukon, Alaska.

Reese followed for a couple of miles, but the machine was just too fast. Confused and lonely, she made her way back towards the dog team that was led by Kona and the human that befriended her friend. She would wait with them. She was sure Phia would be back.

By the time she got there, Francis had already turned his team around and was mushing his way towards Whitefish Lake and the cabin. Reese caught up to them in no time and ran close to the alpha male as they charged north and east.

Francis was relieved to see the wolf again. When she followed Phia and his father, he worried. He knew how much Phia loved her. Now, he worried that he may never see Phia again. He knew that when she and the other survivors were rescued, they would be flown directly to Fairbank, which was their original destination.

"I never got her phone number," he sadly said to himself, which made him laugh, because he didn't even own one, and besides, there was no service out here.

He looked up at the Northern Lights and sighed. And at the top of his lungs, he hollered, **"Good Night Phia…whatever your last name is, I will miss you**." And with an aching heart, he mushed on through the night.

CHAPTER 21

The census in 2010 showed that the population of Fort Yukon, Alaska was a little over 550 residents. The town's fame is that it lies right on the Arctic Circle. It was established in the mid-eighteen hundreds by the Hudson Bay Company as a trading post, when Alaska belonged to Russia. In 1959 Fort Yukon was incorporated and officially became a modern town with an airport. And the Native Americans now dominate the population with the whites tipping the scale at less than 14%. It is a colorful village and a tourist attraction.

A little over three hours later, Phia climbed off the snowmobile covered in frost and her teeth were chattering. Not from the cold, it was from the pure terror of the trip. If she had to choose between taking another ride on a snowmobile, or risking her life in a plane crash, she was leaning towards the plane.

The buildings were predominately single-story log structures. The ones on the river were larger and taller and built with newer construction materials. They were the thriving businesses of Fort Yukon. As one looked north and away from the river, the structures in this area were small houses, log shacks, and then rickety hovels. The uninhabited ones had no smoke rising out of their rusted tin stacks. And there were quite a few of those. The dogs now outnumbered the people.

Frank stopped in front of the Tribal Police Office. They had electric power and a landline connecting them to the outside world. He quickly ushered Phia inside.

The place was quite warm and looked modern. It had some kind of central heating system. Just inside the door, there was a long countertop that had a young Athabaskan woman in a police uniform sitting on a tall stool. There was a post office on the far left end and a sitting area with small tables to its right. This area had a tiny kitchenette with a full coffee pot and brown paper cups next to it. There were two people sitting on wide, padded chairs by a window looking over the frozen river. One was a man reading a newspaper, and the other, a native woman going through her mail. They both seemed to be enjoying their coffee.

Frank pulled off his mittens and unbuttoned his parka. He stepped right to the tribal policewoman. Her nametag said, Grey.

Officer Grey looked up from the paper that she was doodling on and set down her pencil. "Oh, hi Frank. Have you heard from Ruth?" It was a small town, and it was the only post office for miles. Everyone knew everyone. There are no secrets in small towns.

"Oh, she's fine," answered Frank. "Francis found her in our cabin on Whitefish Lake." He was distracted from his mission by her concern for his family.

"Your son is such a sweet boy." She looked at Phia. "Who is that with you?"

Frank pulled Phia up to the counter. "Actually, she is why I'm here, Karen," which was Officer Grey's first name.

Frank turned to Phia and with an excited voice said, "You tell her what happened and that we have a real emergency going on here. You tell her." Frank looked back at Karen, and before Phia could open her mouth, he said, "There was a plane crash. A big plane and there are survivors and they need to be rescued." He turned back to Phia. "Tell them Phia. Tell them about the crash."

Again before Phia could say anything, Frank looked back at Officer Karen Grey. With a nervous frantic voice, he continued, "She was in the crash, and she can tell you everything. Go ahead Phia, tell her."

By this time, the other cop on duty, and several lookie-loos, and their kids, were gathered around Frank and Phia. Phia finally got a chance to repeat Frank's urgent message, and she clarified it. And everyone intently listened to the young girl and her incredible story. Officer James Brook quickly called Fort Greely. It was the closest place with helicopters large enough to rescue more than one person and equipped with military night vision. They agreed to dispatch two choppers immediately to Fort Yukon. The man on the other end of the phone asked for the coordinates of the crash site.

"Somewhere between here and Canada," replied Officer Brook. He was young, new, and a bit nervous. This was his first big emergency.

"That's a bit vague," replied the Greely dispatcher. "Can we narrow that down a bit?"

"Sure," said Brook and he handed the phone to Phia."

"Hello?"

"Hi, I am with the Fort Greely Response Team. Who am I speaking to?"

"Phia."

"Hi Phia. I was told that you could give me coordinates to the crash site. You sound pretty young. How old are you?"

"Fourteen."

"Phia, honey, will you please put the idiot that handed you the phone back on it?"

"Okay." Phia looked back up at Officer Brook. "He wants to talk to you."

"Hello?"

"Will you please put your boss on the phone?" The Greely guy's voice was soft, as he spoke through his clenched teeth.

"He's not here right now, but Officer Grey is."

"Fine, let me speak with him."

"Officer Grey is a her," corrected Officer Brook, as he handed the phone to Karen. She suspected the problem.

"This is Officer Grey. How may I assist you?"

"What can you tell me about the location of the crash site?"

"The girl that you just talked to was a survivor. From her story and the amount of time it took to get here, I am guessing that the plane is south of the Brooks Range and close to the Canadian border."

"Do you have any planes up there that can begin searching immediately? It might save us all a lot of time."

"I'll see what I can do. I'll keep you in touch."

As Karen hung up the phone, the man reading the newspaper folded it and got out of his seat. He walked up to Karen. "Hi, Karen, I couldn't help hearing about the plane crash. Is there anything I can do?"

"Hi, Shawn. Maybe there is."

Shawn O'Malley was a bush doctor, and he had his own plane, and he was instrument certified. That meant he could fly in bad weather. So yes, there was a lot he could do.

Meanwhile, Officer Brook decided to get on the phone with the airline industry. "Phia, what airlines did you fly with?"

"I don't know. My mom bought the tickets."

Since it was flying into Alaska, Officer Brook took a wild guess. "Phia, was there a picture of an Eskimo painted on the plane's tail?"

Phia nodded.

"Good," said Brook. He quickly dialed the head office of Alaska Airlines. Brook drummed the counter irritatingly with the fingernails of his free hand while waiting for someone to answer.

Finally, "Yes, hello. This is Officer Brook of the tribal police in Fort Yukon, Alaska and I would like to report a plane crash." And as an afterthought, he added, "It was one of your planes." There was a pause. "Okay."

The place became quite quiet. All eyes were on Brook. He looked around and smiled. "I'm on hold."

"Ah," quietly murmured his audience.

A few seconds later, "Yes, I am still here. And yes, I can hold." It was quiet enough that the elevator music coming from the phone could be heard by everyone, well except for Ward. He was irritatingly hard of hearing and refused to wear his hearing aids.

Finally, "Yes, I'm still here."

Brook listened and answered, "I am Officer Brook in Fort Yukon Alaska."

Brook again listened. After a few seconds, he said, "I understand that there are no reports of a plane crash, **now**. This plane went down about…" Brook looked at Phia. She shrugged her shoulders. She had lost all track of time. Brook took a guess. "About a month ago."

Another pause while Brook listened. "Yes, I'm sure it was one of your planes."

Brook nodded on the phone, as he listened to it question him again. "It happened somewhere near the border of Canada," he answered. That was followed by more head-nodding and ending with an eye roll. "So, you're telling me that you did lose a Boeing 737 three weeks ago. And you're saying that it can't be yours, because yours went down over Hudson Bay."

Brook incredulously shook his head, as he listened. "I am sorry, if I wasted your time, sir. I just thought you might want to send someone out here on the off chance that it might be yours, especially since your plane has been the only recorded accident this year and it has not been found. I know you don't think that there were survivors, but what if you're wrong?" Brook paused and added, "Have a nice day." He hung up the phone. "Damn bureaucrats!" he swore as he shook his head.

Dr. O'Malley was short with thick gray hair. His father was also a doctor who practiced in Anchorage. The younger Dr. O'Malley took his practice to the bush. He felt that he was needed more out there, and because he loved to fly.

Dr. O'Malley leaned forward and extended his right hand to the young girl standing next to Frank. "My name is Shawn, what's your name?"

"Phia." She timidly shook the good doctor's hand.

"That's a nice name. What does it mean?"

Phia shrugged her shoulders. "It is short for Sophia."

"Sophia, that's a pretty name. Were you traveling by yourself?"

"I was traveling with my mom. She's sick."

"Well, Phia, I am a doctor and I would like you to help me find your mom. Do you think you can help me?"

Phia nodded and a few tears of joy started running down her eyes. "Oh, yes."

"Okay, kiddo. Put your parka on and follow me."

As they reached the door the phone rang. Brook picked it up. "Fort Yukon Police." It was Alaska Airlines calling back. "Just a minute, I need to put you on hold." Brook pushed the hold button and looked up. There were a lot of thumbs pointing at the ceiling.

Brook chuckled and asked, "Do you think fifteen minutes is enough?"

CHAPTER 22

It was an exceptionally-nice, moonlit morning, for winter. The sky was clear, and it was frightfully cold with the temperature hovering deep in the negative numbers. But on the bright side, the visibility was great. It was early, and the only sound in this pristine white world was the crunch on the brittle snow as two pairs of mukluks scurried to a small plane.

Dr. O'Malley's aircraft was parked in front of a small hangar at Fort Yukon airport. The small facility had a paved runway, and it was long enough for commercial planes. The nose of Dr. O'Malley's plane was covered with a heated, insulated canvas blanket that was plugged into the side of the building to keep the engine warm for quick starts. The wings were also covered with a light drop cloth to keep the snow and the frost off of them.

Dr. O'Malley's aircraft was a four-place plane, meaning it had room for four passengers. He had the two rear seats removed, so that he could fit a stretcher on the plane's floor to transfer injured patients. Basically, he had set it up as a flying ambulance.

When Phia saw O'Malley's rescue vehicle, she gasped in horror. The plane was on skis and to her, it looked like a snowmobile with wings.

"What's wrong?" he asked when Phia stopped and stared at his weird snowmobile.

"Nothing," lied the brave little girl, as she stood there remembering her ride with Frank.

"Oh, I see," said Dr. O'Malley as he reached for her hand and led her towards his flying snowmobile. He assumed that since she was in a plane accident, she had a fear of flying. "I promise you that this plane won't crash. These small planes are quite safe. Even if you lose power, they soar like a glider, and you can safely land them."

"It's not a snow machine?" asked Phia. She had never seen a plane on skis before.

He laughed. "No child." And he explained, "In winter my little plane is a sled that flies, and in the summer, when I put on the floats, it is a boat that flies. And for the in-between months, I put on the wheels, and it becomes a regular airplane that needs a runway, which, unfortunately, limits me to where I can land."

Phia studied the winged machine and contemplated what he said about it. She concluded that it would be more versatile this way, and that it kind of made sense. But the boat-plane idea was stretching it a bit.

"Well, okay then," she replied reluctantly.

Dr. O'Malley gave her a confident smile. "Good, this is going to be fun." He quickly began removing all the coverings. He stashed them in a compartment in the plane.

"Phia, please help me turn the plane." He began pushing on the tail of his plane, and with Phia's help, the plane skidded in a half-circle on its left ski. It was now facing the runway. He opened the passenger door. "Hop in kiddo." He started to help Phia up on the wing, but she was too fast for him. She literally hopped in.

"Buckle up."

He walked around the plane and did his preflight inspection. Lastly, he spun the prop by hand. His father had a plane that started that way. He had an electric starter but rotated his prop just to loosen things up. Once satisfied, he crawled up into the plane and put on headphones.

"Here, put these on." He handed Phia another set of headphones. "These are so we can talk. It gets a bit loud in these small planes." He cranked over the engine, and it fired right off, which created a dust storm of snow around the plane. By the time that the engine had warmed, the snow had cleared, and Dr. O'Malley throttled her up. The winged snowmobile began moving slowly at first, and then it quickly gained speed, as it charged down the icy runway.

Phia gasped as the acceleration pushed her back into her seat. Faster and faster the plane slid down the snow-covered runway. At the end of the runway was the wide-open tundra, and it was approaching very fast. All of a sudden she could not feel the chattering of the skis on rough ice. They were airborne. She watched in awe as the lights of town dropped beneath her. She could see the mighty Yukon River turn into a small stream that snaked itself around the low hills of the sparse boreal forests that covered them and the vast tundra below seemed to stretch on forever.

She laughed in delight. It was beautiful up in the sky, and they were on their way to save her mom.

After an hour in their flight, Phia leaned back into her seat and rested her eyes. The view was incredible. The earth was a huge white ball that was dimly lit by a billion stars. It looked cracked, where the dark vegetation ran along the rivers and streams that flowed in their jagged path towards the Yukon River. The dark trees and the shadows of hillsides mottled the landscape beyond the rivers. And the wide tundra seemed to spread its blemished face as far as one could see.

In large jets, as they fly far above the clouds and with their tiny windows, the bored passengers miss this breathtaking view. It is a shame that their destination is more important than the journey and all at the expense of a shorter travel time.

Dr. O'Malley flew over the Chandalar River retracing Phia's journey. When he flew over Frank Jackson's cabin, he pointed it out to Phia. She put her nose close to the window and looked for Francis and his team of huskies, and of course, Reese. But they had already passed them. Phia sighed as she realized that Francis would not reach the cabin for another day.

"Okay now, Phia," said O'Malley through the headphones. "I am now going to fly east. If you recognize anything, let me know."

Phia looked at him and nodded, "Okay." She went back to watching the tiny white world flow silently beneath her.

"I am guessing it will be about three hours from here to where your plane went down. East is a pretty wide destination; it will be like finding a needle in a haystack. Pray that we get lucky."

"Okay," whispered Phia.

When Phia's stepfather started getting physical with her mother, she sought help at a lot of different churches, and each pastor prayed with her for the troubled man that was abusing them. But none of their Gods seemed to work. So, in desperation and the lack of God's help, she took her daughter and ran away to Alaska.

"Doctor, which God do you pray to?"

O'Malley switched on the autopilot and leaned back in his seat. He looked carefully at the young girl. She was still watching the ground. "At times like this, I would have to choose the most powerful One."

Phia turned and looked at him. "Which one is that?"

"Ah therein lies the rub. Each denomination claims that their God is the most powerful One. They also claim that theirs is different than their competitor's God. Some Gods are quite strict and breathe fire and brimstone. And others are gentle and forgiving. If they made a list of all the Gods and sorted them accordingly, one could then possibly choose. But alas, they also believed that there is only one God, and therefore, no need for this list. And to write this list, it would offend all of the gods."

Phia, finding O'Malley answer not all that helpful, again asked, "So, which God do you pray to?"

"Which God?" Dr. O'Malley paused while he thought about how to best answer this philosophical question in layman terms. "The Baptist probably has the easiest God to slip into paradise with. All you have to do is believe in Him. He is a tad strict though in other areas. And the Catholic God, on the other hand, demands guilt. He punishes His followers each Sunday with many genuflects for their sins. Now the Mormons..."

"There, down there." Phia suddenly pointed to a spot below her. "I think that is the place we found Ruth."

O'Malley quickly took back control of the plane and circled lower.

"Yes, we are on course. That was how the Brooks Range looked from here."

Shawn could see no difference in this spot as opposed to any other spot along their trip. He was duly impressed. She pointed towards the way she had come. He lined his compass up with her finger, and at 180 knots, they flew on towards the downed 737 and closer to their rescue mission.

Shortly:

"There, there," excitedly pointed Phia's finger. "That was where Jackson was attacked of a wolverine."

Since there was nothing to see, O'Malley kept flying on their course. But that information rattled him a bit. "Jackson was attacked by a wolverine?"

"Yep."

"Oh my God! Is he all right?"

"Tore his leg up pretty bad."

"It's amazing it didn't kill him." O'Malley paused and looked at Phia. "Why didn't it kill him?"

"I run him off with my spear," said the little warrior proudly. She decided not to tell him that Reese was the actual deterrent. Her life was complicated enough without explaining to him about the wolf she befriended.

"You ran the wolverine off with a sharpened stick?"

Phia shrugged her shoulders and said, "Yep."

"Who are you?" gasped the incredulous doctor.

An hour later, and close to the Yukon Territories, Dr. O'Malley saw a conspiracy of ravens feeding on a caribou carcass. Curiously, he circled lower.

Phia was looking out the other window and didn't see them right away. When they got closer he pointed it out. "The wolves sure didn't leave much for those black scavengers, did they?"

Phia gasped. This could be one of Officer Murphy's kills. She studied the tundra for the lake and for the large, snow-covered fuselage that was the survivor's shelter. She didn't see it. Murphy had to walk a long way for that one.

"We are close. Keep circling," she begged.

With straining eyes, O'Malley flew lower and wider circles. But the last blizzard obliterated the scene below. Jackson's fuel gauge was nearing the half-full mark.

"Half empty," said O'Malley to himself. "I need the rest of the fuel to get back. I will give it one more circle."

CHAPTER 23

Inside the smoke-filled fuselage, the surviving passengers huddled around a very small fire. Decent firewood was scarce and a long way off. The mood was as cold as the outside temperature. And they were running low on meat. Officer Murphy's last couple of attempts ended in a dismal failure. Either he missed his shot, or the animal was not mortally wounded and ran off.

Cheryl noticed Murphy was not warming himself by the fire with the others. He was sitting cross-legged on his sleeping pad with his head lowered in despair. She joined him.

"Murphy, you okay?"

Murphy was holding the 38 caliber revolver in his right hand and a single bullet in his left. He looked up at Cheryl and forced a smile. "I'm fine."

"No, you're not." Cheryl could be brutally honest at times. Everyone was hungry, cold, and on edge. They were either cursing their God, or fervently praying to Him. "What's wrong?"

"This is my last bullet. Our last bit of hope. My last chance. I'm afraid I'm going to fuck it up." He looked at her with broken, sad eyes. "Do you think Jackson is going to find help?"

"Well, you know that he was our best shot at it." Cheryl chuckled, "No pun intended."

Murphy chuckled. She made him feel better. He loaded his revolver. "I guess this bullet isn't doing much good in here." He climbed to his feet and put on his wool cap and mittens. "Wish me luck."

"That's the spirit," she said, as she followed him to the frost-frozen blanket-door. "Wait," she gasped and grabbed his shoulder. "I think I hear a plane."

Suddenly, several pairs of ears perked up. It was definitely the hum of an engine, and it sounded like it circled right over them. The place emptied in an un-orderly fashion, more like a Chinese fire drill. Whooping and waving, they excitedly ran under the small plane that was circling just over their heads. Jackson had made it. Bless his ornery big heart.

Dr. O'Malley roared in laughter when he saw all the survivors. "We did it, Phia, we did it." The good doctor quickly dialed up his satellite phone and called Fort Yukon.

Officer Karen Grey answered the phone on the first ring. She was just about to leave. Her shift had ended.

Dr. O'Malley was excited. "Hi, Karen. We found them."

"Oh, thank God."

"Okay, write this down." O'Malley looked at his GPS and rattled off his position. "Call Fort Greely and relay the coordinates to the dispatcher there."

Karen handed the coordinates to Brook, and he picked up the other line and began relaying the message.

"How are the survivors doing?" asked Karen.

"I am still in the air. I see a lot of hands. I am going to see if I can set this thing down."

"Don't crash," joked Karen.

"Good safety tip. I will call you when I am back in the air." O'Malley put the satellite phone back in its slot. He banked in a wide sweep and lined his plane up with the small, frozen lake under him. He adjusted his throttle and slowed down to 90 knots. He lined his nose up with the lake's center and descended between two scrub trees growing at his end of the lake. The plane hopped a bit when his skis hit the hard ice of the windswept lake. He reversed his prop to slow down the plane, as he approached the other end of nature's frozen runway. Once he got close to the Boeing fuselage, he turned his tail rudder to a hard left, spinning the plane in a half-circle, and he shut her down.

He turned to Phia and said, "You can unbuckle your…" Her side door was open, and she was already gone. Dr. O'Malley chuckled and climbed out his side door. He was immediately engulfed with hugs and inundated with questions. Most of them were the same.

"Yes, I brought food," he said as he opened the cargo door. He had a case of canned peaches and a case of Bush's Baked Beans. The men quickly took them inside, where it was warmer. Dr. O'Malley followed with the can opener.

The excitement inside was even greater than the time that they had discovered all the extra rolls of TP in a small cabinet on the plane. As fast as the cans were opened the survivors devoured them cold right out of their metal cans.

Murphy and Cheryl worked their way over to the pilot. Cheryl asked first. "Where's Jackson? Is he alright?"

"As far as I know, Jackson's fine. He is holed up with his grandson in a cabin south of the Brooks Range."

"Fine?" asked Murphy. "What happened?"

"He tangled with a wolverine. I guess it chewed up his leg pretty bad."

Cheryl became quite concerned. "How bad is it?"

"I don't know. I am a doctor, and I'm going to check in on him on the way back."

"And when is rescue?" asked Cheryl.

"Helicopters should be on their way. I called them the second I found you. They're several hours out. We are a long way into nowhere."

"How did you find us?" asked Murphy.

"That girl that was traveling with Jackson, she showed me."

"Phia?" questioned Cheryl.

"Yes, Phia. She's quite canny. She was like a homing pigeon. To tell the truth, I thought I was wasting my time. This country is huge."

"Wow!" Murphy dropped his jaw, "Inconceivable!" He took a quick breath, "She left two days after Jackson did. We all thought she died somewhere out there by herself."

Cheryl, when she heard, was beside herself in relief. She looked over at the blanket covering Phia's mom, Amy. And there was Phia squatting next to her mother and gently stroking her cheek.

As Cheryl made her way to Phia, she heard Murphy ask O'Malley, "So, she talked to you?"

In all the excitement, no one noticed the young girl in Jackson's parka as she scurried inside and rushed up to her mother. Amy's breaths were shallow and ragged. She wasn't getting any better, but at least she wasn't any worse.

"Mom," softly whispered Phia. "Mom, I'm back. And I brought a doctor."

Amy's lips cracked into a relaxed smile. Her eyes slowly opened and brightened. "Sophia, my baby, it really is you."

Sophia nodded with tears in her eyes and had to wipe her nose. She used her sleeve. "I will be right back."

Phia jumped to her feet and ran over to Dr. O'Malley, latched on to his coat sleeve, and dragged him back to her mother. "**Fix her,**" she demanded.

Dr. O'Malley got down on his knees and studied Amy's face. He turned to Phia. "Behind my seat in the plane is a small red box with a white cross on it. Please, fetch it for me."

Before he finished saying the word 'Please,' Phia was already out the door. "That kid sure is fast," commented the good doctor.

Murphy and Cheryl nodded their incredulous heads in agreement.

The doctor-pilot carefully examined Amy. And it was a severe case of pneumonia. "Her lungs are pretty full," he said as he took off his stethoscope. "Help me get her into the plane. I have oxygen in there. I need to get her to a hospital."

Dr. O'Malley had a stretcher in the plane. Murphy quickly retrieved it and the doctor gently strapped her into it. Several of the men helped to carry Amy to the winged, snowmobile-ambulance. He hooked the oxygen mask over Amy's nose. "Hop in little girl and buckle up."

Dr. O'Malley did a quick preflight, crawled in, and mashed down on the starter button. The Cessna roared to life. The crowd cheered a "thank you,' and waved. Phia smiled. Murphy gave him a thumbs-up and waved back. Dr. O'Malley adjusted the pitch on his prop to full bite, and the plane headed down the lake, lickety-split. When they were airborne, he dipped his left-wing, and they banked west. By the time they had leveled out, the Northern Lights dropped out of the heavens and began escorting them towards their destination.

"Oh wow, there really is a powerful God out there," whispered Phia as she put on her headphones.

After almost two hours of flying time. Dr. O'Malley engaged the autopilot and crawled between the seats to check on his patient. She was sleeping. Her color looked good. And her vitals were acceptable. "Good," he mumbled. He crawled back up to his seat.

"Phia, your mother is resting comfortably, and if it's okay with you, I would like to check in on Jackson?"

Phia looked at the doctor. Her second favorite person in the world, excluding a wolf, was Jackson. "I would like that. I worry about him."

"Excellent," said Dr. O'Malley. He altered course slightly and began humming a tune that Phia had never heard before. It was kind of a catchy tune, and before long, she was happily humming along.

Dr. O'Malley would regularly pick up his mike and radio his position. If there was another plane in the area, it would answer and relay back theirs. It was a safety thing. If they were on a collision course, they would know it immediately and adjust their courses accordingly. And it was nice to know that someone else was out there.

After one of these radio reports, and with no answer, Dr. O'Malley replaced his mike and wondered why the rescue helicopters had not answered. He figured that they should be close enough to hear his signal. "They probably got off to a late start," he said to himself. He resumed humming. At this time of the year, it was not uncommon to be the only small plane out there.

Phia again joined in the hum. She was happy that the grueling ordeal was over with, and that they were on their way to a hospital with her mother. She could see the Brooks Range through the frosted windscreen, and she smiled thinking about the small cabin they were flying towards and that it contained Jackson, and Francis, and Reese.

Shortly, she noticed that she was humming by herself. She looked over at Dr. O'Malley. He had a frown on his clean-shaven face.

"What's wrong?"

"Nothing," he calmly said as he tapped on a round, glass-covered gauge. His finger seemed quite nervous.

Phia looked at the instrument panel and all the needles were pointing at *normal,* and the one that he was concerned with was the fuel gauge, and its needle was pointing straight up at the *halfway mark.*

Phia looked back up at Dr. O'Malley. "Is something wrong with the gauge?"

"It seems stuck. It hasn't moved since we left the crash site." Dr. O'Malley looked over at Phia and gave her a confident smile. "Even if it's not working, I know we have enough gas to get to Fort Yukon, and I can refuel there."

Phia relaxed, a little. Neither of them went back to humming.

The plane flew fine for the next fifteen minutes, and then it didn't.

CHAPTER 24

After Francis and Phia left the old trapper's cabin on their rescue mission, Ruth helped Jackson hobble back inside. She sat him on one of the cots and set two coffee cups on the rough-sawed table. In a far corner of the cabin and in an old crate stuffed with old snowmobile parts, she produced the hidden bottle of cheap whiskey. She poured a generous amount in one of the cups and handed it to Jackson. He filled his mouth and swallowed it slowly. His eyes watered and his beard separated into a wide smile.

"Thank you kindly, Ruth." He took another sip. "Please join me."

Ruth filled her cup with tea, and she sat on the cot across from Jackson. They both sipped in silence and nervously stared at each other like shy teenagers. When Jackson finished his cup of pain medicine, Ruth refilled his mug.

"Is your leg feeling any better?"

"A mite, now that you mentioned it."

"Good," she smiled and sipped her tea. Finally, she had to ask. "Why does your son hate you so much?"

"Ah, you're feeding me a truth serum." Jackson chuckled. "That's getting a little personal, ain't it?"

"I don't think so. He is my son-in-law and has lived with us longer than with you." She looked him in the eye, "He is my family, now."

Jackson studied the old woman. She was fairly short and a bit round, but sitting there in that soft green dress, she looked quite fetching. Jackson's chest tingled and he started to feel fond of her. Or maybe it was the whiskey.

"Yes, you are family," agreed Jackson. "And we are related. We have a handsome Grandson that shares both of our blood." Jackson drank the rest of his whiskey and handed the empty cup to Ruth. "But it's going to take another shot of medicine to loosen my lips, Ruthie."

Jackson leaned back against the cabin's log wall while Ruth filled his third cup. After she handed it to him, she leaned forward with her elbows on her knees and her hands under her chin, in anticipation. "Well?" she said.

Jackson took a deep breath, shook his head, and spit it out. "I was unfaithful to his mother."

"You bastard!" she scowled.

Jackson bowed his shameful head, and his eyes watered. "I know." He took a sip. His heart now hurt worse than his leg.

"Well?" demanded Ruth. "Go on."

"You want the gory details, do ya?"

Ruth nodded. She was now sitting up straight and all ears.

"It happened in Anchorage. It was during the Fur Rendezvous. I had a good year on my trap line, and I knew I could get more for my prime pelts in a big city. It had been an extremely cold winter, and my furs were thick and with good color.

"I scheduled a meeting with a fur buyer. He was from Seattle and was looking for raw furs to take back to his company. Turns out the salesman was a woman. A snappy dresser, too. She really liked what I had shown her and wanted to see the rest of my furs. She bought them on the spot and offered to buy me dinner to celebrate and wanted to do more business with me."

Ruth scoffed, "A snappy dresser?"

"Yep. She had on a low-cut blouse that was pleasantly filled with…nice puppies."

"Pig!"

"It was just a one-time thing, Ruthie. I regretted it and never went back. Sold my furs locally after that." Jackson started getting a little melancholy. "My wife forgave me, but my son never did."

Jackson's eyes glazed over, and he leaned back against the cabin wall. Ruth took the empty cup from his hand and carefully stretched him out on the cot. He had passed out.

Ruth had purposely over-medicated Jackson with whiskey, so that she could clean and doctor up his leg. The confession was a bonus. Ruth carefully rolled Jackson onto his belly. And with a devious grin, she tied his wrists together. When the knot was good and tight, she roped him securely to the bed. Once she was satisfied that he was properly restrained, she retrieved her sewing kit. She threaded a long curved needle with black thread. She chose black, because her old eyes could find the stitches better, when it came time to remove them. She poured some of her hot tea water over the needle and thread, and over Jackson's sharp pocket knife to sterilize them. She found a clean towel and laid out her crude surgical equipment on it. She was ready to play doctor.

She hung a lantern over her patient, pulled up a chair, and sat in it. Carefully she slid up Jackson's pant leg and gently removed the dirty, bloodstained handkerchief that Phia had tied around it. "Whoa," she gasped when she saw what was left of the mangled muscle. It was starting to turn green, and the smell was quite sour.

Ruth shrugged her shoulders and went to work. She had seen worse patients. First, she had to clean this mess and then sterilize it. She fetched a bowl of hot water and a clean washcloth. She dipped it in the bowl and began scrubbing the wound like a dirty dishpan. She got an instant response.

Jackson screamed in pain and tried to move. He spun his head towards whatever wild creature was attacking him and saw Ruth. She smiled at him.

"Jesus Christ, old woman, what the hell are you doing?" Jackson squirmed and fought his restraints with murder in his eyes. "Untie me right now and I promise I won't kill you," he growled.

"Liar," she said calmly and continued cleaning the dead tissue.

Jackson cursed, took a breath, and passed out from the pain.

Ruth painstakingly cleaned the injury and was pleased with how well the wound had clotted. There was very little blood. When she first saw the damage, she thought she might have to cut off the leg. She had sterilized a small bow-saw just in case.

While she inspected her work, Jackson regained consciousness. With gritted teeth and with tears in his eyes, Jackson demanded more whiskey to kill his pain.

"Whiskey, right good idea," nodded Ruth. She picked up the bottle and removed the cap, and with a professional look on her face, she said, "Disinfectant," and poured what was left in the bottle on her patient's leg."

That was followed by a helpless scream, and then her patient again passed out.

Jackson dreamed. It was short but revengeful, and it involved Ruth.

Ruth studied the wound for a minute, while her patient was temporarily unconscious. She became satisfied with how well it now looked. It was time to sew him up. She took two flaps of skin and pulled them together, and suddenly realized she needed another hand to hold the needle. Ruth found another bottle of whiskey and took a sip to disinfect her mouth. She placed the needle between her sterilized lips, and now, once she had the loose skin in position, she could hold it together with her left hand and take the needle with her right one. She took her first stitch and Jackson woke with a piercing cry of pain.

"Keeehrist!" hollered Jackson. "What the hell are you stabbing me with, you old crone."

Ruth tied the thread into a knot and neatly cut it with the pocket knife. As she put the needle between her lips, she scolded, "It's not nice to name-call someone, who has complete control of your pain." She snatched two opposing leg skins and yanked them together and that was followed by a quick needle threading and a snug knot.

"**Ouch**! Oh hell." yelped Jackson. "Okay, I'm sorry," He took a deep breath and decided that Ruth had a good point, literally. He calmed a bit and asked, "Where did you learn how to stitch up a leg?"

Ruth was gentler on the next stitch. "Grey's Anatomy."

Jackson began crying. "I will be lucky, if I don't lose my leg and you end up cutting it off."

"I can do that too. I saw also that episode," she proudly said, as she began her third stitch.

Jackson would have passed out again, but he was afraid that if he did, he might wake up to find her sawing off his leg with a chainsaw, a chainsaw that had its wide, chisel-teeth dipped in whiskey.

When Ruth finally finished her stitching, she wrapped Jackson's leg in a clean cloth. Relieved and exhausted, her patient fell deeply asleep. She untied him and slid her cot next to his and curled up on it. A lot of disinfectant had passed through her lips and when her head touched the pillow, she instantly fell asleep.

Ruth woke up warm and contented. The cabin was dark, and she had no idea what time it was. But she felt rested. She had a good night's sleep. She suddenly realized that she was snuggled up next to Jackson. She quickly threw off her blanket and hopped off the cot. The fire had gone out during the night, and it was damn cold inside. Freezing cold. Her source of heat had been Jackson. "He was a survival thing," she rationalized. "It was definitely not some sort of affection for him." After all, she had slept with a few dogs before in order to keep from freezing. "He was just a big, scruffy dog," she told herself.

After she lit the lantern that was hanging from a beam in the cabin's center, she quickly laid a mound of tinder in the wood stove and put a match to it. As the flames flared high she added the kindling. The fire grew, and with the small logs that she added, the quaint, little log-hovel warmed up. She put the coffee pot on the woodstove. She had filled it the night before, and it was now frozen solid. It was going to take a while.

Ruth slid her cot back to where it was originally positioned and sat on it, and she studied her patient. She wanted to shave his face to see what he really looked like. She decided against it. Cutting off a man's leg was one thing, but removing his beard might piss him off worse.

While she pondered this matter, Jackson rolled over on his back and began blinking the sleep out of his eyes. He was slightly taken aback, when he saw Ruth staring down at him. He sat up. "What?"

"You need to shave."

"I need to pee," he countered. Yesterday's nightmare suddenly came to mind. He quickly checked his legs and was pleased to see both of them. "My leg feels much better this morning. I hope I didn't say anything to offend you last night."

Ruth shook her head, "Nope."

Jackson knew she was lying. His feelings towards the woman that probably had saved his leg were warming up, but not enough to shave for her. "Help me to my feet, so I can go outside and pee. My bladder is about to explode."

Ruth scoffed, "No. you will tear your stitches loose. I will get bucket." Ruth went outside and dumped the snow and ice out of the bucket that they used to get lake water. She brought it inside and placed it between Jackson's knees. "Do you need help with your pants?"

"No! Turn around." Jackson found that he could not stand for fear of popping a couple of stitches in his leg. He had to sit on the edge of the cot and pee. So he wiggled and squirmed and tugged and pulled, but his pants fought back hard and held firm. His bladder was getting impatient and informed him to go for the offered help, or else it was going to pee down one of his legs.

"Um, Ruthie," mumbled Jackson. "Maybe I do need a little helping hand here."

Ruth held a serious look on her face and said, "Okay." It was tough, she really wanted to snicker.

She had Jackson put his hands on the cot and push up in order to lift his torso and his old ass up off the bed. She gently pulled his pants to his knees.

She couldn't help herself, "Nice boxers."

"I said no looking." Jackson quickly covered his manhood with his hands while Ruth sat back on the other cot and stared at the ceiling. Jackson took aim at the bucket, and with a relieved sigh, he peed.

Again, Ruth couldn't help herself. She peeked.

Francis and his team of huskies ran all night. He was worried about his new grandfather, and needed to get back to check in on him. When he got to the end of White Fish Lake, he stopped his team by the trail leading up to the cabin and buried his snow hook. He quickly ran up to the cabin with the first aid kit that his father had given him. When he burst through the door, he was stopped in his tracks.

"What the hell are you two doing?"

CHAPTER 25

The prop on Dr. O'Malley's plane stopped spinning and ended with one of the blades pointing straight up, like an angry finger. Phia looked over at O'Malley for assurances. After all, he had said that he could land this thing without a working engine and now was a good time, because the engine wasn't working.

O'Malley quickly scanned the moonlit, snow-covered ground for a good spot to set her down. Since he was flying at a low altitude, he didn't have much choice. They were in the foothills of the Brooks Range with its scrawny black spruce thinly scattered over the hillside. He picked a wide spot between the trees and lowered the plane's nose, and with the help of gravity, he maintained airspeed. He had to slow the plane down enough to land and yet keep it above stall speed. And true to his word, the plane performed flawlessly. He glided in for a smooth landing. Since he couldn't reverse his prop, he could not slow his plane down, but with the tail rudder, he could control the direction of the plane. His vehicle was now a sled with wings.

His runway was rough, and it flowed downhill. It became a terrifying ride as he dodged tall mounds, trees, and a browsing moose. The slope flattened, and the plane slowed in the deep snow. They were going to make it. The plane finally slid to a stop between a tall alder tree and a long snag of a dead spruce tree that had blown over and got hung up on another tree at a 45° angle. When the plane hit the snag, it shattered the windshield of Dr.

O'Malley's plane causing severe damage to the plane and to the poor doctor. Dr. O'Malley lost his head.

Light snow solemnly floated down from the heavens. Mother Nature sadly was covering the airplane/snowmobile/boat/coffin with her best white flakes of snow. He would be sorely missed.

Phia gagged when she saw O'Malley's headless torso. She quickly gathered her senses. She didn't have time for this. The sky was clouding up, and, without the moon and stars, the winter's four month-long night becomes as black as writer's ink. She needed to find shelter for herself and her mother. And find it very soon.

"Mom," softly called Phia. "Are you okay?"

Amy had slept through the landing and the thrilling sled ride. She blinked a couple of times, and when her eyes focused on Phia, she smiled. "It is so good to see you," she said, and then she realized that the engine was not vibrating under her. So, she asked, "Are we there?"

Phia shook her head. "We're not there yet." Phia could not bring herself around enough to tell Amy that she had been in another plane mishap, and especially, the part that involved Dr. O'Malley.

"Well, where are we, and why is it so quiet?"

Phia's brain was screaming, 'Sugarcoat it, sugarcoat it, …' "We had a little engine problem, and so Dr. O'Malley decided to land here and check it out."

"Where's here?"

Phia shrugged her shoulders and changed the subject. "We need to get you out of this plane. Do you think you can stand?"

Amy nodded and sat up. Phia put her arms around her mother and gently slid her out on the wing. She carefully crawled around her and gently slid her down to a standing position. "Hold on to the wing, mom. I have to get your stretcher."

Amy nodded and hung on with both hands.

Phia retrieved the flat-bottom, fiberglass stretcher and positioned it on the snow just under the wing. "Okay Mom, put your arms around my neck."

Amy smiled. It felt good to hug her daughter again. "You are such a strong little girl. I am very proud of you."

Phia carefully lowered her mother onto the stretcher. Phia took all the blankets that she could find and covered her mother with them. Amy was exhausted and fell back asleep, without asking any more questions.

"I love you, mom."

Phia searched the plane for rope, or anything else that she might need. She stashed everything in a gunny sack. If she would have grabbed the satellite phone, she could have called for help, but she didn't know what it was or how to use it. But she did find a flashlight and stuffed that into her parka. Right now, she needed to find a shelter, or her mother was going to freeze to death.

Phia tied the rope to the front of the stretcher, and with the other end she made a harness that slipped over her shoulders. As she looked towards the mountains, they began disappearing behind a thick snow cloud. But she quickly got her bearings and started trudging through the deep snow that was falling heavily around her. She was now pulling her mother towards… God knows what?

The snow thickened, and their world darkened. Phia could not see anything. She moved by instinct. As long as she climbed, she knew that she was going in one direction. On and on she stumbled through the deep snow and around broken stumps and along downed trees. She was mindlessly towing a sled that her sick mother was laying on, while looking for anything that could act as a windbreak, and as protection against the harsh elements that had engulfed them.

The hill steepened, which made pulling the make-shift sled impossible. Phia turned downwind and began tugging her mother around the side of the steep hill. The pulling became easier, and she was now able to catch her breath. The direction she was headed began to swing into a small valley. The howling wind now seemed to be blowing above her. The steep hill became a shield from the blizzard's fury. Phia stopped to rest and explore. She found that the hill beside her was cliff-like. It was on the lee side of the storm, and it would be a good place to try and shelter them.

She quickly dragged her mother up close to its protected edge. After Phia made sure she was tightly covered, she took her flashlight and began looking for spruce trees. She planned to cover her mother with the green boughs and use dead ones to start a fire. When she turned on the flashlight, all she saw was blinding snow. She went back to her mother.

Phia shined the light against the cliff wall to see if she could find a better spot. She crawled along the steep, rugged, basalt wall until she found an opening. "Perfect," she exclaimed, "Just perfect."

She quickly got her mother and slid her into its protection. Phia crawled in and found that it went a long way back. She shined her light at the cold stone walls and then back at the entrance. The cave had leaves and needles and dried tundra grass scattered just inside the opening that the wind had blown in. She gathered them and made a nest for herself and her mother. She slid her mother into it and covered her in the dry debris as added insulation. With a relieved sigh, she curled her exhausted body up close to her mother and they both slept like hibernating bears.

The storm blew itself out in seven hours. After the wind died, the moon and stars proudly peeked back down at the earth. And with the fresh snow, the northern world was once again effectively lit up. The critters that call this harsh climate home began chewing, and gnawing, and browsing away again.

Phia heard the silence and decided it was time to build a fire for her mother. Without the blanket of snow clouds to insulate the ground beneath it, the temperature began dropping. Her mother was still sleeping, so Phia carefully wiggled away and sat up. The cave entrance was dimly lit by the midnight moon.

Phia quietly found the sack of stuff that she had salvaged from the plane. She pulled out an insulated metal coffee cup that had a plastic lid for traveling, some thin rope, a cigarette lighter, a large tin can that had once held coffee, a pair of sunglasses, a wool hat, and a screwdriver. Since the sun would not be up for another three months, she shook her head and threw the glasses across the cave. She picked up the tool and looked at it and laughed, the nearest screw to be had was…well she had no idea. Phia cocked her throwing arm. It held the useless tool that was tightly clasped in her hand. She paused and changed her mind.

She put the lighter in her pocket and crawled out of the cave. It was time to find some firewood. There was a thick stand of willows and a couple of birch trees just below her.

Phia worked her way through the snowdrifts to the willows. She dug down into the snow and found some dry moss. She snapped off dead branches from old trees for her tinder and gathered some spruce branches that still had green needles on them. As she worked her way back, she came across a set of rabbit tracks. They had crossed her tracks; they were fresh. She stopped and quietly set the firewood on the ground. Well, all but one of the longer willow-sticks, that one she kept in her mitten-covered hand.

She listened, and ever so slowly, she followed the tracks. Shortly, a large snowshoe hare stood up on its back legs with its head above the deep snow and began sniffing the air.

Phia froze.

Hares have eyes that are positioned on the sides of their heads and this enables them to see 360°, and they can run very fast. As a prey animal, this is an excellent advantage for survival. But this eye advantage has one flaw. They can't see much detail, so they rely on movement.

Phia waited perfectly still. The snowshoe hare dropped back down and dug in the snow looking for dried grass. Phia crept closer.

Hare heard and popped back up. He sniffed something. He panicked, but did not know which way to run. It was a standoff. Phia waited. This reminded her of stealing candy from Jackson. She loved that game. They each waited for any kind of movement. Both were poised to pounce.

And then it happened. Hare blinked and Phia made her move. With the hard willow stick, she swung. Hare never had a chance.

When Phia got back to the cave with breakfast, she laid out her fire near the entrance, so that most of the smoke would flow out of the opening. She pulled out her lighter, but before she lit it, she felt something was wrong. She quickly crawled back to check on her mother. The blankets were there, but Mom was gone.

A cold fear gripped her heart, as she scrambled out of the cave in search of Amy. She saw her mother's tracks in the snow. She could see the yellow snow, where she had squatted and peed, and Phia saw where Mom's tracks came back inside. Phia crawled back to the blankets, where her mother had slept, and retrieved the flashlight that she had left there for her mother. Amy had to be in the cave, and she was without her blankets. She would shortly freeze.

"Mom," call the daughter, "Mom, where are you?" Phia crawled in a circle shinning her light on every granite nook and basalt cranny in the cave. The cave was larger than she thought. Finally, she saw the back of her mother's thick coat. Her mother was laying on a very large, furry rock.

Phia gasped when she got a closer look at the strange rock. It was a huge, hibernating brown bear.

Well, fortunately for her mother, she was warm but Phia now had other concerns. At least hypothermia was not one of them.

CHAPTER 26

Francis slept on the cabin floor between his grandparents. It struck him as funny that these two living relatives of his were strangers.

He crawled out of his sleeping bag and lit the candle on the table. The candle had an empty whiskey bottle as its holder. He added a little more wood to the wood stove and added a little lake ice into the coffee pot and put it on the stove to thaw. He pulled out a paperback novel and sat at the small table in front of the candle. While he waited for the water to soften, he liked to read.

Ruth was the next to stir. She slid out from under her thick wool blanket and made the bed. She sat on it and began weaving her long, gray hair into two braids.

Jackson was busy snoring.

When Ruth finished braiding her hair, she joined Francis. "Good morning, sweet boy, what-cha reading?"

"Stephan Hawking," replied Francis as he dog-eared the page and closed the book. He looked up at Ruth and waited for her questions.

"Who's Steve Hawkins?"

Francis smiled at his sweet grandmother. "It's Hawking, Grandma. And he is a physicist, a scientist, kind of like Einstein."

"I've heard of Einstein. He invented gravity, right."

"Close enough, Grandma."

Grandma Ruth picked up the well-worn book and read, "*The Universe in a Nutshell.*" She snickered, "That's funny. The universe is too big to fit in a nutshell."

"You have no idea how big it is, Grandma. Our sun has eight planets that circle around it, which is called a solar system. And our solar system, along with a million other solar systems, circles around a black hole at the center of our galaxy. And there are millions of these galaxies out there, and they all orbit around the heavens with each other. And some are so far away and so big that the billion stars in them look like a single star from here on earth."

"Wow," said Grandma Ruth. She looked up at the tiny cabin ceiling trying to form a mental picture of the immense sky and dropped her jaw in awe. "We sure **are** pretty little."

Yes, we are, Grandma. Almost little enough to fit into a nutshell."

"You're so smart," proudly uttered Ruth as she stood up. "Our water is boiling." She hugged her grandson affectionately, and then she made her way to the stove. "I will make the coffee now." She poured a handful of ground coffee into the old percolator. After she put the lid on it, she looked over at the box that Francis had brought in from his sled, when he had arrived the night before. She asked, "Did you bring anything good to eat?"

Francis picked up his book and leaned back in his chair. "You betcha. I brought a lot of bacon and sourdough starter for pancakes. I mixed it up last night, so it would ferment properly." Frances pointed to a large, covered tin can by the stove. "I set it there to keep it warm."

"Not only are you pretty, but you are also half smart." said the grinning Grandmother. She picked up the batter and smelled it. "She nodded approval. "Do you know the history of this sourdough?"

"I heard tell that it came from the Klondike Gold Rush. I got it from my father who got it from a seedy old man that used to trap somewhere around here. I also heard that he was a cussed old bastard."

"Did you ever get his name?" asked Ruth as she checked the coffee's progress.

"I never got a name, but I suspect that the cussed old bastard that my father was referring to is sleeping over there." He pointed to Jackson and chuckled.

Grandma Ruth laughed at the sweet boy's remark. She leaned over and hugged him. "You know you are my favorite. But don't tell the others."

Grandma had told each of her grandchildren that same line but this time, she really meant it.

The coffee started perking; it was almost time. Ruth waited five minutes and removed the metal filter. She took two mugs off the pegs over the small counter and poured two cups and set one in front of Francis. She found the bacon and sliced it moderately thick. She neatly lined up the slices in the hot iron skillet and the pork bellies began wiggling in its own fat.

"Is that bacon, I smell." This was a redundant question, because Jackson's nose never lied to him. He swung out of his cot and stood up. Francis closed his book and helped his grandfather to a chair at the table. Jackson was wearing a faded-red, Duluth union-suit. Ruth brought him the other cup of coffee. She snickered at the one-piece, pink, underwear with a buttoned-up back door that he was wearing.

Jackson took a sip. "What are you laughing at?"

"Nut and honey."

Francis roared in laughter.

Jackson scoffed. "Don't call me honey."

When the pieces of bacon were brown and crispy, Ruth put them on a plate. She found the ladle and dipped it into the sourdough batter. She took a generous helping of the thick batter and poured it into the skillet full of bacon grease. And the dollops of sourdough were formed into perfect little round cakes. Small tiny batter-bubbles floated to the surface and screamed in delight. Ruth could tell right off that it was a good batch of sourdough starter.

Jackson looked at his grandson and asked, "What-cha read-en?"

"Stephan Hawking," replied Francis as he dog-eared the page and closed the book, and waited for his questions.

Jackson's first question was interrupted by a short howl by Francis's half-wolf lead dog. And that was followed by the rest of the huskies excitedly barking.

"Someone's coming," said Francis. He got up and went out the door to take a look, because there were no windows in the small cabin. Shortly the faint buzz of a snowmobile engine could be heard. Francis came back in. "It's dad. I wonder what's going on." Francis looked at Ruth, "This ought to be interesting."

Jackson leaned back in his chair. He hadn't seen his son for years, and it had been even longer since they had spoken. For him to come within cussing distance of Jackson, it had to be pretty important. Probably, bad important.

Ruth set another plate at the table and finished cooking her pancakes. She put the stack on the center of the table. They stood taller and prouder than the candle on the whiskey bottle. She had three hungry men to feed, in fact, three generations of them. She felt needed again. She felt good. And she was dying to hear what was going to happen next.

Frank parked his machine on the lake ice next to the path that led to the cabin. He took off his goggles and hurried towards the cabin. At the door, he stomped the snow off his mukluks and went in.

"Hi dad," greeted Francis. "What's up?"

"Hi, son," greeted Jackson.

Frank ignored him.

"Frankie, I made pancakes. You want some?" greeted Ruth.

"Sure, that sounds good." Frank sat on the farthest chair away from Jackson.

Ruth poured him some coffee and topped off the other cups, which emptied the pot. She quickly added coffee and melted snow-water to it for a second pot. She didn't want to miss a thing.

"Hi son," said Jackson again nicely. "I guess you didn't hear me the first time."

Frank looked at Francis, who was sitting next to Jackson. "Tell your grandfather that I am still not speaking to him."

"Okay, dad." Francis turned to Jackson. "Dad says hi."

Under lowered eyebrows, Frank threw a cold eye dagger at his son.

Ruth came back to the table and began dealing the pancakes onto each plate, just like she was shuffling cards. She emptied the deck and sat down.

Frank took a nervous sip of coffee and burned his lips. "Ouch." His eyes watered. "It's about Dr. O'Malley. His plane is overdue."

"So, did he find the survivors?" asked Jackson.

Frank ignored him.

Jackson repeated the question to Francis.

Francis scowled at his father, "Dad, survivors?"

"Yes, he found them and called in the location to Fort Greeley, and they sent helicopters."

Jackson turned to Francis, "Ask him if everyone was all right."

"So far as I know, they are." Frank's response was directed to Francis.

"And, what do you mean by: Dr. O'Malley's plane is overdue?" asked Jackson.

"He had to fly through that snowstorm we had yesterday. And they figure he had to set it down somewhere and wait out the storm. He was on skis, so he could land anywhere, and he is probably in some remote valley and out of radio range. His emergency locater beacon was not activated, which means he didn't crash, and if they were in trouble, he would have activated it manually."

"Who's they?" nervously asked Jackson.

"Yes, dad, who's they?"

"He was headed back to the hospital in Fort Yukon with that girl and her mother."

"What girl and her mother?"

"The girl that rode with me into Fort Yukon. I think her name was Phia."

Both Jackson and Francis gasped. They had developed a fondness for Phia, and now they became very worried and began feeling quite helpless.

Frank dug into his pancakes. He saw the book on the end of the table. "What-cha reading, Francis?"

Ruth answered first, "It's a book written by Steve Hawking."

Frank smiled at his mother-in-law. "You know that Francis owns a 45-70 Hawkins rifle. There're good guns. Is it about hunting?"

"**Hawking**," corrected both Francis and Ruth. "And, no."

CHAPTER 27

Phia was witnessing something that she was sure no other person had ever seen before. "How am I going to get my mother off that sleeping bear?" She was befuddled to say the least. This was not where she expected to find her mother. The longer she stared at this dilemma, the less time she had to save her mother. If she did nothing, her mother was dead. If she did anything, they both were dead. The former was not an option.

Little did she know, she was about to witness something else that no other person had ever seen in the wild.

"Mom," softly whispered Phia, "Mom." Her mother stirred and snuggled in closer to the warm bear.

Phia froze as she watched the bear blink a few times. He reached towards Amy and pulled her closer to his chest. The bear was now spooning her mother. Amy had just snuggled herself out of the frying pan and into the fire. At least she looked comfortable.

Phia propped her flashlight against a rock with it pointed at the cave ceiling. It now cast a dim light over the hibernating bear. Slowly, and ever so cautiously, Phia worked her way around the deadly teddy bear.

Phia crawled up to her mother and gently put her hand over Amy's mouth. "Mom," she softly hummed, while trying to mimic the sound of the wind, "Mommm."

Amy opened her eyes and saw Phia with a finger across her lips. She was confused, but stayed quiet. She saw the cave ceiling that was lit up by the flashlight and noticed how sturdy and safe it looked, and she felt proud of her daughter for finding such a good shelter.

Amy was still waking up and started to sit up, when she felt a thick arm around her waist. Still half asleep and confused, she reached for the arm and was going to shove it off her, when she noticed that the fingernails on the hand were pointed and about six inches long. Now she was uncomfortable.

Amy looked at her Daughter with panic in her eyes and then back at the claws. She was helpless and became very afraid for her Daughter. "Run Phia," she whispered, "Run like the wind."

Phia shook her head and put her finger back on her lips. "Ssssh!"

"Don't you shush me," demanded her mother in a loud whisper. "I am the mother."

And that was when it happened. Teddy grunted, sat up, and shoved Amy off his lap. He leaned forward and moaned. Phia quickly reached for her mother, and before they could escape, she witnessed it. Teddy gave birth.

The little critter was hairless and probably didn't weigh a pound. Teddy was a mother. The helpless new life squirmed around the cave floor looking lost. Amy's mothering instincts kicked in, and she quickly cradled the infant. It was a lot smaller than Phia was at her birth, and its mother was a lot bigger than Amy. She became jealous of this and of the injustice of it. The toughest mammal on the planet gets to have painless childbirth **and,** while she is sleeping. "What was God thinking?"

Amy gently nestled Teddy junior up next to a nipple. It latched on and ate like a hungry bear. It made Amy smile.

"Mom, for Christ's sakes," whispered Phia. "Mom, we have to go, now, hurry."

Teddy, now Tedalina, leaned forward and grunted again. She became the mother of twins. Midwife Amy couldn't help herself. She caught this one before it hit the ground and lovingly put it on another nipple.

Phia latched on to her crazy mother and dragged her away from the bear. Female bears are called sows, and for all she knew, Tedalina could be having a litter of ten.

As they made their escape, Phia noticed that her mother seemed more alert and stronger. "You're feeling better, aren't you mom?"

Amy took a breath. It was a little less ragged than before. "I think so." She was pleasantly surprised. "And I think that I am hungry. In fact, I think that I'm hungry enough to eat a horse."

"Would you settle for rabbit?"

"Rabbit's good," she said, while she hung onto her Daughter, as they scampered to their side of the den. She was still quite weak, but on the mend.

The bear relaxed and went back to its hibernating state and seemed to be contended nursing her new cubs. Phia did not want to look for a new shelter and decided that they could share this humble home in the wilderness. That is if she could keep her mother in their part of the cave.

Phia built a fire near the cave's entrance. She took the large empty coffee can and filled it with fresh snow and placed it on the edge of the fire. Now she needed to skin the fat, white rabbit. She remembered the screwdriver. She studied the flat end on it. She began rubbing one side of the screwdriver back and forth on the hard granite floor to try and sharpen it, and it seemed to work. It took an hour of grinding, but she did end up with a crude knife that had a very tiny cutting edge.

The round-handled screwdriver-knife actually worked quite well. Phia was able to skin the large rabbit and roast it on their fire, and her mom feasted on it like a true carnivore. When the snow in the large coffee can melted and boiled, Phia poured some of the hot water into the Starbucks travel mug that she had scrounged off the plane. She added a sprig of spruce needles like Jackson had done to his grog and let it steep for a minute. Phia took the leftover meat and bones and dumped them in the coffee can's remaining water. She slid it back in the fire. She was making a rabbit stew, and she wished that she had a carrot to add to it, which would have been quite fitting.

"Mom, I need to get some more firewood. I shouldn't be gone long."

Amy nodded as she took a sip of her tea. It made her lips pucker. "This stuff is quite bitter. While you're out and about, see if you can find me some honey for it."

Amy studied her mother for a bit of dementia and saw a hint of a smile. "Okay, Mom." Phia then asked, "Can I have the keys to the car?"

Amy laughed at her humor. They hadn't been this close for years. And to think all it took was a little plane crash. Amy gave a fake scoff and added, "You know you're not old enough to drive."

"Well mom, you can't blame a girl for trying."

Phia threw on her parka and crawled out of the low cave entrance. She poked her head back in. "You get some rest. I will be right back."

Amy nodded.

"And stay away from the bear. You have a fire to keep you warm now."

"You sure have gotten bossy in your old age."

The moon was up and shedding her cool, white light on the cold world below. Phia smiled at it and said, "I sure miss your big sister." She looked down the valley for any signs of a man-made shelter, or a road. She wanted to see the twinkle of a fire coming through a cabin window. But the black and white world was empty and still. It was cold, and nothing was stirring.

Phia could see her breath, so she pulled her hood over her head and decided to climb the highest point on the hills that corralled this remote valley and see what was on the other side. And like a deer, she loped towards the tallest hill.

She stopped at the top of it and threw her head back howled long and clear. "Please, Reese, please answer me."

She waited for a couple of minutes and called again. This time she was answered. But she didn't recognize the voice. It sounded like a male wolf answering her challenge. She was in another wolf pack's territory and his howl was a warning.

Phia understood and stayed quiet. She began gathering firewood. She needed a lot of wood to keep her mother warm, while she was gone and looking for help. She knew that she might have to travel far and long.

After gathering an armful of firewood, Phia took the thin, strong cord that she found on the plane and tightly cinched it around the bundle. On the other end of the rope, she made two loops as shoulder straps. She hoisted the bundle on her back and began retracing her steps back towards the cave.

The lone wolf that had answered her call, howled again. This time it was a lot closer. Phia gasped and began running. And she ran like the wind, as her mother had so recently ordered.

The wolf caught wind of the trespasser. It was human, and he hated all humans more than trespassing wolves. Humans had shot members of his family recently, and he was out for blood. He ran even faster towards the scent.

Phia caught glimpses of movement coming up the valley as she approached the cave entrance. It was going to be close.

It was a tie.

Phia spun her back towards the wolf as he leaped.

Snarling and snapping his sharp teeth viscously, he bit into the firewood on Phia's back and pulled it to the ground. Phia slipped out of the rope straps and dove into the cave. She scrambled for her screwdriver-knife and jumped in front of her sleeping mother. The fire was down to smoldering coals and was now of no protection.

The old wolf spit out spruce bark and leaped through the low cave entrance. He was enraged and going for the kill. He had the horrid human trapped. Once inside, he saw that there were two of them, which delighted him even more. He stopped and growled, and leaned back on his powerful back legs. He paused before he leaped, something was not right. His nose got a whiff of a bear, a sow with cubs. The most dangerous of all bears. And that was followed by a very low, nearby growl.

In a corner of the cave, a large Brown Bear stood up on all fours and began pawing the stone floor with its six-inch claws. It curled its black nose and bared its long teeth. It gave out a low, bone-chilling snarl.

The wolf whimpered and quickly slunk out of the cave.

Phia wet herself.

The Brown Bear sniffed the air. She had grown accustomed to the smell of the strangers, while she was hibernating and now accepted it as friendly. Her cubs started crying their tiny, baby-bear cries. She scooped them up, as she laid back down and pulled them close to her chest, so that they could nurse. She curled protectively around them and went back to sleep. She seemed fine with her two new roommates.

"Oh, hi, Phia." Amy stretched, yawned, and sat up. "Did I miss anything?"

CHAPTER 28

The saying goes, '*There are old pilots and there are bold pilots. But there are no old, bold pilots.*' George Boatman was a bush pilot and a good friend of Dr. O'Malley. He was the first to volunteer his services, when he found out that the good doctor's plane was missing in action. Everyone that knew George Boatman just called him, Bo. If it wasn't addressed as Bo, he would throw the letter away, or ignore the text, or not answer the door. It seems that he was a little behind on his taxes. The IRS and a few smaller government agencies had been trying to get a hold of him for years.

Bo's super Cub had an oversized prop with a lot of bite on it. His cruising speed was a little slower, but his take-offs were short and fast. It was a perfect bush plane. In the fall and before freeze-up, with his floats on, he could land his clients on remote beaver ponds and in excellent moose country. Bo was still young.

Bo flew his plane fairly low over the ground. After the snowstorm, he knew that O'Malley's plane would be covered in snow and hard to see. He flew in a zigzag pattern between Fort Yukon and the Brooks Range. When he flew over Frank's old trapping cabin, he saw smoke coming from the cabin's tin chimney. He circled for a better look and saw Francis' dogs staked near the cabin. And on the edge of the lake, he saw Frank's snowmobile.

"Do you suppose Frank has seen anything?" Bo talked to himself a lot. "Well, I guess there is one way to find out." And he also answered himself a lot.

Bo circled to the far end of the lake and cautiously dropped down onto its frozen surface and taxied up to the snow-packed path that led up to the cabin. He was greeted by eight barking dogs.

By the time that he wormed his way out of his plane, Frank had joined him. "Hey, Bo. What brings you to my neck of the tundra?"

Bo shivered and pulled the hood of his parka over his head. "I saw some smoke and figured ya might have some coffee brew-en."

"Yep, just put on a fresh pot."

"I see Francis's dogs are here. Are you two trap-en? I hear rumors that there is a big wolverine up this way. Been stealing critters right out of traps."

"No, we are not trapping. But I know that wolverine that you're talking about. In fact, he tangled with my father. Tore up his leg pretty bad."

"Jackson's here? I thought he was in Florida with your Sister." Bo stopped and faced Frank. "I thought you weren't speaking to him, or are you now?"

"Keep walking, Bo. The coffee is getting cold."

Bo chuckled and continued up the snow packed trail. "I take it that is a no."

Bo was pushing forty and a good friend of the Jacksons. He was shorter and rounder than Jackson and his thick, dark hair was already turning gray. He had a walrus mustache that he constantly stroked, when he was telling a good story.

Bo walked into the cabin, hung his parka on a peg, and turned to Jackson. "Well, you old son-of-a-gun," he said with a laugh. "Did you get kicked out of Florida? Or did you just miss me?" Bo worked his way to the woodstove and warmed his hands.

Jackson chuckled. "I thought that was your plane that I heard buzzing us. You still patch it with Duct Tape?"

Bo poured himself a cup of coffee. "Naa, been using Gorilla Tape. Seems to be a tad stronger."

Francis got up and offered Bo his chair. When Bo sat down, Francis found an empty crate to sit on. He slid it next to his grandmother.

"Well, Hi, Ruth," said Bo. "What is this some kind of a family reunion?"

Ruth shook her head and asked, "What are you doing out this way? I know hunt-en season is over."

"I don't know if you heard, but O'Malley's plane has been missing over twenty-four hours now. A lot of small planes are looking for him. I volunteered to search this area. But it's hard to see anything with all that fresh snow we just had. O'Malley is a good pilot, a bit bold at times. I'm guessing that he had to set his plane down, when the snows came. He's probably in some valley with a dead battery"

Bo turned to Jackson. "When did you get home?"

Jackson chuckled. "I left a month ago, and I still ain't made it home."

"What, you walked from Florida?"

Bo sat quietly stroking his bulky mustache as he listened to Jackson's incredible story, and about going for help for the surviving passengers, and about the young girl that had followed him, and of course, about the wolverine. He rolled up his pant leg and proudly showed him the stitches.

"Wow," explained Bo. "Who sewed you up?"

"Ruth."

Bo turned to Ruth. "Where did you learn doctoring?"

"Grey's Anatomy."

Bo nodded in complete understanding. "Yea, that's one of my favorite shows. Did you get to see the last episode? Dr. Grey sewed some guy's head back on. Them doctors sure are good. They haven't lost a patient yet."

Ruth shook her head, paused, and with a concerned look, asked, "Did you know that there was a young girl and her mother on the plane with O'Malley?"

Bo sighed and nodded. "I heard that he was headed to the hospital in Fort Yukon. "I've searched from there to here. I am guessing he lost electrical power around here, and that is why his radio does not work. He has survival gear onboard. He should be fine for a little while." Bo looked over at Frank. "You know, another set of eyes on board wouldn't hurt."

Frank agreed.

Ruth went through Francis' grub box and packed a lunch for Frank and Bo. They wasted no time. They put on their parkas and they were soon airborne.

Francis looked at Jackson and sighed. "I feel so helpless just sitting here."

Jackson leaned back in his chair holding his coffee with both hands. "You want to take the dogs and look for her, don't you?"

Francis nodded.

"You know that it will be a complete waste of time. Bo's plane in the air can cover a hundred times more area than you on the ground."

Francis nodded.

Jackson leaned forward and whispered, "But if it were me, I would be stupid enough to try it."

Francis grinned and jumped to his feet. He put on his mukluks and threw on his parka. Ruth stopped him at the door. She had already packed him a lunch, several of them, in fact. "You use your heart. It works better than compass. You will find girl."

"Thank you, Grandma." Francis kissed her on the cheek, and then he looked over at his grandfather.

Jackson lowered his eyebrows. "Don't even think about it!"

Francis couldn't help himself. He kissed the old man on his forehead and was out the door before Jackson could put up a fuss.

Jackson scoffed and he smiled. He turned to Ruth, "Say, Ruth, is there any whiskey left?"

Amy sat close to the fire. The cold, dry air seemed to agree with her, and her breathing was becoming relaxed and full. The pneumonia had run its course. Amy was pleased to see that Phia had become her old self again. Her sassy little girl was back, and she was becoming a young woman. Amy formed a broad smile, as she watched her daughter on the other side of the hearth fire. She was tediously working on the rabbit pelt that she had skinned the day before.

"What-cha making, Phia?"

"A sling."

Amy paused, "A toy?"

"No, a weapon," said Phia. "If David could kill Goliath with one, surely I can use it to kill a bunny."

Amy was intrigued. "How does it work?"

Phia had cut an oval patch of rabbit hide to form a pouch. She fastened a thin cord to each end of it. One end of the rope had a small loop in it, and the other end had a large knot on it.

Phia picked up a small rock from the cave floor and said, "I will demonstrate." She placed the rock in the leather pouch. She hooked the pointer finger of her right hand through the loop, and then she brought the other end around and held the knot tight with her thumb against the finger that held the loop. This was the quick-release mechanism.

While holding the knotted line, she began swinging the weapon in a circle. Centrifugal force kept the rock that was in the pouch in place. And at the right moment, Phia would lift her thumb and the rock would be set free and fly towards the target cracking Goliath on the head, or that of a rabbit's. Theoretically.

Phia pointed to a rock that was sitting on a ledge near the cave's entrance. "See that rock over there, Mom?"

Amy nodded, and quickly, she covered her ears.

Phia laughed. "It's not a gun, Mom."

"Sorry, I guess you're right."

Phia began spinning her projectile around her right side. Faster and faster she spun it, till all you could see was a blur. She figured the faster that she spun it, the faster it would fly towards its target. It was now going fast enough to completely take off Goliath's head. She took aim and lifted her thumb.

The small stone shot out of the pouch and hit the ceiling above her head. Her release was a bit too soon. The rock ricocheted, and Phia ducked out of the way as its course had changed towards the entrance wall. And with a cracking noise, it slammed against the wall and picked a new direction. It flew back in towards Amy. It was like watching billiards in 3D.

Amy ducked, just as the rock whizzed closely past her uncovered ear, and it finally rolled to a stop. She shook her head and pointed at the target. "Perhaps, I should stand over there."

"Sorry, Mom, I will practice outside."

"Good safety tip, Phia."

Phia practiced and practiced, until she thought her arm was going to fall off. When she began tiring, she relaxed a little and let the sling swing in an arch behind her. And with a quick snap, she swung it over her right shoulder and released it, like she was throwing a baseball. The rock accelerated in the long arch, and it flew true and straight. It still missed her target, but not by much. This quick launch worked much better.

Since Phia's targets were going to be small game, she started putting several smaller rocks in the pouch at the same time. Kind of like a shotgun that uses small bb-shot for upland birds and waterfowl. She found that it worked quite well. And on ninety percent of her throws, she was able to have at least one of the rocks connect to her target. She began to feel very confident with her new weapon.

That night they celebrated with the rest of yesterday's rabbit stew and the bitter tea. When it's cold outside, and you share a cozy den with a bear, and you have worked up an enormous appetite, everything tastes great.

Amy looked at her daughter and smiled.

"What," said Phia.

"I love you."

CHAPTER 29

Under the full moon, Francis hooked up his dogs. He had good visibility, and he wanted to use every inch of it, while he could. The moon would only be up for another four hours, so he had to hurry. When he snapped on his lead dog's harness, he noticed that Kona seemed a little upset.

Francis knelt down and gently stroked the dog's thick fur. "What's wrong, Kona?" That was when he realized that the she-wolf was gone. Francis jumped to his feet and swore in disappointment. He spun in a circle looking for the wolf. His plan was to let the wolf run and follow her. If anyone could find Phia, it would be her wolf friend, Reese. He dropped his head and said a prayer, but his tone sounded a little like a curse.

He knelt back down in front of Kona and looked into his sad eyes. "It's up to you now. Do you think you can find the wolf?"

Kona's eyes brightened, and he barked. He understood and leaped against his harness. His canine crew obeyed, and they were off. They yanked the pronged snow-hook out of its icy bed, and Francis barely caught the back of the sled, as it flew by him.

Kona found the tracks of the she-wolf and began following them. The northern lights came out and flashed their stunning, green curtain of light. It was as if Francis's prayer had been answered.

Kona began running his team over the tracks that she had made in the snow. Reese was looking for Phia and was covering a lot of ground. She was running in ever-widening circles and sniffing for the faint scent of her friend. Kona followed but, was hours behind, and Reese was moving faster.

When the moon went down, Francis stopped his dogs. It was dangerous to run in the dark. He fed them dried salmon, and after they were fed, he rummaged through Grandma Ruth's packed meals. He chose one of her sandwiches. He took a bite, while trying to decide whether, or not, to continue on in the sky's weak starlight. He walked to Kona and tossed him part of his sandwich.

"What do think, Kona? Should we keep going?"

Kona listened to his soft words and wagged his tail.

"Yes, I know we shouldn't."

Another tail wag.

"Was that a 'we should?' Or were you just begging for another piece on my sandwich?"

Kona looked at him confused and barked.

"Okay, if you insist. We will go on a little longer. You're the one that can see in the dark, so I'm depending on you."

After a short rest, they were back on their mission. On and on, and over hill and dale, and down into the tundra they ran. Francis blindly held tightly onto the sled's handlebars. It was a night run that he would never forget.

Jackson set down his coffee cup with a bang, which startled Ruth. They had been quietly sitting at the table and sipping coffee all morning. The only thing making a sound was a couple of mice scurrying around looking for crumbs. Silence is a wonderful thing, when one is meditating, or stalking game, but in a cabin with another human being, it is deafening and just wrong.

"Jesus Ruth, I just realized I ain't had a bath in a month."

"Ruth blinked out of her far away thoughts and focused on Jackson. She sniffed him and said, "Only a month?"

"I think that's all it has been. Why, do you think I could smell worse?"

"I didn't want to say anything, but God, I hope not."

Jackson stood up and put a little weight on his injured leg. It complained, but it held him. "Where do you live, Ruth?"

"I have a small house just outside of Fort Yukon. Why?"

"Does it have a shower?"

Ruth was starting to feel where he was going with his interrogation, "Maybe."

"What say you and me go for a snowmobile ride?"

"I don't think so. It's cold out there."

"I could bring it inside," said Jackson with a chuckle, as he sat back down. "Ya know, Ruth, we are getting pretty low on grub and firewood. We cannot leave this cabin empty of food and wood to start a fire with. This cabin might mean survival for the next poor bastard that gets stranded out here. We have to leave him something; that **is** the code up here in the north, Ruth."

"But, what about Frank? If we take his snow-go, how will he get home?"

"We leave a note. He can fly back with Bo. Or if Francis is here, he can ride with him."

Ruth stared at her empty coffee cup. She hated it, when a man was right, especially if the man was Jackson. So begrudgingly, she said, "I will think about it."

"Good," said Jackson. He took that as a yes. He handed her his empty coffee cup and stood up. "You wash the dishes, and I am going to gather my things."

Ruth stood up with the stained cup in her hand, and as Jackson turned, she saw the spot on the back of his head where she wanted to throw it. "Who would really know, way out here, if I killed him?" she said to herself. She took a breath, and with great restraint, she put the dirty cups on the counter. "Screw the code of the north. They can wash their own cups." Ruth put on a parka and was ready to go. She had no, 'things to gather.'

Frank's machine fired up on the third pull. Ruth crawled on behind Jackson.

"It's been a while since I have driven one of these things. They don't have them in Florida."

"Really?" sarcastically, said Ruth.

Jackson put on goggles and tightened his parka hood. "Hang on," laughed Jackson with an evil tone. He revved up the engine and cackled, "God, I've missed this."

Ruth no sooner got her arms around Jackson, when the machine leaped forward, making it quite necessary to hold on tight. That old man drove as crazy as his son.

But on the other hand, she realized, she liked holding a man again. She was becoming fond of the crazy old bastard, and it perplexed her.

A lone raven circled high looking for a meal. He saw a large wolverine lope up to a small cabin on a frozen lake. The wily predator seemed to be searching for something. Perhaps, he thought, it got a taste of something it liked and wanted more.

While the raven circled south, he saw a snowmobile, as it wildly ran down the Chandalar River. There were two humans riding the metal beast. One was singing in satisfaction, and the other was trembling in terror.

"Old people!" incredulously croaked the Raven, and then he laughed.

"Shhh," Phia interrupted her mother's story. "I hear something."

Amy strained her ears. "I think it's a plane."

Phia scrambled to her feet and squeezed through the cave entrance and out into the cold night air. And there it was. A small plane with a very large prop was flying right over her. Phia waved and hollered and jumped up and down, but the plane flew on. It was devastating, but at least it meant that someone was out there, and that they were looking for her.

She crawled back inside.

"Was it a plane?"

"Yes Mom, but it didn't see me. What we need is a torch."

Phia picked out a piece of firewood that was suitable as a handle of a torch. She wrapped dried moss around one end of it and lashed it on with strips of rabbit hide.

"It won't burn long, but it will burn brightly for a few minutes, which should be long enough to get someone's attention. Even if I have to throw it at them."

Amy went back to telling her story.

The next day, Phia decided to go back to O'Malley's plane and look for a flare gun. Before she left, she made sure her mother had plenty of firewood. She strapped on her white, snowshoe hare backpack, hung her sling on her side, filled her pockets with rocks, and grabbed a long pole that she sharpened as a spear.

"Behave yourself, Mom. I might be late."

"Not even a small party with the three bears?" she joked.

"Nope!" Phia sternly shook her head.

Amy couldn't help but notice that Phia left looking just like, Ayla, the girl from the 'Clan of the Cave Bear.' And she was sure that her daughter was now just as cunning.

When Phia found the plane, she took off her pack and set it on the ground. Carefully she crawled inside and searched for its emergency flare-gun. But she never found one. During her flare gun search, she did find other useful items. She tossed them towards her backpack, as she discovered them.

Phia looked closely at the poor doctor; he was frozen to his seat. He looked even worse than he did, when he was newly dead. But by now, Phia had grown a tolerance for survival and its harshness.

She noticed the nice parka that O'Malley was wearing. "Oh, Shawn," she softly said. "I need your coat for my mom." She looked at his feet. "And your mukluks." Phia went around the plane and opened the pilot-side door. She unhooked his seatbelt and lightly tugged on him. He was frozen in pretty tight. She yanked harder, and he moved slightly. Finally, she had to crawl back to the other side of the plane and sit in the passenger seat. She faced him and put her feet against his right shoulder and used her leg muscles to try and break him free of his seat. She pushed. He moved a little. On her next shove, he toppled out the door, slid down the wing, and landed on the tundra. "Sorry," was all she could say.

Phia worked her way back to the good doctor, and as reverently as she could, she removed his parka and his mukluks. She put the parka into her pack and tied the mukluks to the side of it. She went back and went through O'Malley's pockets. His left pocket held a lot of cash. She put the money in her pocket as paper to start fires with. When she put her hand in his right pocket, she gasped and quickly pulled out a pocket knife. "Thank you, Shawn," she uttered as she kissed it. She next removed his thick flannel shirt and added it to her pack.

Phia went back to searching every compartment in the plane for anything useful. Finally, in a grocery sack hidden under the pilot seat, which O'Malley had stashed for himself, Phia found heaven. There were two cans of sweet potatoes, one of corn, and one can of cranberry sauce, and joyously, a small can opener.

"Oh my God," screamed Phia in delight. "He was picking up things to take home for thanksgiving." She blew O'Malley a kiss and said, "Thank you, Shawn, thank you." It was Christmas and thanksgiving all rolled up into one.

When Frank and Bo returned, Frank left a note for Francis in their small cabin on the lake. He told his son that it was time to go home. Tomorrow was Monday, and he had to be back in school. This was his senior year.

He placed the note on the table and went back to the plane. He climbed into the passenger seat of the running plane. Bo gave her a little gas, and the plane sprung to attention. Its long prop grabbed air, and the plane left the ground before it reached the center of the small lake. They were headed for their homes in Fort Yukon.

The moon had gone down. The sky was clear, and the stars were twinkling brightly. The black and white world below them was surprisingly clear. The airport in Fort Yukon had runway lights, so if they ran into a high overcast, landing there would be no problem.

Bo flew west until he found the Chandalar River, and that was his road map south to the mighty Yukon River and home. As Bo flew along this river, a movement below him caught his eye.

"Frank, is that your son running those dogs?"

Frank looked where Bo was pointing. "That looks like his team. He sure is a long way from the cabin. He is pushing his dogs pretty hard. He knows better than that."

Bo circled lower for a better look. "Jesus Christ, Frank. There is a pack of wolves biting at his tail." Bo quickly lined up with the river and began his descent. Frank retrieved the rifle from its rack behind them. He worked the bolt and slid a live round into the chamber. Bo set his plane down on the river behind the wolf pack. His skis touched the middle of the river, and the fast sliding plane caught up to, and surprised, the running wolves. They scattered like popcorn.

Francis pulled his tired team to a stop. Bo taxied up to him and shut down the plane. When it slid to a stop, Frank replaced Bo's rifle and crawled out of the plane.

Francis sat on his sled to catch his breath. He was exhausted from the adrenalin rush of fear.

"Francis," scolded Frank. "You just scared the hell out of me. What the hell are you doing out here?"

Francis stood up and checked his pronged parking brake, even though the dogs were dog tired and lying on the snow panting. "I was looking for Doctor O'Malley," he explained, "and that girl."

"That girl!" scoffed Frank. He took a breath and remembered his first love and some of the stupid things he did to impress her. "I am sorry son." Frank walked up to his son and gave him a hug. "The idea of something happening to you…well, it just scared the hell out of me."

Frank turned to Bo. "You can go ahead without me. I'll ride shotgun with Francis. We will see you in town."

"What about Grandma Ruth and Grandpa Jackson?" asked Francis.

"They already left."

"How?"

"They took my snowmobile, while I was flying with Bo."

Francis thought about it for a minute, and the mental image of it caused him to burst out laughing.

"It's not funny, Francis. If I were speaking to him, I would give him a good piece of my mind."

That remark made Bo laugh.

"Okay Bo, you can leave now."

Bo climbed back into his plane and restarted it. He waved at the man and his son, as he throttled her up.

On a hill, not too far away, a lone wolf watched the noisy bird take to the air and wing its way south. When it was out of sight, she looked back down at the team of huskies, and especially at the handsome lead dog in front. Reese sighed, turned toward the tundra, and loped off. She had gotten a slight whiff of her human friend. It was time to go back to searching for her.

CHAPTER 30

Phia found a blue plastic tarp far back in the fuselage of the Cessna. It was torn and full of holes. She carefully doubled it over and placed it over O'Malley's remains, and she tightly tucked it under him. She bowed her head and prayed. "Rest peacefully, Shawn. You deserve a place in heaven and a seat beside your God." Phia quickly buried him with snow, hoping to keep the ravens and animals off of him.

She had been gone a long time. She threw on her full backpack and started retracing her steps towards the cave. With all the can goods she was carrying, her pack was now quite heavy.

In the flat tundra, and excited with her find, she made good time. As she worked her way up the steep foothills, she began sweating, so she stopped to rest. She took off her load and sat on a log to catch her breath.

She had adapted to her environment, which meant she was on constant alert. When a slight movement caught her eye, she froze and reached for her spear. The dim black and white world around her concealed both its predators and its prey equally well. She carefully studied the last place that she had seen movement. It wasn't very far from her, so she was guessing a snowshoe hare. She remained motionless, while patiently waiting for it to make the next move.

It moved again. It had a dark eye with a red patch over it. It was small, and pretty soon she saw a black beak and white feathers. The plump little bird was a type of grouse that is brown in summer, and when winter comes, it puts on its parka of white feathers. It is called a Ptarmigan and they are quite tasty.

Phia slowly unhooked her sling with one hand, and with the other, she retrieved several small rocks from her parka. She put three stones in the sling's pouch and slowly stood up, as did the Ptarmigan. Phia lowered the sling to where it almost touched the snow. She swung it behind her, until it lined it up with her target. And with a quick snap, she swung it in an arch over her head and released her thumb. The three projectiles were right on target. The bird didn't have a chance. It flopped over on its side, flapped its wings for a second, and died.

Several other Ptarmigans stood up from their beds and looked for the danger. But until one of them flew and gave a direction, they stayed motionless. Phia killed three, before the covey took to the air.

Phia now had a proper Thanksgiving feast to prepare for her mother. She had no idea what day it was, or even how close to Thanksgiving it really was. But in the wild, who cares?

Amy had a nice fire crackling away by the time her daughter returned. As Phia pulled out each can, her mother clapped her hands and giggled in gladness. "Is it really Thanksgiving, Phia?"

Phia nodded. "And that's not all. We have turkeys." Phia showed her the Ptarmigan. With the white feathers, they looked like miniature, farmed turkeys.

Amy helped Phia pluck the birds. They saved the feathers to stuff in the linings of their parkas as extra insulation. The miniature turkeys were skewered and roasted to perfection. The yams and the corn were cooked in their metal containers, and the Cranberries were thawed and warmed up in their can.

And then they feasted.

They went to sleep that night with full bellies and dreamed of warm places. As the fire died down, the sky darkened, and a soft snow began silently falling. It was a fitting end to a proper Thanksgiving Day.

Phia woke up and opened her eyes, and she saw nothing. The cave was as dark as a black cat locked in a closet. She fumbled for the flashlight fearing blindness. She flipped it on, and the magic of light filled the cave. She shined the light towards the cave's entrance. It always had a little light bleeding in it.

"Oh, wow," she exclaimed, when she saw that the snow had completely covered the cave's entrance.

The hearth was cold. She had to build a new fire. She crumpled up a few twenty-dollar bills and added tinder. She reached into her pocket and pulled out her precious Bic lighter, and lit the greenbacks. The cave brightened, she added small sticks and dried tree branches, and the fire added some heat to its dancing flames.

Phia suddenly realized that the cave was filling up with smoke. The entrance was sealed with snow. Phia quickly crawled to the opening and dug a small tunnel at the top of it to let the smoke out. As she backed out of the snow chimney, a dead rabbit came out with her.

Phia picked up the rabbit and inspected it. "Where did you come from, little fella?" It was too dark to see. She brought it closer to the fire.

Amy was just getting up. She added more wood to the fire. After warming her hands, she noticed that her daughter was holding something. "What do you have there?"

"It's a rabbit, Mom."

"Where did it come from?"

Phia shrugged her shoulders as she inspected it closely. When she saw the teeth marks on it, she gasped. "It's a gift Mom. It's breakfast." Phia dropped the rabbit and ran. She hit the snow-drifted entrance, and it exploded open, as she came out the other side. "**Reese,**" she cried. "Reese, where are you?"

The wolf was curled up in a ball under the snow, and when she heard her friend, she leaped up and puppy-attacked her, and they both rolled over into the deep snow. Phia hugged her tightly. "I missed you."

Phia crawled back into the warm cave and coaxed Reese towards the cave. The cautious wolf stopped at the entrance. She smelled bear and refused to come any further.

"It's alright, Reese."

Reese sniffed again and backed up two steps.

Phia laughed, "Coward."

"Who are you talking to?"

Phia turned to her mother, "Reese."

Amy jumped to her feet and scrambled towards the entrance. "Who's Reese? Are we rescued? Did somebody find us?" When Amy saw who it was, she fainted.

Phia caught her mother and held her in her lap. "Mom, Mom, it's okay."

Amy slowly opened her eyes and gazed up at her daughter.

"It's okay, mom. Reese is my friend."

Amy sat up and looked at the wolf and then back at her daughter. "I have no idea why that surprised me, especially after everything else that you have done." She looked back at the wolf. It seemed harmless enough. "Well, are you going to introduce me?"

After two weeks looking for Dr. O'Malley, the woman, and her daughter, the search was suspended. Along with the local bush pilots, there were small military spy planes that used the latest in night-vision goggles, and they had thermal-view body-heat sensors on board. Their sophisticated instruments only found animal forms that browsed or chased prey. Their devices do not penetrate cave walls.

The man, the woman, and the child were now presumed dead.

But our intrepid cave dwellers survived and thrived.

Amy took over the job of collecting firewood, and each day, she had to search further and further, and each day she became stronger and stronger.

Phia and Reese hunted and provided meat, and they explored in an ever-widening circle each day. Before long, they had gotten as far as the Chandalar River, and Phia recognized it. It was the one that Frank and she traveled on by snowmobile on their wild rescue run.

The bear cubs were growing like weeds. They each had gained ten pounds by the end of the first week. The second week they had hair and were moving around. By the third week, they were exploring the cave. Amy named them and started giving them a little meat. And best of all, their rough and tumble play was a constant source of entertainment.

Reese still was a little shy about sharing a den with a bear. She slept near the cave entrance. But the curious cubs eventually found the wolf and began playing with her as one of their own. Reese just tolerated them at first, but eventually, she remembered playing the same games as a puppy herself.

Phia looked up from stitching up something in the rabbit leather and smiled at her mother, who had one of the cubs in her lap. "Mom?"

Amy looked up, "What, honey?"

"I think I know where we are, and I think I can find the small town where Dr. O'Malley lived."

Amy became curious and a little apprehensive.

Phia took a breath and asked, "Do you think that you are strong enough to go for a long walk?"

Amy's eyes smiled. "When do we leave?"

Phia shrugged her shoulders. "I am not sure how far it is. It might take us a week to get there. We would be sleeping on the snow. I need to know that you are up for it."

"Oh, I'm up for it, Phia, and I am ready to leave, right now."

Phia laughed. "Okay, Mom, good. We should get some sleep, and when the moon comes up, I say we go for it."

"Good," said Amy as she went back to scratching one of the cub's fat, little tummy.

Phia went back to her leather. She was just finishing up a small double-pack to strap on Reese.

Phia and Amy did not sleep much that night in excited anticipation. It was like the thrill on Christmas Eve.

In fact, Christmas was fast approaching.

CHAPTER 31

Jackson was drinking a beer and watching an episode of *Grey's Anatomy* with Ruth when the phone rang. Ruth still had a landline and refused modern technologies, like cell phones and the internet. The TV didn't count. "TV's," she explained, "are just motion pictures, and they have been around a long time."

Old people are stubborn.

Ruth has been taking care of Jackson for almost four weeks now. They tolerate each other fine, and it beat living alone.

The phone rang again.

"Ruth, are you going to get that?"

"I can't. Dr. Meredith is right in the middle of her surgery."

The phone rang again.

"You can pause it, Ruth, that way you don't miss anything."

Ruth scoffed. "You get it. You're not watching it anyway."

"But my leg." Jackson had been milking the pain in his leg to no end and Ruth knew it. Now it was just a pain in her butt."

The phone rang again.

"Ruth?"

"Fine," said Ruth, even though it wasn't. She scrambled to her feet and answered the phone. "Hello." Pause. "Just a minute." Ruth looked over at Jackson and growled, "It's for youuu,"

"Me?" Jackson scrambled to his feet and took the phone from Ruth, and he walked towards the kitchen for privacy, bad leg and all. She wanted to brain him with the receiver.

"Hello?" Jackson listened. It was Officer Murphy on the other end.

Ruth went back to her TV.

Officer Steve Murphy leaned back on his chair and put his feet on his desk. "How's the leg doing, Jackson?"

"Coming along fine, Murph, just fine."

"You on any medicine?"

"I take a shot of single malt in the evenings; sometimes I need to increase the dosage a bit. How you do-en?"

"I'm doing fine," answered Murphy, "The reason I called is that we are throwing a party and we need you to come."

"A party? Where? When? Why?"

Murphy took his feet off his desk. "You remember the two couples from first-class, Ed and Ron, and their wives? Well, they want to throw a Christmas party for all the survivors of the crash. And since you are the one that saved us, you are the guest of honor."

Jackson reached for his bottle of pain killer and pulled the cork out with his teeth. He took a quick swallow from the bottle. "I don't know?"

"What do you mean you don't know? You have to go."

"I don't know, Murph. I'd have to take the plane to Fairbanks and this leg ain't quite up to it yet."

"Ed and Ron rented the town hall in Fort Yukon. They invited the whole town. And it is also going to be a wake for Dr. O'Malley. I know he was a good friend of yours"

Jackson took another drink and tightened his lips in nervous anticipation.

"Jackson, hello, you still there?"

Jackson nodded and remained quiet.

Murphy could hear Jackson breathing on the phone. "What's the matter? Are you coming or not?"

"On one condition, Murph. I will go and be your guest of honor as long as I don't have to give no damn speech." Jackson listened as he waited for a reply. "What's so damn funny, Murph?"

"You, you old cuss. Christ, you head out in the wilderness by yourself, on foot, in winter, and have to fight off a wolverine to get help for the rest of us, and now you are afraid to say a few words at a function to honor you? You just leave me speechless. Okay fine, you don't have to give a speech."

Jackson set down the bottle. "So, when is this party. I need to check my busy schedule."

"What the hell do you have to **do** between now and spring besides watch old episodes of *Grey's Anatomy*?"

"Oh, I do things," indignantly replied Jackson. "I do lots of things."

"Okay, this function is scheduled for the Saturday before Christmas. I know that it is next week and such short notice, but I would be honored if you can fit it into your tight schedule."

"I can hear the sarcasm in your voice, Murph."

"Good," said Murphy with a hardy laugh. "I look forward to seeing you." Murphy hung up.

Jackson poured a little of his Scotch whiskey into a glass. He looked at Ruth who was still intently watching TV. "Ruth, you want a beer?"

"Sure," she said.

Jackson poured her beer into a glass, picked up both drinks, and went to the couch and sat beside her. He handed her the beer. "Say, Ruth, you want to go on a date next Saturday night?"

Ruth choked on her beer and promptly turned off the TV.

With packs packed, three female mammals crawled out of the security of their cave in excited anticipation. Reese stood guard while Phia and her mother completely repacked the cave entrance with snow. When they had finished, Amy wrote, 'do not disturb,' in the snow.

"Nice touch mom," said Phia as she adjusted her mother's pack. "Are you sure that you're up for this?"

"Just the thought of peeing in a real toilet… Hell, I could walk to the moon for that."

In single file, they began their journey. Reese led, followed by Phia. They were breaking a snow trail for Amy so she didn't have to step so high. For most of the journey, they stuck to moose trails, which snaked around a bit but the walking was faster and easier.

As they worked their way down and out of the foothills of the Brooks Range, and down into the flat tundra, they were paid a visit by Miss Aurora Borealis.

She felt like dancing.

She put on her finest, long skirt. It was trimmed with florescent, moss-green pleats, which had ripples of pink and purple colors flashing richly through it.

And she danced.

She picked up her dress like a flamingo dancer and began whirling and twirling her long skirt all over the huge northern sky.

The half-moon cocked his head and smiled at her as Miss Aurora proudly performed her nightly show, each one was a little different and her audience was never bored.

The three females stopped and watched. "Wow," whispered Amy. "God sure favors his northern children, doesn't He?"

"Jackson told me that Aurora has a twin sister at the South Pole. And that she lights up her sky at exactly the same time and with the same show," added Phia.

They continued on through the frozen world around them each in deep silent thought. A lone wolf howled and sent a shivering chill through Phia. She looked at Reese and could see the concern in her eyes. She quickened the pace.

"I got nothing to wear!" Poor Ruth was beside herself. "I hate men. They put on a white shirt and a tie, slick back their hair and they look good. No muss, no fuss!" Ruth gasped as she realized, "And, now I need to do something with my hair."

Jackson chucked, which was a very bad mistake. "Ruuuthie, put that coffee cup down. Someone could get hurt."

They fought like an old married couple. It was kind of sweet in a gothic sort of way.

Old people, …ah!

Jackson took Ruth shopping and then to the hair salon. Ruth mellowed and agreed to let Jackson back into her home. Plus now, she was getting a little excited about going to a Christmas party. And as the date of the guest of honor. She suggested that he wear a tux.

"Over my dead body, woman."

"That can be arranged, old man," countered the sassy Grandmother.

Alaska Airlines agreed to fly the survivors to Fort Yukon for free. It was the least they could do. And, there was also going to be a monetary settlement given to each of the survivors and to the relatives of those that had died in the crash. The attorneys for both sides were already working out the details and the amount of money given to compensate for their suffering. Apparently, the attorneys had suffered the most.

The plane arrived on the Friday before the gala. The hotels in town were sparse and many of the guests were put up for the night in the homes of the local people. Flight attendant Cheryl had been chosen to stay at Ruth's humble home. She had no idea that Jackson was also living there.

From the airport, Cheryl took a cab. Lyft and Uber hadn't drifted this far north yet. The driver was Indian. He was foreign, not domestic, which surprised her a little.

"Hi," Cheryl said as got into the cab. "I am looking for the home of Ruth…" Cheryl started searching her purse for the address and the last name.

"Vetty good. I know where Ruth lives. Please fasten your seat belt." The India, Indian, quickly sped off.

Ruth's home was on the outskirts of town and near the river. When they arrived, she paid the driver his fare and added a good tip. He helped her with her luggage. He carried to the front door; there was too much snow on the walkway for the tiny wheels to work.

Ruth answered Cheryl's soft knock; she didn't have one of those fancy door chimes. The cabbie left.

Cheerfully Cheryl introduced herself. "Hi, I am Cheryl. I am your guest," She added a friendly smile. But she was a little apprehensive when she saw the native woman in front of her. "You must be Ruth." The old native woman was smiling, which was a good sign. "Do you speak English?"

"Yes," laughed Ruth. "Please come in. Can I make you a cup of tea?"

"That would be great." Cheryl took off her thick fur coat and hung it on a peg, and she followed Ruth towards the kitchen.

"Who is it, Ruthie?" hollered Jackson.

Cheryl recognized the voice and excitedly detoured toward it.

Jackson stood up from the couch to see who it was, just as Cheryl threw her arms around him. Jackson lost his balance and toppled back on the couch with Cheryl on top of him. She gave him a big kiss on the lips.

Ruth gasped and became instantly jealous. It was a good thing that she wasn't holding a coffee mug.

CHAPTER 32

A second wolf howled, long and loud. This one was closer. "That one sounds awful close," said Amy.

Phia put a finger to her lips and whispered, "Best not to talk. On these clear quiet nights, your voice travels."

Amy understood and nodded. They hastened.

The still, calm air was cold, damn cold. Puffs of frozen moisture exhausted from each exhalation, as Phia and Amy followed Reese across the tundra and onto the frozen Chandalar River. It had been an hour, since they heard the wail of the wolf. Now it was the cold that concerned Phia.

The river bottom contained a layer of hoarfrost. This frozen cloud of fog covered the trees, on both sides of the river, in thick white foliage. Reese led them down to the center of the river. The ice was wind-swept and free of the deep snow, which made walking much easier.

Phia decided to stop, so that her mother could rest a minute.

Amy looked like an Ewok. She had a dirty brown scarf that covered her face, and her hood was cinched tightly over her head, and she was wearing the oversized parka that once belonged to O'Malley. Her mother's image made her snicker.

"What?" whispered Amy.

"Oh, nothing. Are you warm enough, Mom?"

Suddenly, two short howls signaled that one of the wolves found something. Several other wolves answered the call.

Reese wined anxiously.

Amy understood the urgency. "I'm fine. I think we should keep moving."

Phia set the pace, and Reese disappeared into the tundra. She needed to find out what the pack behind them was up to.

It didn't take long before Reese found out that they had been discovered. She rejoined her human family. The pack of gray wolves was closely following her. They began running down both sides of the river, as they completely surrounded them. They were about to close in for the kill.

Phia stopped. 'If you run you are prey.'

The pack closed in on the three trespassers. The large, dark, Alpha wolf sniffed the air looking for fear, as he sized up the small group of intruders that were in his territory. The pack circled and waited for their leader. The Alfa male snarled and bared all of his teeth and slowly inched his way forward. He was surprised that they didn't run and that their two-legged leader held her ground. When he realized that they were ready to fight and not run like scared rabbits, he paused.

Phia handed her mother the spear that she was carrying and unstrapped her sling. She reached into her left pocket and retrieved three small stones. She had filled her pockets with these rocks at the cave to hunt rabbits and grouse. She looked at her mother, who proudly held the thin spear and then she loaded her sling.

She took a step towards the large wolf and shouted, **"With sticks and stones, I will break your bones."**

The old wolf laid back his ears and crouched, he was ready to spring at her. He accepted her challenge.

And in a quick blur, Phia spun her sling and the three small stones shot forward. Two of the stones missed but the third one hit the wolf on his black, cold nose.

He yelped a loud wolf curse and leaped and spun in a complete summersault, and landed on his feet. He shook his bloody nose, growled, and charged.

Phia quickly reloaded and launched three projectiles with all her might but she missed.

The large wolf leaped for Phia's throat.

Reese hit the angry predator just behind his shoulder knocking him to the ground, and Amy raised her spear high and hit him over the head as hard as she could.

The wolf was stunned. He staggered to his feet, and he backed off. He had had enough. This was the far edge of his territory, and he decided that they could have it. He slowly trotted off into the tundra, and his pack followed.

Amy was proudly beaming at their victory and Reese's tail was happily wagging up a storm. They had conquered.

Phia turned to her mom and grinned, "You know Mom, that is not the proper way to use a spear. You are supposed to use the pointy end."

"Well, now you tell me. You could have passed that information on a little earlier," laughed her mother.

The tenacious three made good time traveling down the flat, winding, frozen river.

By late afternoon, Phia could see that her mother was tiring. She decided to make camp for the night. She picked a spot along the river that had a high bank for a windbreak to set up her campsite. It had enough drifted snow against it to dig a snow cave. She sat her mom on a backpack. After she made sure her mother was warm and comfortable, she made her way to the trees along the top of the riverbank to gather firewood. Reese went looking for dinner.

Shortly Phia returned with a load of firewood and a pocket full of tinder and dry moss. "Are you warm enough, Mom?"

With chattering teeth, Amy lied. "Yes."

Phia began setting her fire.

"Are we sleeping here?"

"Yes, Mom. I will dig a snow cave, and it will be snug and warm." Phia tried to sound enthusiastic.

Amy sighed, "Will it be as snug and as warm as that cabin, over there?"

Tucked into the trees and covered in deep snow, sat a rundown old trappers cabin. They could not have been happier, even if they had found a five-star hotel. Well, maybe a little happier.

The door had a large timber propped against it to deter bears. Phia quickly removed it and went inside. It was like walking into an inkwell. She quickly pulled the Bic lighter from her pocket and flicked it on. There was a candle on the table. She lit it, and the light from it was almost too bright for their eyes, which for months now, were only accustomed to the brightness of a full moon.

The small log structure had a river rock fireplace for heat and for cooking. Phia quickly started a fire and sat her mother on an old rickety rocker in front of it. "Maybe I can find some tea, mom."

As the place warmed and the snow melted into tea water, Phia gathered more wood for the night. Before long, Reese returned with a fat snowshoe hare. And there was tea. The three of them ate and relaxed as they sat in front of the fire, while silently soaking up the heat. That night they slept peacefully, for the first time since that fateful day, when Alaska Airlines flight *AS2511* went down.

Christmas was in the air. It was Saturday morning, and the town was lit up like Macy's in downtown New York City. The proud black spruce trees were trimmed with a rainbow of colored lights that sparkled magically through their frost and snow-covered needles. These same lights also adorned doors and windows all across town. Yesterday was the winter solstice, and today was the town's Christmas festivity, and tomorrow was Christmas Eve. It was the best week of the year to hunker down and party.

Ruth was in the kitchen making coffee and cleaning up last night's dishes. Jackson was watching the national news on the TV via satellite. Fairbanks news was also piped in as local news. The actual local news for Fort Yukon was a weekly paper.

Jackson was comfortably slouched on the center of the couch with his injured leg propped up on the coffee table. "Ruthie," he called, "would you mind bringing me a cup of coffee."

Ruth scoffed and reached for a clean cup for the *cripple*. As she poured, Cheryl came out of the spare bedroom. She was wearing a thick yellow robe, and for someone who had just gotten up, her hair was surprisingly well-kempt.

"Good morning," chirped Cheryl.

"Here, give this to Jackson." Ruth handed her the full cup.

Cheryl put it on a proper, small saucer and walked into the quaint living room. "Good morning Jackson. How's your leg?"

Jackson quickly took his leg off the table and sat up. She was looking pretty good this morning. He smiled and answered. "It feels a damn sight better this morning. Seems to be healing up nicely."

Cheryl set the coffee on the table in front of Jackson and sat down beside him.

Ruth scoffed and mumbled to herself in a mocking tone while rocking her head side to side, "Seems to be healing up *nicely*." She filled two more cups and brought them into the living room. She set one of them on the coffee table in front of Cheryl and walked around the small table and sat next to Jackson. It was the side with his bad leg.

"Thank you," politely said Cheryl as she reached for her cup.

The three of them quietly sat there and watched the weather report. It called for continued cold with a chance of snow. It could have been a recording, because it hadn't really changed for the last two months, and would probably be the same weather report for the next two months. Jackson picked up the remote and hit the *off* button.

Cheryl took a sip of the strong coffee and turned in her seat towards Ruth. "Jackson told me that you saved his life."

"Really?" said Ruth a little surprised, as she turned and faced Cheryl.

Jackson slouched back on the couch, so they could see each other a little better.

"He said you saved it twice, actually," added Cheryl. "Once when you found him in a blizzard and took him to your cabin, and then when you sewed up his leg."

"He told you that!"

"Yes I did, Ruthie. Don't sound so surprised."

Ruth gave Jackson a warm smile and patted him on the leg.

Cheryl bit her lower lip. She had a delicate question to ask. "How did you know that Jackson was lost in that blizzard? And why were *you* walking in a blizzard?"

Jackson became a little curious himself, as to how she was going to answer that one. He was sure that she was just ending her life, because she was a burden to her family. He never confronted her about it. It is a very private thing, and he completely understood the feeling of being useless.

"If you must know, Cheryl," Ruth paused to sip her coffee and form her words. "I walked out into that blizzard to talk to God. There are much fewer distractions when it is snowing," she clarified. "And that's when He spoke to me."

Cheryl stopped drinking in mid-sip. "Wow, what did He sound like?"

Jackson couldn't tell whether she actually believed Ruth, or was just mockingly being polite.

Ruth continued, "It was more like a suggestion, a whisper, a feeling in my heart that a poor, old, Christian man was out there and needed my help."

Jackson became impressed with her story, well, except for the 'old' part.

"Then what happened?"

"I asked God to show me where to find him."

"And did He?" asked Cheryl.

Ruth solemnly folded her hands. "Yes, He did. He sent a white dove, and I followed it. The dove led me to Jackson and just in time. He could not walk another step. I was able to support him, until I could get him to my cabin and doctor the ugly wound on his leg."

Jackson scoffed, "A white dove?" He figured she overdid it.

"Yes, I know, it was probably a ptarmigan. It was snowing pretty hard, and I may have been mistaken."

Jackson was impressed with her recovery. He had always added a little spice every time he told one of his stories. Ruth was the goddess of embellishments.

Cheryl snickered and climbed to her feet. "Let's go to breakfast. I'm buying. After living in a broken plane and dieting with a very limited menu, I just can't seem to get enough to eat lately."

Cheryl turned to Ruth. "Maybe at breakfast I can hear more about your encounters with God and with Mother Nature."

"I'd be delighted to, Cheryl."

CHAPTER 33

Darker than dirt was the sky, and softer than snow were the clouds, and the temperature was tumbling. The moon was full and was hidden behind the high scattered clouds. It was a dandy night for traveling down nature's frozen highway in the far north.

Mom and Daughter and wolf made their way down the ice-covered Chandalar River. They were now near its end. Near where it dumps into the mighty Yukon River. They were close to town and getting their second wind.

"How are you doing, Mom?"

"Good, this fresh cold air seems to agree with me."

"You seem to have gotten your strength back."

"Maybe, or maybe I'm an old horse getting close to the barn and a hot bath in a large tub."

Phia chuckled, "And a tub with lots and lots of bubble-bath bubbles."

"And a long-stem glass full of red wine," added Amy.

The night wore on, and the moon rolled west and was about to set, when they reached the end of the river. It was going to be very dark soon. But even in the dark, the wide frozen highway would be easy to follow.

Phia walked out to the middle of the Yukon and looked in both directions. She was not sure which way to go. When she was riding the snowmobile with Frank, she was busy holding on for dear life and didn't see which direction he took. She knew the town was not far up, or down, the Yukon River, as least by snowmobile. She was hoping to see the white haze of the town's lights.

Amy took off her pack and sat on it, "Which way Phia?"

Phia took off her pack and set it beside her mother's.

Reese sat on the thin layer of snow between them.

"I'm not sure mom." Phia opened her pack and took out some dried, smoked rabbit, and handed it to her Mom to eat. "Wait here. There should be some snowmobile tracks going towards Fort Yukon. I'll see what I can find." Phia tossed Reese a large piece of dried rabbit. "You stay with Mom."

Phia did find a lot of snowmobile tracks that were running both up and down the river, and a few went up the Chandalar River. The tracks were of no help. Phia had to guess. If it was wrong, she would know by the end of the day. They would then just sleep along the river and change direction the next day, adding a precious day to their journey. She was pretty sure that the town was less than a day's walk from here. "But Frank's snow-go was pretty fast," she said to herself. "Maybe it's a two-day walk."

Phia looked up at the moon for help. It winked at her through a break in the clouds just before it ducked below the western horizon, and then everything turned very dark. "Oh, great!" she sighed, even though it wasn't. Phia decided to let her mother pick the direction. She had always been pretty lucky.

Phia took a last look upriver. As she started to turn, a dark shape came around a bend in the river. With the moon gone, the world was a dark gray with even darker shadows. "It's probably a moose," she mumbled. She began walking upriver to get a better look.

The dark shadow made its way to the center of the frozen Yukon and was coming her way. It was tall and had no horns, but then so is a cow moose walking towards you. Phia loaded her sling and cautiously ambled towards it. As she closed the distance, it began looking and walking more like a man.

Phia stopped and waved. "Hello," she called. This startled the man and he stopped moving. Phia was close enough to see that it was definitely walking on two legs, and he was carrying something under his left arm.

The man was a giant. He was wearing a fur parka with matching pants. His fringeless hood was small and pulled tight around his head, and his reddish beard completely covered his face, and it was the same color as his parka. "Wow, he looks like a yeti," she said to herself.

"Sir, can you tell me which way to Fort Yukon?"

The startled man was tall and barrel-chested with thick legs and dark eyes, and his parka seemed to be a one piece furry union suit. He quietly studied Phia for a minute.

Phia now had a good idea of how David felt, when he confronted Goliath. She readied her sling and said, "Hi, my name is Phia. What's your name?"

The huge man looked towards the mouth of the Chandalar River and saw Amy and the wolf. He looked back at Phia and smiled, which revealed very large, terrifying teeth. He said something. His voice was more of a growl and not very articulate.

Phia wasn't sure what he said. It sounded like he was speaking in the guttural German language. She guessed he was new to Alaska. The guttural noise of his name sounded something like, Gary. Phia relaxed her sling. "Hi, Gary, can you tell me which way to town?"

Gary nodded and pointed towards the direction he had come from, which was upriver.

"Thank you, Gary."

Gary grunted again. It sounded like, *Merry Christmas*. He turned and began walking his big feet down the Yukon River. He still had the package under his arm. It was beer.

"Merry Christmas to you too."

Phia put her sling away and walked back towards her mother. All the way back she was thinking, 'Wow, it's Christmas…it's Christmas!'

When Amy saw her daughter coming, she put her pack on and met her halfway. "My God Phia, that guy you were talking to was huge. Did he tell you which way town is?"

Phia nodded and pointed. "Upriver. That way."

"Did he say how far it was?"

"I didn't ask. He was hard to understand. He had a terrible accent. But he did wish me a Merry Christmas."

Amy gasped. "Is it Christmas? Wow, I guess it could be. I completely forgot…" Amy stopped walking and threw her hands in the air. "I haven't done any Christmas shopping." Amy was beside herself.

Phia laughed. "Keep walking Mom. We can do some shopping when we get to town."

"I don't have my purse!" Amy panicked. "All my credit cards were in it!"

"Well, Mom, we could turn around and go back and look for it."

Amy looked her daughter in the face and laughed at her suggestion. "Sorry, old habits. I always panic at Christmas time." She grabbed her daughter's hand and squeezed it. "Let's hurry, it's Christmas."

"Mom, is Bigfoot real?"

Amy shrugged her shoulders. "Why do you ask?"

"Hurry up Jackson, you're going to make us late," scolded Ruth.

"It's this confounded tie." Jackson was standing in front of the bathroom mirror. "I tried every knot that I can think of, and none of them look proper." Jackson opened the bathroom door. He stepped out with the collar of his white shirt up and a red paisley tie draped around his neck.

"Do you know how to tie these stupid things? I think they were invented by women to keep men on short leashes."

Ruth looked up at Jackson. "What happened to your face?"

"I shaved, so what?" scoffed Jackson. "Are you going to tie my tie, or not? Jackson handed the tie to Ruth and paused as he looked at her from head to toe. "Oh, you look nice, Ruth."

Ruth was wearing a traditional Athabascan soft-leather top over a dark red skirt. From shoulder to shoulder was a wide band of green and blue beads with dangling white quills. The intricately decorated band looped down across her chest. The leather top was embroidered with different colored beadwork. A long thin seashell hung from each ear. Her dark gray hair had two braids with long white Ptarmigan feathers clasped at the bottom of each one. Grandmother Ruth did look quite fetching.

Jackson's complement made Ruth blush. "Sorry, I don't know how to tie a tie." Ruth turned towards the kitchen and hollered, "Cheryl, can you tie Jackson's tie?"

"Sure," she said. "Be there in a minute." Cheryl was standing in front of a large mirror that was attached to the inside of the door to the hall closet. She was doing the final touchup on her face. She turned and faced Jackson. "Wow, you shaved!" Cheryl slowly walked around him while slightly nodding her head. "I think you have just shaved off twenty years."

Cheryl looked nice too. She was wearing a dark blue cocktail dress. It was sleeveless with a low-cut V-neck and slit up the left side from floor to hip. She had dyed her hair blond, and it draped down around her right shoulder. She also looked twenty years younger.

Yes, she looked very nice, and I have to add, very sexy.

Jackson was just as stunned, when he saw her. Literally, she was stunning. He closed his gaping mouth and said, as casually as he could, "You look nice."

Cheryl laughed. "You clean up pretty good yourself." Cheryl took both ends of the tie and put it around his neck. She adjusted the front end of the tie, so that it was a little longer. She took the wide end and spun it around the thinner end. She wrapped and tucked and slipped it under a loop and pulled it tight. She folded the collar back down, and after a small adjustment, she stepped back. "All done. And now you look pretty."

Ruth shook her head. "Oh my God, you're teenagers. If you think that you both look pretty enough, we need to get going."

"I can see the lights of town," gasped Amy. "Hurry." Amy took the lead.

They had no idea what time it was. Since the sun never rose, their days were dictated by the rise and the fall of the moon. Phia was guessing that it was close to the time for the moon to be coming up, which was the beginning of their day, but on clock time, that meant the beginning of night.

They finally strolled into Fort Yukon on Saturday, the 23rd of December in the late afternoon. The town was lit up with Christmas lights and traffic lights. Both of which, melted Amy's heart. They had made it.

"What do we do now?" asked Amy. "We don't have any money."

Phia remembered the two nice police officers, Karen Gray and James Brook. Phia pointed to a large building on the edge of the river. "That's the Police Station. They will take care of us."

The first thing Amy felt, when they went inside was the blast of warm air. It was truly happening. The place was empty. The police part of the building was closed up, and there was a sign on the door. The Post Office part also was closed except for the individual, locked Post Office boxes. Since the place was empty, Phia let Reese follow them inside.

Phia saw that the coffee pot was on and the pot was half full. "Mom, how would like a cup of real coffee?"

"We have no money."

"It's free, Mom." Amy pointed to the small counter with the coffee maker and paper cups. While Amy poured herself a cup, Phia sat at a table. It was the one that she sat at, when she first met Dr. O'Malley.

Amy came back with two cups. "They also had hot chocolate." Amy took a quick sip of real coffee and giggled in contentment. "We can sleep here. I may never leave this building…ever."

Phia picked up her cup and walked over to the thick glass door on the police side of the building and read the note. "Mom, it says, 'If you have an emergency call 907-555-8711. We can also be reached at the Town Hall.'"

"Where's the Town Hall, Phia?"

Phia shrugged her shoulders, came back to her mother, and sat down, and sipped her hot coco. "Wow, this is the best cup of Chocolate that I have ever had in my life, Mom. How's your coffee?"

Amy smiled. "It's even better."

CHAPTER 34

The town hall in Fort Yukon had a modern kitchen in it and was set up for formal functions. Deborah and Stephanie, the two wives of the oil executives that had sat in first-class, personally sponsored this event to honor and thank Jackson for his heroic efforts.

This function was going to be the *coup de grâce* of all Christmas parties. "Even," bragged Stephanie, "if I have to spend every last dime of my husband's money to do it." The two women were so happy to be back in the city that had shopping malls, and central heating, and Starbucks, and especially, to be in charge again. "We all deserve this," added Deborah.

They hired caterers and had an open bar. The tables were covered in white table cloths and each had its own ice-filled bucket that cradled a bottle of expensive Champaign. And there were a lot of waiters.

There was a table set up in front for the guest of honor and his date, Ruth, and the hosts. Murphy and Cheryl also sat at this table, since they were the two leaders that had taken charge of the stranded passengers and kept them as comfortable and as safe as they could, while Jackson had trudged off into the harsh elements in search of rescue. There were also two empty chairs that sat at this table. One was designated for Dr. O'Malley, who had lost his own life in his part of rescuing the fateful survivors, and the other vacant chair was for the passengers that had lost their lives in this tragic event.

After cocktails were served, Murphy stood up to say a few words. "Merry Christmas," he spoke it loudly to get everyone's attention.

The guests hushed and turned their eyes on Murphy.

"Today we are here to celebrate a second chance at life, and to mourn those who did not get this chance. And to honor the man who gave his life for *our* new lease on this life, Dr. Shawn O'Malley. And, of course, to honor Jackson. If it wasn't for his gallant efforts, none of us would be here to celebrate anything today."

Everyone stood up at their tables and applauded. Jackson blushed.

Murphy continued. He was Irish and a teller of stories. He held the microphone tightly, as he recalled the lighter events of their time in the cold wilderness while waiting to be rescued. The food began arriving, and Murphy held the floor. He was good with words and elaborated on the lighter incidents and detailed the funny happenings of the whole ordeal. As Murphy told his tail, the gala turned quite festive.

And finally, Murphy ran of words, and he finished with, "I want to thank you all for coming here tonight, and especially, to thank Edward and Deborah, and Ronald and Stephanie, for sponsoring this fine evening." Murphy turned and looked at the four sponsors and began clapping.

The tables of eaters stopped chewing and joined in. They clapped their hands, long and loud.

When the applause finally subsided, Murphy added, "Oh, one more thing. My good friend, and the real reason we are all here tonight, would like to pass on a few words to you." Murphy handed the microphone to Jackson and quickly sat down to enjoy his cold meal and to watch Jackson squirm.

The Irish are evil that way.

Jackson looked up from his plate and scanned the room. It became church-quiet and all eyes were on him. Jackson gulped in panic.

Ohhhh, he so wanted to stab Murphy in the heart with his soup spoon.

Jackson forced a smile towards his audience, downed his cocktail for courage, and climbed to his feet. When he stood, his ears were greeted by rousing applause.

"Thank you," said Jackson humbly into the microphone. He turned to the Irish cop and grinned, "And, thank you, Murphy. I have a personal surprise for you, when I catch you alone." He turned to Stephanie and Deborah and softly said, "You two have outdone yourselves. This place is fit for a king. Thank you very much."

That was followed by more clapping and a few whistles.

Jackson cleared his throat and scanned his audience. "Murphy pretty much said it all. So I will keep this short. I just want to add that I am not the real hero here. There is a young girl that should be sitting in my chair. If it weren't for her, I wouldn't be here, and for that matter, neither would you."

Jackson paused and tried to quell the emotion that was swelling in his heart. He took a couple of deep breaths and continued on with his part of the story "If it hadn't been for Phia and her wolf, I would have died out there. And if it hadn't been for Ruth," Jackson paused and pointed to her. "If she hadn't found us in that snowstorm and led us to a cabin, I don't think we would have made it." He looked back at Ruth, "Please stand up."

The shy Athabaskan woman stood up and turned red. The building vibrated in applause just for her.

Meanwhile:

Amy and Phia sat enjoying their hot drinks in the warm Police and Post Office Building with Reese lying on the vinyl floor between them.

Suddenly, the wolf perked up her ears and growled softly. The entry door opened, and a blast of arctic wind blew in, and that was followed by a bent-over old man with a white, tobacco-stained beard. He stomped the snow from his boots and rolled back his parka hood. His hair was as white as snow and very thin on top.

The old man pulled out his mailbox key and began walking towards the Post Office end of the building.

When he saw Amy and Phia, he stopped in his tracks. "Lordie," exclaimed the startled old man. "I weren't 'specting to see nobody here. I thought everyone was at the fancy shindig in town." He studied their faces for a second. "Say, I don't know you two. You're new." The old man looked at Reese lying between them. "Oh, they don't allow no dogs in here. Dem's the rules."

Amy gave the old man a warm smile. "I'm sorry. But we have been on a long journey, and we need to rest awhile and warm up, and so does our dog."

"Oh, it's alright with me. I just didn't want you nice folks to get into any kind of trouble. It's good to see new faces in town, especially ones as pretty as yours. Don't mind me, I just come ta get my mail." The old man's beard separated into a warm smile. He turned and wandered towards a wall of small, mailbox doors.

"Say, mister," interrupted Phia. "What's this shindig thing that you spoke of, about?"

He stopped and turned. "Well, I was told it is a Christmas party, and it is a celebration, and it is a wake, all rolled into one. I was invited, but it sounds like an oxymoron to me."

Both Amy and Phia looked at each other in a surprised grin, because of his use of such a big word.

The old man continued on to his mailbox. He inserted his key and opened the door. He pulled out a stack of envelopes and Christmas catalogs. After closing the small door, he set his mail on the counter by the coffee pot. He went through it. He put one letter in his pocket and dumped the rest in the trash.

He looked back at Amy. "Couldn't help but notice, but it looks to me like your dog's got a lot of wolf in him."

"Yes, she does, mister," said Phia proudly, and then she asked, "What's your name?"

"Ward."

"Say, Ward, who's the wake for?"

"It's for Dr. O'Malley and some other people I don't know. O'Malley's plane went down some time past." Ward sadly sighed, "They never did find him or his plane."

"I know where it's at," said Phia enthusiastically. "I can take you there."

The old man paused and scratched his head; he thought that he didn't hear the young girl right. He asked, "How can you know where the plane is at, little girl?"

"Because me and my Mom were on the plane, when he landed it."

Ward gasped. "What happened to Dr. O'Malley?"

"The plane ran out of gas, while we were flying, so Dr. O'Malley landed it in the tundra. But it was dark, and he didn't see a leaning tree, until it was too late."

Ward sagged his thin shoulders and shook his head, "That's too bad. He was a good doctor and my friend." Ward looked quizzically at Phia. "Well then, if you were flying with the doctor, you probably know Jackson."

Phia and Amy gasped and grinned. "We sure do. Is he here?"

"Well damn, girls," said the grinning old man. "Jackson's at this shindig. I can take you there, if you two want to go."

"Great," said Amy.

"Do they allow dogs?" asked Phia.

Ward shook his head. He paused, and with a stroke of his stained beard and with a coy smile he said, "But they never said anything about no wolves."

Meanwhile:

Jackson had found his tongue. Apparently, he also has a little Irish in him. He definitely has some Scotch in him. He was on his third glass.

As he finished up his tales of survival, dessert was being served. It was a dark, rich chocolate cake that was drizzled with a raspberry sauce. Jackson thanked everyone for coming and sat down in front of his dark desert and picked up his fork.

The old clock chimed twelve times marking midnight. It was officially Christmas Eve. Jackson looked up at the clock, but became distracted, when he saw three late-comers come through the hall's arctic entry. He recognized Ward and saw that he came in with two women wearing thick hooded parkas. And there was a chocolate-colored Gray Wolf standing between the two women.

Phia anxiously searched for Jackson in the crowded room. In his suit and tie and with a naked face, he looked like a stranger to her, a stranger who was staring intently at her. Suddenly, Phia recognized his eyes. She smiled.

Jackson blinked several times at her. He thought his old eyes were playing tricks on him. But each time he blinked she was still there. He put down his fork and stood up. He snatched his cane and slowly worked his way towards her. His heart was about to burst with joy as tears flooded his eyes.

Everyone in the building hushed and watched him closely, as they tried to understand what had suddenly happened to him. He had his free hand on his chest and was breathing heavily. They became concerned. Was he having a heart attack?

Amy didn't recognize him at first, but when she did, she gasped and ran up to him. And she threw her arms around him and started to cry.

Phia walked up to him and shook her head. "What happened to your face, old man?"

Jackson laughed and reached over with his right arm and pulled her in. It became a three-way hug.

And one by one, as each passenger of Alaska Airlines flight *AS1125* discovered who had arrived, he would join in with the group hug.

CHAPTER 35

Jackson threw another log into the stone-faced fireplace and pulled up a thick-cushioned, well-worn, easy-chair in front of the cracking fire. On the table beside the comfortable chair was a full glass of scotch and a phone. It was Ruth's old landline phone. He slid into the soft chair and exhaled a comfortable sigh. It was the one-year anniversary of the plane crash.

Jackson was still a guest at Ruth's house. He had sold his small place in Fairbanks and decided he wanted to live closer to his son and grandson. Ruth offered him her home to stay in temporarily, until he found a place of his own.

By nature, Jackson was not a procrastinator. But he got very comfortable living with Ruth and showed no signs of leaving. And she was, for the most part, a sweet and a good housemate. But on some occasions, Ruth could become quite ruthless, literally. On these days, Jackson would spend the night at his son's house, which turned into a good thing. He and Frank were now speaking to each other, thanks to his grandson, Francis.

Francis finally got fed up being used as a talking device between the two stubborn jackass Jacksons and threatened to leave them, if they didn't behave themselves and act like reasonable adults. They agreed that it had been long enough, and so they had a couple of beers to seal the deal.

But after the night away from Ruth, Jackson would pick up a bottle of wine and some flowers, and crawl back and humbly apologize for whatever dastardly deed, that he might have done to upset her. The sweet old Athabaskan woman would always forgive him, and they would drink the whole bottle of wine. After that, Ruth would invite the old reprobate to her warm bed.

And so it was, Jackson continued his procrastination. The cold winter was coming.

Jackson took a sip of his scotch and picked up the phone. He dialed up Murphy, who answered on the third ring.

"Officer Stephan Murphy, how may I assist you?"

"Murph, Jackson here. Do you know what day it is?"

Murphy paused and looked at his calendar. Today's date was familiar for some reason, and then it hit him. "Wow, Jackson, it's been a year. It doesn't really seem that long." Murphy leaned back on his chair and put his feet up on his desk. "How's the old leg doing?"

"It's still weak, but there's no pain anymore. I do have a hideous scar, so I don't wear shorts in public."

"Shorts? I didn't know you even owned a pair."

"I don't, but that not the point, Murph." Jackson picked up his glass of scotch with his free hand and took a large sip. "Say, Murph, whatever happened to your prisoner? What was his name again?"

"Bobby, Bobby Walker." Murphy laughed in remembering. "He went to trial, and the judge fined him a $100,000 for his crime, but was lenient on jail time, because of the time he spent in custody during the plane crash. He figured that his time out there was incarceration enough.

"Ole Bobby paid the fine and started up his own business. He's got a kid now, and he is walking the straight and narrow."

Note:

Alaska Airlines had settled with the surviving passengers for five-hundred thousand each and a million dollars to the relatives of the ones that died. The attorneys of the living complained that it was unfair. The insurance companies offered a compromise, a half-million now, or the full million to their relatives after they died. All chose the former.

"Well good for him," said Jackson. "So, he has a kid already. Who did he marry?"

"Kayla. But they're not married. They're partners in a business. She came up with half of the money."

"Who is Kayla?"

You remember when Bobby's arms were in a splint?"

"Yes," replied Jackson. "Oh, I remember. Kayla was the one that helped him pee?"

"That's the one. They pooled their settlement money and bought a topless bar. They renamed it *The Survivor's Pub*."

"A bar? Well, I'll be damn." Jackson shook his head and laughed.

"And, here's the best part, their son was born about nine months after the plane crash."

"Well I'm guessing," chuckled Jackson, "that she ran out of pills and the temptation while lingering under a warm blanket, was too much for them."

"She wasn't the only one, Jackson. You remember the two women in first class?"

"You're kidding? One of them got pregnant too?"

"Actually, both of them did. Debra had a boy, and Stephanie had a girl. She named hers, Frances, after you."

Jackson laughed and raised his glass, and he took a hearty drink of scotch to his namesake. "What about that other girl that was traveling with Kayla? What's she doing now?"

"That was Barbara." Murphy chuckled. "Yep, she got pregnant too."

"Really, who was the father?"

"Jesse. He was that young fellow from the farm, who was visiting his brother. Jesse and her paired up for the warmth in the wild and love bloomed. Those two actually married and bought a house with their settlement. Jesse now works construction with his Brother, and Barbara tends bar occasionally at the *Survivor's Pub.*"

Jackson leaned back and smiled. "What about you, how are you doing?"

Murphy took his feet off his desk. "I'm doing good."

"How about Cheryl? Do you hear from her?"

"Actually, we are dating."

"Dating?" Jackson leaned forward. "Is she pregnant too?"

"Heaven's no! We never slept together."

"Liar."

Murphy chuckled. "Well, at least not out there." He then steered the subject in another direction. "Do you remember Albert Evans?"

"No, there were a few out there that didn't talk very much, plus I wasn't out there as long as you were.

"So, what about this Albert Evans," asked Jackson?

"Well, that poor man was down and out. He confided in me that he had no idea where he was at. He said he bought a plane ticket on the first plane out of New Jersey and didn't care where it was going. He said he was running away from a job that he hated, and that he had five kids and a nagging wife and thought that he couldn't bear it any longer.

"By the end of the first week, he was terribly homesick and missed his family something awful. He swore that, if he ever got back home, things were going to be different.

"After we were rescued, he bought a plane ticket back to home. He got his life back and wanted it to stay that way. When he got his settlement check, he tore it up. He was afraid it might change things."

"He tore it up?" exclaimed Jackson. "Wow, he's a bigger man than me."

"I know. I found out, when his wife called me. She was beside herself and didn't know what to do about it. 'We could really use the money,' she told me. But she was afraid, if they kept it, that she might lose him again. So, I told her to have the airlines write the check to her personally, put it in a secret bank account, and just use it for emergencies. She took my advice. She said that she handled their money anyway. She paid off the house first thing, and a couple of months later, she bought a new car. They now go on regular family vacations.

"I suspect Albert knows," chuckled Murphy. "So, how's Phia and her mother doing?"

"Good," said Jackson. "You know, she and Amy each got a check, and so they went shopping for a house. They bought a nice place on the river. It sits on a high bluff and overlooks the Brooks Range. Amy bought a new SUV to drive to its remote location in summer and a snowmobile for the winter. She seems happy, and she now works for the Police Department as a dispatcher.

"Phia is a junior in the high school. It is the same one that my grandson was going to. They went to the senior prom together. Francis is now in Fairbanks. He's a freshman at the university there.

"Oh, and do you remember Phia's wolf?"

"Sure," answered Murphy.

"She had a litter of pups. It seems that Francis's lead dog was the father. His dog was half wolf, and the two seemed to have pair-bonded.

"Phia and Francis and the wolf family spent the summer together on the tundra. By fall, the family of wolves migrated north to start their own pack. Sometimes Phia runs with them. She's also free and wild just like them and is accepted as a member of the pack."

Murphy listened silently on the edge of his chair. He remembered Phia being timid, and shy, and speechless.

"When school started," continued Jackson, "She tamed back up, hopped the bus, and went back to school. She's a very bright little girl, top of her class. But I hear tell she keeps a sling in her backpack. She used it once on a senior. He played football. He got a little forward with her and as he was strutt'in away from her, she nailed him a good one on the butt."

"Ouch," laughed Murphy.

"Well, I gotta go Murph. Ruth just got home. It's been good talking to you. Say hi to Cheryl for me."

"I'll do that. You take care. Bye."

Jackson threw another log on the fire and Ruth poured herself a glass of wine and joined her roommate.

The new season's snow was falling. The days were now very short. It was time to hunker down for the winter. Jackson put his arm around Ruth, and they sat there silently watching the fire, without a care in the world and nothing pressing, as they quietly waited for the coming of spring.

And they lived happily ever after.

That was how I wanted to end my story. After what Phia had been through in this short part of her life, she deserved that. But alas, life is not always fair. Phia was about to find that out. Before very long, she would don her parka and be off on another quest to save the lives of the loved ones around her.

It will be another harrowing adventure for her that will involve a conspiracy of evil men, and they will be too much for her to handle by herself. Phia will have to seek help from a very unlikely source. I don't want to give it away, but he has very large feet, and his name is Gary.

www.ingramcontent.com/pod-product-compliance
Lightning Source LLC
Chambersburg PA
CBHW031006190726
48286CB00003BA/714